T0374276

Pathways

Ron Bruce

WestBow Press books may be ordered through booksellers or by contacting:

WestBow Press
A Division of Thomas Nelson
1663 Liberty Drive
Bloomington, IN 47403
www.westbowpress.com
1-(866) 928-1240

ISBN: 978-1-4497-7544-5 (e)
ISBN: 978-1-4497-7545-2 (sc)
ISBN: 978-1-4497-7546-9 (hc)

Library of Congress Control Number: 2012921296

Printed in the United States of America

WestBow Press rev. date: 11/28/2012

Chapter 1
Mike

Mike Larson stood on the mound. The warm late summer breeze blew in lightly from centerfield. Mike knew that this might be his last chance to impress the coaches. He had begun to labor through the sixth inning of his final start of the 1998 Class A baseball season. Mike knew that if he could not leave a positive impression on the final start of his second season that he may not be invited back to The West Michigan Whitecaps for a third season. The game had started well for Mike. He took a shutout into the fourth inning before giving up a two run home run. Mike recovered to retire the opposing team in order in the fifth inning. The fifth inning's reprieve had faded into a nightmarish sixth inning. Mike gave up a lead off home run, and then got the next hitter to ground out before giving up back-to-back singles and a walk to load the bases. He knew a double play or a strikeout would save him. The batter took his spot in the batter's box and Mike stared in, he wound up and delivered a fastball outside for ball one. Mike looked in again, got the sign from the catcher, and delivered another fastball on the outside corner for a called strike. Mike then proceeded to throw back-to-back split finger fastballs that missed the strike zone. Mike was behind in the count 3-1. He knew he had to throw a fastball, so did the batter, and so did everybody in the stands. Beads of sweat began rolling down the back of his neck, as he stood on the mound ready to deliver the next pitch. Mike wound up and threw a fastball as hard as he could. Mike watched in what felt like slow motion as the ball traveled to the middle of the plate, and then a loud crack rang out as the batter hit the ball. The next thing Mike saw was the ball landing somewhere over the left field fence. Mike put his head down; the manager came out from the dugout and signaled for a relief pitcher. Mike handed the ball to the manager, took the obligatory pat on the back, walked back to the dugout, found a quiet spot at the end of the bench, and put his head down. Mike sat at the end of the bench fearing that his pitching career had ended. About a half an hour after the game, he received confirmation that it had.

Mike's life seemed like a bad dream. This dream did not boast the hideous monsters of famous bad dreams, but instead featured tiny jabs of torment that left the dreamer in a dazed delirium. Mike lived each event of each day hoping for improvement but always meeting with disappointment. He was tall and gangly, with shoulder length greasy hair. He was a skinny young man blessed with a metabolism that allowed him to eat large amounts of fast food and not gain an ounce. He still had a small amount of acne left from a big breakout in the tenth grade and lasted through much of his high school career. Mike wore glasses for nearsightedness, which he always felt, lowered people's perception of him, even though the glasses were thin and did nothing to draw unwanted attention to him as an adult. He never quite got over the four eyes insults in the third grade. Nobody accused him of being the most attractive young man but nobody considered him ugly either.

Mike lived and grew up in the small suburb of Roseville Michigan. Roseville is a small suburb just a few minutes north of Detroit almost touching Lake St Clair but blocked from doing so by the city of St. Clair Shores. Mike grew up in a blue-collar neighborhood. Many of the people in his neighborhood worked in manufacturing jobs either for one of Detroit's Big 3 or a supplier for one of Detroit's Big 3. He worked a menial factory job at a plastic injection-molding factory in the neighboring suburb of Warren. However, the job didn't pay Mike enough money to move out of his parent's basement, a rather disheartening place for a man of twenty-four years old to be living in the spring of 2002. He went to school pursuing a degree in business but no matter what he did or how many classes he took, he never seemed any closer to being finished. In high school, he had grandiose visions of making a name for himself. He thought that, by this time, he would either be a pitcher in the Major Leagues or have a high paying job that would afford him all that he ever wanted. Since both of those dreams still resided in either the distant future or a fairy tale, he was not the happiest person on planet earth. Nobody ever accused Mike of being outgoing. Introversion hindered his ability to make friends. He knew people at school, work, and the bar he frequented, but they were more acquaintances not friends. They were people that he could talk to about music, television, sports, alcohol, schoolwork, and partying, but never anything deep. In fact, Mike didn't understand that real friends help each other out with life's difficulties. Instead, Mike believed he only needed to talk about the superficial, and kept all real emotions bottled up inside in a metaphorical box under lock and key. A box in which nobody but Mike had permission to look inside. After many years, Mike's box of pent up emotion had reached a tipping point. It was ready to burst yet Mike kept wrapping more chains around the box in a vain attempt keep the contents locked tight. This extraordinary effort to contain all pent up emotions began to wear away on Mike. He became more tired, stress mounted which in turn increased the number and severity of colds, and flues Mike got. Still, he trudged through his routine silently sporting the mantra "play through the pain." Mike believed all adults should and did follow the motto. Mike's stress needed an outlet and that outlet became drinking. Drinking helped relieve the stress temporarily. It made him temporarily numb to his parents' urgings to finish school and get a "real" job. It also gave him his parents as an outlet, to blame someone else for his own problems. Mike thought that if they had helped him more, he would be in the Major Leagues or already be embarking on his career of choice. It had to be their fault. There could be no other explanation. To the untrained eye Mike may have seemed like an ungrateful alcoholic, however, as always, much more lay beneath the surface. Much more that would soon flood to the surface as he came realize that maybe his purpose remained undiscovered.

Mike wanted nothing more than to move from his blue-collar hometown in the Detroit suburbs. Mike hated the area, found it constricting and uncivilized. People, he thought, were too wrapped up in themselves and too selfish to care about anyone but themselves. Mike had seen it firsthand; girlfriend's who cheated on him because someone else was better looking, employers who passed on him time and time again because he was too genuine and real to succeed in business. Sure, they'd always tell him something like "We need someone with more experience," or "We really liked you but decided to go in a different direction." Mike heard it all and grew tired of it. He knew the real reason. Genuine people like him always got the shaft. He lived in a dog eat dog world that punished being genuine. Just be a cookie cutter of everybody else and success will follow. Mike tried that it only increased his depression. He struggled constantly to achieve whatever he wanted but he seemingly could never get the things he really wanted. No matter how hard he tried at a career, a home, a relationship, or at baseball, he could never seem to get over that invisible hump. Mike had to blame others. The metaphorical box that he had built inside himself started to overflow and could hold nothing else without exploding and causing Mike a breakdown. Therefore, Mike began to blame others for his failings. Blaming others always gave Mike an avenue to keep his box of emotions from exploding.

Mike's biggest failure in his eyes was baseball. He had played baseball since he was six years old and truly loved the game. He played in little league, on school teams, and in city leagues since he started playing tee-ball at age six. Then in 1996 when he graduated high school, he decided he wanted to try for the big time. He wanted to prove to all his coaches who would always let another player pitch over him that they were wrong in their assessments of his talents. Mike knew he had a great fastball, a serviceable slider, and a dominating split finger fastball. He believed that would be enough to make him successful at the A-ball level. At that point, he figured a pitching coach would help him develop an off speed pitch or curveball to compliment his hard stuff.

Mike left to try out for The West Michigan White Caps in the spring of 1997. He knew his chances of making the team weren't the best as an open try out, but at that point in his life; he had confidence in his pitches. Sure enough, Coach Dave Hamilton and Pitching Coach Randy Cotts noticed something in him that they liked and gave him a contract. They told him that he would come out of the bullpen and be a reliever until he developed an off speed pitch. Coach Cotts said he would work with him every day in practice until he achieved command over a devastating curve ball. Mike was ecstatic. He felt that he had made it and he would have a chance to prove everyone wrong. He felt that he would finally prove to everybody that he did have talent. He couldn't wait to go back to his old high school and rub it in his former coach's face. He would say "look coach, I'm playing pro ball now, I have coaches that work with me, and believe in my abilities. Aren't you sorry now that you didn't let me pitch more? Maybe if you did we would have won that state championship instead of losing it."

Mike was referring to the 1996 Michigan High School Baseball Championship. His team led 7-6 heading into the bottom of the ninth inning. Mike had been warming up in the bullpen on and off hoping to come in. Karl Dawes, the pitcher who had pitched the seventh and eighth inning told the coach his arm was sore and that he was tired. Karl's exact words were "Coach, I don't have much left in my tank."

Mike started to get ready to enter the game. However, the coach, said to Karl, "Nonsense, Dawes, this is your game. I don't want Mike in there; he doesn't have the stuff for this order. You do, even if you're running on empty."

Then the world began to crash down around Mike. He wanted to be in the game. He knew he could get the final out. In addition, there were pro scouts in the bleachers. He knew if they saw his fastball and split finger that they would be interested in signing him. Instead, Mike sat on the bench and put his head down. His day only got worse a few minutes later when Smith High's Chad Downing hit a walk-off, three run home run to win the game. Mike wanted to tell off the coach. He figured, "hey, I'm out of school now. I can't play another game. Why shouldn't I tell him exactly what I think of him?"

Mike worked up the nerve and walked over to the coach who stood in the middle of the other players talking. Mike stood up, and walked over ready to let the coach know how he felt, but as he got closer, he lost his nerve and returned to the corner of the locker room and sat down. That is when the coach began a speech that would scar Mike for many years. The coach said, "Men, you played a great game, and should be state champs right now. Heck, you would be state champs if Mike could get off his lazy, untalented duff and learn how to throw a halfway decent off speed pitch." The entire team started ragging on Mike. He heard cheap shots and took physical abuse the entire bus ride home. Mike wanted to disappear. This event began Mike's emotional lockdown.

That's when he got the idea for A Ball. The insults Mike endured on the way home from the state championship lit a fire inside him that only revenge could quench. He trained and worked out for months leading up to the 1997 tryouts and it had just paid off.

Not only was Mike successful, but also Randy Cotts would train him. Cotts had been one of his heroes growing up. He watched him for years pitch for his hometown team The Detroit Tigers. In his prime, Major League hitters feared Cotts more than any other pitcher. He had a great fastball, slider, sinker, and one of the best curveballs in the history of baseball. Mike figured if anyone could teach him to throw a curveball, it would have to be Cotts. Not only did hitters fear his pitches but also Cotts stood an imposing six foot six. Many hitters used to say that just seeing Cotts' huge frame on the mound was enough to scare them into taking a pitch they could hit. His short black hair by now had begun turning grey but he still had that huge imposing frame. Cotts probably could have been a successful forward in the NBA, lineman in The NFL or defenseman in the NHL. He had that rare combination of size and athleticism that could make him successful in whatever sport he chose.

Mike also thought highly of Cotts because of a chance meeting as a young boy. When Mike had his appendix taken out, Cotts happened to be in the hospital doing volunteer work. Mike's mother saw Cotts at the nurses' station near Mike's room on the way back from the cafeteria. She asked him to come meet her son who had just had his appendix removed and Cotts did. He not only came to see him but Cotts gave Mike an autographed picture and baseball to boot. That made Mike forget all about his appendectomy and caused him to idolize Cotts. Mike decided that he wanted to be just like Cotts when he grew up. However, he could never get that curveball down. It didn't matter to Mike that he had never conquered the curveball. He figured he had his hero training him he would master it in no time.

Disappointment struck Mike when he mentioned the incident to Cotts and Cotts didn't remember. Even when he showed Cotts a picture of the two of them in the hospital, the autographed ball, and the autographed picture,

Cotts didn't remember. Mike was surprised to realize that the moment that changed his life wasn't even a blip on his hero's screen. It didn't bother him too much though, he figured Randy Cotts had probably met a number of similar kids over the years and couldn't possibly remember them all.

For the first month of training, Randy kept his promise and worked with Mike every day. Mike even started to get the hang of how to throw the curveball. However, he still had trouble throwing it over the plate.

When the season started, Mike came out of the bullpen 3 times in the first week and did pretty well. He only gave up one run on two hits in five innings of work. He threw the curveball sparingly because he knew it was still learning how to throw the pitch. He mainly relied on his split finger fastball to get batters out. He continued to have trouble getting his curveball over the plate.

Mike began to get a reputation among the hitters as a guy without a good breaking pitch. Players began sitting on his fastball, just crushing it. By the end of May, Mike's ERA climbed over nine, not a good number at any level of pro ball, especially Class A.

Then in mid June, things got even worse. The White Cap's Major League affiliate drafted a hotshot college pitcher whom they wanted to begin grooming immediately. When he came in, Mike started to lose playing time. In fact, he pitched only once the entire month of July. That still was not the worst thing however. When the Detroit Tigers drafted Todd Keel, signed him, and designated him to West Michigan, Coach Cotts stopped working with Mike entirely. Mike would show up every day for their personal workout but Cotts just told him to go pitch in the bullpen, while he concentrated on Keel.

The season ended in late September. Mike had a dismal first season. He finished with two wins, eight losses, and an ERA of 9.57. After the last game, Coach Cotts called Mike into his office. Mike thought this would be an encouraging sign, but when he got in there, Cotts was drunk. Cotts ripped into Mike and told him he'd never make it. Cotts told him he had no talent, and that he wouldn't waste anymore of his time with a failure.

Mike's world seemingly came crashing down around him All light that he had seen at the end of the tunnel vanished into a pitch-black darkness.

His boyhood hero had just called him a failure in a drunken stupor. This may not seem like much but boyhood heroes are something special. To a young boy they offer models of professionalism, and adulthood. Athletes are especially easy to idolize because they do things all little boys dream of doing themselves. Whether it be hitting a home run in the World Series, scoring the winning touchdown in the Super Bowl, or scoring the winning goal in overtime of game seven of the Stanley Cup Finals, athletes do the amazing. Mike had thrown a rubber ball against his brick house many times trying to emulate Cotts. He tried to copy his delivery and his release. He imagined himself striking out the final batter in the World Series for The Detroit Tigers and getting a congratulatory phone call from Cotts himself.

All of that seemed lost now; his hero had called him a failure. His parents echoed the sentiments when he came home for the winter. They told him to stop wasting his time and get a real job and an education. They told him to stop following pipe dreams and settle down. Mike didn't know what to do. He still felt he had baseball in him. But how could he go back to the White Caps? Then right before New Years, he got a phone call from Coach Hamilton. Coach Hamilton said he wanted Mike back. Mike relayed his concerns about Coach Cotts. Coach Hamilton told him not to worry; Coach Cotts had left a local bar and hit a minivan killing a family of four. The police arrested Cotts and charged him with vehicular manslaughter. The White Caps had no choice but to fire Cotts and hire a new coach. The team hired Dave Cleary two weeks after Cotts' arrest. Cleary had been an ace for The Chicago Cubs in the late 1970s until a torn rotator cuff ended his career. Cleary had a reputation of being extremely good at developing young pitchers, plus Hamilton and Cleary wanted Mike to start.

Mike couldn't say no, against his parents' wishes began training like a maniac, and went back to West Michigan for the 1998 season. Mike enjoyed working with Coach Cleary and found him to be much more helpful then Coach Cotts. Coach Cleary also gave him life advice and tried to help him become a better person. Still despite the shame, Coach Cotts faced from his arrest over the winter and his drinking problem, which he hid for years but with his arrest, was now in the public's eye, Mike couldn't help but idolize

Coach Cotts somewhat. In fact, despite the horrible things that Coach Cotts said to him, he still kept the autographed ball and picture as a memory of his hero.

As Coach Hamilton promised, Mike began the season as a starter. Coach Cleary continued to work with him on his curveball. In his first start, it seemed to pay off. He pitched seven shut out innings and struck out career high eight batters. He was very excited. He continued that success into his next start, once again pitching seven innings but this time giving up two runs and walking four. Not a bad outing but could have been better. Coach Cleary continued to focus Mike on working on his curveball. However, the rest of the year, Mike struggled; no matter how much Coach Cleary worked with him, he couldn't consistently control his curveball. Mike finished the 1998 season with a record of eight wins, fifteen losses and an ERA of 8.03. Coach Hamilton and Coach Cleary kept him in the starting rotation for the entire season. At the end of the season Coach Hamilton called him into his office and said "Sorry son, you're a great kid but I'm afraid we won't have a roster spot open for you next year."

Mike knew now that his world had officially ended. There would be no spring training at the end of this winter. In fact, Mike didn't even know what he would do. He had no job, no prospects, no contacts, and not even a single lead. He had gambled all of his chips on baseball and just lost. He Mike had a full house but baseball had a straight flush. Mike had officially washed out. He sat at his locker and cried for three hours. Players came and went throughout that time, a few offered up some sympathy but most went about their business without even noticing.

Finally, Coach Cleary came up and sat down next to Mike. He was holding a book in his hand but Mike didn't bother to look and see what it was. For a moment, Coach Cleary didn't say anything, then he turned to Mike, "Rough day huh kid?"

Mike tried to fight back the tears. He fought valiantly but could not fight them all back. When he had fought back most of them he replied, "Yeah. I've had better."

"I understand. I remember when I tried to come back from my rotator cuff surgery. I had hurt my rotator cuff in May of 1980. They said I would be out the rest of the 1980 season and probably at least the first half of 1981. I had the surgery the first Tuesday in June of 1980. For the entire summer I had to keep my pitching arm immobile. I hated it; I stopped watching my team's games as they made me jealous and angry. I'd sit, watch, and think that I should be out there playing. Why did this have to happen to me? God must hate me."

Just then Mike interrupted Coach Cleary, "Yeah I think that sometimes to."

"Let me finish son. I felt that way all summer. As a result, I began treating my wife and kids badly. I would yell at them for no particular reason and say very hurtful things to them. Luckily, by late September I had healed enough to begin light workouts at the team facility. I purposely began seeing doctors far way from home so I didn't have to be around my family as much. As horrible as it sounds it probably saved my marriage. In the spring of 1981, I was able to train with the Cubs at their spring camp in Mesa Arizona. The excitement of a new season grew larger by the day. The excitement faded when they told me I would have to begin the season on the disabled list. During the first part of the season, I flew all over the country looking for a doctor who would clear me to begin a minor league rehab stint. It took me until early May but I found one in Pittsburgh. I began my minor league rehab starts a week later. My shoulder was still a bit sore when I pitched but I was getting hitters out and that was all that mattered. I didn't bother to notice that I had lost almost 10mph on my fastball. When I got back to The Cubs, major league hitters feasted on my pitching. I could barely hit 85 mph. The first two starts we attributed to rust but after five bad starts in a row, we knew something wasn't right. However, I was convinced that I would be fine. I shot my arm up with cortisone before my next start and pitched well. My fastball got back up to 90 mph and I got a win, that win would be my last. The next morning when I woke up my arm hurt like you wouldn't believe. The slightest movement caused excruciating pain. I went back to a reputable doctor; they took x-rays and came back with bad news. They told me that I had come back too soon and caused irreparable damage to my arm and I would never pitch again. For the next year I lived in a deep depression, I became an alcoholic, I ran through most of my family's savings. Finally one Saturday night in November 1982 my wife gave me an ultimatum, either you quit drinking, come to church with your family, and look for a job, or we're leaving. She took the kids to her mother's that night but before she did, she threw a bible on the table in front of me with some highlighted passages. The bottle landed right next to an open bottle of Jack Daniels. As she was walking out the door, she said, "Make your choice."

"At first I sat in stunned silence. Then I reached for the bottle and took a sip. Then something inside me told me to reach for the bible and give it a chance. I opened and began reading through the highlighted passages. I sat there for several hours as when I looked up I noticed that it was after one in the morning. I looked again at the bottle, and then again at The Bible. I then grabbed the bottle, and dumped its contents down the sink. Then I went to the refrigerator and dumped all the liquor that was still in there. Then I made my way to the liquor cabinet and repeated the same process. Then I sat back down in the living room for about an hour and cried. I thought about how selfish I had been. How I had hurt my family even though I loved them more than anything."

"Even baseball?" Mike asked.

"Even baseball. I picked up the bible and read some more. Then I noticed light was coming into the room. I went into the bedroom, put on my best suit and tie, and waited at the door for my family. When my wife walked in I hugged her stronger than I had ever before. Jamie instantly knew that I had chosen her and the kids over alcohol and began to sob uncontrollably. I sobbed with her. It probably took us an hour to compose ourselves. After we did, we went to the late service. At the service, there was a principal from the local high school. I told him who I was and asked if they needed any help coaching baseball. He informed me that their varsity coach had quit and I told him that I would be interested in the job if it were available. I interviewed that week and got the job. Two years later I was coaching minor league baseball in The Cleveland Indians organization and I have been coaching ever since. So you see Mike when God closes a door he will open a window, you just need to climb in and not worry about what's on the other side."

"Thanks. But right now I think I'm out in the middle of nowhere with no windows in sight for miles."

"I figured that might be your reaction. Always remember that God will lead you to that window. Here is a favorite passage of mine from that fateful night my wife left me with the bible. I must have read this passage twenty times that night, and I still read it in times of struggle. I have printed out a copy for you and I hope that it helps you. It's from the Book of Matthew."

> *So don't worry about these things, saying, 'What will we eat? What will we drink? What will we wear?' These things dominate the thoughts of unbelievers, but your heavenly Father already knows all your needs. Seek the Kingdom of God above all else, and live righteously, and he will give you everything you need.*
>
> *Matthew: 6:31-33*

Mike took the piece of paper from Coach Cleary and said "thank you. I'll definitely look at it." Mike had no intention of looking at it religion wasn't his thing. However, he admired Coach Cleary and didn't want to offend him by not taking the verse.

"On the back of that verse is my phone number. Call me if you need anything. Remember, it's a big world out there. Baseball may not be your thing, but something is." Mike looked up and then turned away. Coach Cleary continued "Mike, there is something out there that you will be better at than anyone and people will praise you for it. I'm just sorry to say for you that it's not baseball. I wish it were because I know what kind of passion you have for the game." Mike kept his head down. Then Coach Cleary helped Mike gather his things, walked him out of the building, and put him on a bus heading home.

By now, Mike was twenty years old and didn't know what to do. He followed his parent's wishes and went to college for business. He never really liked business but he knew he could make money in it and show everyone that told him he was a nobody that he was, in fact, a somebody. He kept Coach Cleary's number but never called it, and certainly never looked at The Bible verse. He thought about calling Coach Cleary now and then but each time put the phone down and thought to himself, "No Coach was just being nice. If I call him he's just going to yell at me and hang up."

Mike went on like this for quite a while. Mike's poor self-image made it difficult for him to communicate with others. Why should he call anybody? In his own mind Mike wasn't important so why would people want to waste time talking to him on the phone. Why should he go talk to that girl? Mike's not important or attractive enough for the girl to give him some of her time to get to know him. Why should he try to get a better job? Mike believed nobody good would hire him. Therefore, why waste the effort in trying if the outcome would be rejection? Mike would lie in bed thinking about these things every night. These thoughts led Mike to begin drinking much more than any man should. The alcohol blocked such thoughts from his mind temporarily, and that solved his problem.

All of these years of rejection and degradation had taken their toll on Mike's self esteem. Mike began to think that all people were out to get him in some way, even the ones that treated him well. Mike met many nice people at college but he never bothered to get to know them because he felt they were hollow people who in the end would only make fun of him. He even felt that way about his parents, all they did was criticize everything he ever loved. They criticized his inability to pick a major in college, and then when he did pick one, they criticized that. They criticized his jobs, no matter what job he had; in their eyes, it wasn't good enough. They criticized his lack of friends, and that just pushed him further away from ever making any friends.

"Why don't you go out and make some friends?"

"Why don't you try networking as they call it?"

"Maybe you can finally get a good job and start making a life for yourself."

"Why don't you find a nice girl to settle down with? A nice girl that will take care of you, people are meant to go through life two by two, not by themselves."

Mike heard all of these criticisms and tried his best to ignore them. He knew he was a good person inside and that his time would eventually come, and then he'd show them all. They would line up to praise his success.

However, during his first three years of college not much went right for Mike. He achieved good marks in his classes and managed to hold a 3.2 grade point average, not a bad average for anyone. Still his parents would nag, "If you don't have a 4.0 you will never get a great job." That pressure did push Mike but at the same time made him so nervous that when he would study he focused more on his parents' words than on the material, and ultimately his grades suffered. The lower grades only brought more nagging from Mike's parents.

Other problems plagued Mike as well. He struggled at finding and holding jobs. He went on countless interviews with major corporations but never got the job.

"You're too young."

"We're looking for someone with experience."

"Your skills just aren't what we're looking for."

"Sorry we've decided to go in a different direction."

Mike heard all the excuses, and eventually became numb. He took his factory job out of desperation. Even though it really wasn't what he wanted to do, it would at least give him enough money to get a decent car and eventually an apartment. At least then, he wouldn't have to listen to so much of his parents' nagging.

So Mike trudged into work at 7 AM every morning, he punched a card, then sat down at a machine, and assembled small parts for eight hours. As Mike sat there, doing his monotonous job day in and day out he began to think that this was no life for him. Ordinarily that kind of thought would motivate someone, but Mike's life was devoid of motivation so the situation seemed increasingly hopeless.

Mike would sit at his machine mindlessly checking parts for defects. The work bored him. Even the inside of the factory bored him. The inside had stale white lighting, bland white walls, a grey floor that looked like the bleakest winter day that you could possibly imagine, and ugly puke green machines that looked like vomit that was never even anything good when it was still food.

The days would pass by seemingly endlessly for Mike. He would spend half of his day thinking about how he wanted to get out of his menial factory job, and the other half lamenting his failed baseball career. He would think that nobody ever believed in him, and that maybe with a little more encouragement, help, and opportunity he could have made a career out of the game. Then Mike would think that it was actually *almost* nobody that ever believed in him. He would often think back to his Grandma Sophie. She was his biggest fan in his early years of T-ball. Grandma Sophie would go to all of his games and cheer for him no matter what. Even if he got out, she would always say something encouraging from the bleachers like "good hit," or "nice try," but always something positive. Mike loved Grandma Sophie. Perhaps even more than he loved his parents at that young age. He loved going over to her house. He would then remember fun times at her house when she would give him all the cookies, ice cream, and pop that he could handle then let him stay up much later than his parents ever would.

The only problem with remembering Grandma Sophie would be that he would begin to think about her death. Her passing had been Mike's first experience with death. He still remembered it like yesterday. The saga began on a warm and humid July morning. Mike had a tee-ball game at 10:30, and looked forward to seeing Grandma Sophie in the stands. When Mike and his mom arrived at the game, he did not see his grandma. He didn't think much about it as he figured that she was running late and would be there before the end of the first inning. This happened sometimes, after all most grandmas didn't move as fast as young people. However, by the end of the game Mike noticed that she still had not arrived. On the way, home he asked his mother if he could call her when he got home and she said that would be fine. Mike got home and dialed his grandma's phone number. "Hi Grandma, it's Mike."

"Oh hello dear, sorry I missed your game, but grandma wasn't feeling well this morning. I wanted to come but thought that it was best for me to stay home and rest. Once you get to be grandma's age, colds and flus hit you quite a bit harder."

"That's all right Grandma, you'll be at the game next week."

"You know me Mike, I'm your biggest fan, and I won't miss two in a row. How did you do today sweetheart?

"I got a triple Grandma! My first one ever! It was awesome, everybody cheered and clapped."

"That's wonderful sweetheart! I wish Grandma could have been there to see it. You'll just have to hit me one next week."

"I will Grandma! I promise."

"Very good dear, now could you put your mommy on the phone for a minute? I'd like to talk to her."

"Ok Grandma."

"Thank you dear. Grandma loves you more than anything."

"I love you too Grandma, here's mom."

"Thank you dear."

Mike never talked to Grandma Sophie again. The next morning Mike was surprised to see that his dad had not gone to work that morning. It was summer vacation and Mike's dad was always gone for work before Mike got out of bed. Mike remembers walking into the kitchen, seeing the expression on his parents' faces, and knowing instantly that something was wrong. Mike's parents then sat him down and told him that Grandma Sophie's heart had broken and stopped working. They didn't know how else to explain a heart attack to a seven year old. Mike went catatonic after that. He didn't know how to understand death. What seven year old does? For that matter, what adult does when it's a beloved family member? Mike emulated his dad in the coming days. His dad remained stoic and quiet during the entire funeral process. Mike figured that was how he needed to behave even though secretly he wanted to cry like a baby because he would never see his grandma again. However, he never did, he remained stoic and unfazed like the other men.

Mike had thought many times about that conversation. It always made him sad. Thinking of her always did. It got so hard to think about her at the factory that he would purposely try not to think about it but the monotony of his job some days made that almost impossible. However, Mike trudged through them like a good soldier does, following the example that his father had always set for him.

Mike still attended classes but to Mike they began to seem hopeless. However, now twenty-four, something was about to change his life in a way he could not imagine.

Chapter 2
Sarah

Sarah loved life. Life seemed to always return her affection. She had bright blonde hair that went half way down her back. She had very full hair, the kind of hair that most girls would kill to have. Sarah also had two bright blue-eyes to go along with her blonde hair. These features alone made her the prototypical American girl. She had a natural light tan that always seemed to glisten in the sun. She was thin but not so thin that she looked like a toothpick. She was by all definitions a very attractive young woman. Sarah seemed to radiate hope and happiness. People often told her that they felt better about their own problems in her presence. Such compliments gave Sarah an intense feeling of satisfaction. She desired nothing more in life than to help other people and make the world a better place.

Sarah grew up in a white-collar neighborhood in Sterling Heights Michigan. She grew up in a neighborhood where doctors, auto executives, and lawyers often lived. People in Sarah's neighborhood always stressed family, education, hard work, and social graces. Sarah's childhood environment had a profoundly different effect on her than Mike's had on him.

As a young child, her parents had nurtured her and made her believe that she could achieve anything. This encouragement always made Sarah feel like anything was possible in life. One day when she was eight years old, she told her parents that she wanted to be the first woman president. Her parents' response to her was "When you are we want to live in The White House."

Eight-year-old Sarah agreed and for the next few months Sarah's life plan was to be president and give her parents a room in The White House. However, during the next school year there was a career presentation made at Sarah's school. The mom of a sixth grader in Sarah's school was a pediatrician and told all these great stories about helping kids recover from illnesses and become regular kids again. Sarah knew at that exact second that a pediatrician was the job for her. She worried as she walked home that her parents would be disappointed in her. She asked her mom, "if I become a pediatrician instead of the president will you and daddy be mad that you won't be able to live in The White House?"

Sarah's mother picked up her little girl, put her on her lap and replied, "Honey, no matter what you decide to do with your life, your father and I will always support you and always be proud of you. We might miss the deluxe accommodations of The White House, but it will be worth it to see our little girl doing something she loves."

"But then I'll be a big girl, not a little girl."

"Yes you will be, but to your daddy and I you will always be our little girl."

From that point on Sarah knew that she would be a doctor. She even started a phase at school in which instead of writing Sarah McDowell on her papers to turn in she would write Dr. Sarah McDowell. Both Sarah's parents and her teacher got a good chuckle out of Sarah's new name.

While in high school she sang in choir, acted in many plays, and became an active member of the school debate team. Sarah was always outgoing and popular yet not so conceited that she would alienate people. She would associate with anyone who took the time to get to know her, which wasn't very hard considering she was very friendly.

She enjoyed going to movies, to concerts, to art shows, and even the occasional night of cruising Gratiot with friends. She loved animals and became an animal rights activist, and cared deeply about saving the rain forests. She was very active in her local church, singing in the choir, and volunteering at many church functions.

Sarah got almost straight A's in high school. She got the occasional B from time to time. She graduated in the top 30 in her class and began attending college right out of high school. Sarah started a pre-med program at The University of Michigan. Sarah felt on her way to achieving her childhood dream of becoming a pediatrician.

Sarah came from a pretty well to do family. Her father was an engineer and always made a good living. Her mother while not having to work did so anyway so her family could have more for themselves. However, her mother worked as a journalist for a local newspaper and as a result was able to do most of her work from home. She only had to go to the office once a week to turn in articles and tie up any loose ends. She worked diligently to accomplish this while Sarah was at school and always made it home before Sarah. In fact, Sarah used to try to race her mother home but her mother always won. Sarah would say, "One day I'm going to beat you mom," but she never did.

When Sarah returned home from school she would always have a nice long talk with her mother. Her parents were always supportive and she always felt comfortable talking with them. Being a girl, she felt more comfortable talking to her mother than her father because she could talk about "girl things" with her mother. Her father whenever he heard the mention of such things always found a reason to excuse himself. He'd make up many different excuses such as "Gotta go work on the car" or "There's a game on that I want to see" to get out of the situation. Sarah and her mother didn't care however; they always enjoyed their "girl talk." They would talk about boys, marriage, things happening at school, friends, college, the future, and of course would share beauty secrets and what not. Sarah treasured these conversations her entire childhood.

When Sarah began her first year of college in the fall of 1996, her excitement was uncontrollable. Her mother even made intimations of giddiness. An entire new world started opening up before her, and she really couldn't wait to be a pediatrician and help those little children. She even pictured herself doing volunteer work in Africa for The Peace Corps. She thought that would be a great way for her to give back.

Her first year of college couldn't have gone better. She earned straight A's in her classes, made the Dean's List, and met a young man named Steve whom she quickly fell in love with.

Steve Sheridan was a year older than Sarah and an Environmental Law major. He wanted to be an environmental activist and make the world a cleaner place for future generations. Sarah loved how goal oriented Steve was;

yet he still had a soft side that only Sarah knew about. That is what attracted Sarah to Steve. He wouldn't let others see it but when they were, alone he always talked about helping the environment. To everyone else he wanted to be the next Al Gore. He only got sentimental about that in front of Sarah. Sarah saw Steve as her ideal. Not only did they both care deeply about helping others, and the environment but both shared common interests and goals as well. Both wanted to eventually settle down and have a family. Both wanted to live in a big house, both were very religious and involved in their own local Catholic churches. They both believed strongly in family values. They both enjoyed cider mills, dining out, going to symphonies, hiking in the woods, and sailing. Also, both Sarah and Steve wanted three children.

Sarah seemed to be living in a dream world. Everything she had ever dreamed of and wanted was at her fingertips. Soon, she thought, soon I will have a great career, a husband who loves me, and children who I will love more than anything.

Her second year of college was a carbon copy of her first. She again got straight A's in all of her classes, she again made the Dean's list, and she again spent every possible free moment with her true love Steve. Sarah never felt better then when she was with Steve. He made her feel like the most important person in the world. He made her feel like the most beautiful girl in the world, and above all, he made her feel loved.

Sarah came home over the summer after her sophomore year and brought Steve with her. Steve met her parents, and the rest of her extended family. They loved him immediately. They saw how happy Steve made Sarah and were happy that she had found someone so special.

Then on July 4, Sarah's dreams came closer to becoming reality when Steve proposed. Steve did this in front of Sarah's entire family at a barbecue. He stood up made a toast to Sarah, and directed everyone's attention to the sky where a sky writer spelled out the words "Sarah, I love you more than anything. Please be my wife" Sarah was so overcome with happiness and joy she couldn't get out an answer, all she could do was nod her head, cry, and fall into Steve's arms.

The two had talked about marriage and decided it was what they both wanted. However, Steve had told her he would not tell her when he would propose. He only told her it would be when she least expected it. He kept true to his word. She never suspected that it would be in front of her family, and she definitely never expected the skywriting. She felt like the luckiest girl in the world to have Steve go to so much trouble just for her. She knew Steve really loved her and she really loved Steve.

Steve would graduate with his degree at the end of the upcoming spring semester. They planned to marry the next summer even though Sarah still had a year of college left. Steve had a good internship lined up for after graduation that he knew would turn into a great career. He would make enough to support both himself and Sarah while she finished her last year of school.

Sarah's happiness continued for the rest of the summer. She had something new and exciting to talk about with her mother. And talk they did, every day until Sarah went back to school they talked and planned next summer's wedding. They were even able to get it set up for Fourth of July Weekend, the anniversary of Steve's proposal. When Sarah left her mom promised that every time she came home for a break she would be waiting for her to plan more of the wedding.

The fall semester was a dream. Sarah became the envy of all of her friends. She had a great fiancé, she was near the top of her class, she was accepted into medical school, and she had a beautiful ring that made all of her friends envious.

When she came home for Christmas things only got better. She had more talks with her mom, and even spent part of the holidays with Steve and his family. Sarah and Steve's mother even began talking the same Sarah talked with her mom. While it was never the same as talking with her mom, she enjoyed this time too. She left Steve's parents house thinking how lucky she must be to have two great maternal figures willing to talk to her and help her.

The second semester went just as well as the first. Sarah again got straight A's. Best of all, she was selected to give an address at a conference of doctors at the end of the semester. Thousands of students, from across the country applied, and were interviewed but Sarah received the honor over all of them. She flew to Washington D.C. to give the speech. She impressed the doctors with her knowledge. At the end of the speech, several doctors approached her and offered her a job when she finished medical school. They all gave her their cards and told her to keep in touch through medical school. She reveled in the accolades so of such highly by such prominent physicians. The entire plane ride home she could barely sit down. Her excitement burst from every pore, in two months, she would be married to her dream man, and with his job, and her prospects they would have that big house in no time. She couldn't wait to tell Steve all about it, and she would. Nevertheless, before that there was someone more important she had to tell. Above everything else, she knew her mom would be waiting for her. They had talked on the phone a week ago and her mom said that she would be right at the kitchen table waiting for her when she got back from the conference.

Sarah literally ran into the house wanting to tell her mom all of the great news. However, when she got in the house she noticed an empty table. She didn't think much of it she just assumed her mother was in the bathroom and would be out in a minute to greet her. She sat down and waited. Five minutes went by and still her mom remained unseen, she began to think that something might be wrong. The door being open and nobody being or coming into the kitchen left Sarah with an ominous feeling.

Finally, she cried out "Mom, it's me; I'm home, everything all right?"

About thirty seconds later her Aunt Mary emerged from the back of the house

"Sarah, you'd better sit down."

Sarah turned pale; she knew something bad had happened. She knew her mother wouldn't have missed her homecoming, especially with the wedding coming up in two months. They had so much to plan and do.

Aunt Mary continued "Sarah, for about the last three months your mother has been having terrible headaches. The doctors couldn't find any cause for them. They prescribed pain medication and that seemed to help. However, two days ago your mother collapsed at home. Your father found her when he came home from work. He called 911. An ambulance came and rushed her to the hospital. The doctors found a large tumor at the base of her brain. There is nothing they can do; the cancer is too advanced for chemotherapy and radiation, and too big to remove. She will pass away within the next month."

A glazed look fell over Sarah's face. She didn't know what to say. She didn't know what to do. All she could do was sit at the table and cry. She began thinking about all of the things her mother would miss, her wedding, her graduation, her children, everything. Everything she and her mother had talked about and planned over the years her mother would now miss.

After several minutes, she picked her head up and cleared away enough tears to talk coherently. "Where's my dad?"

"He's at the hospital sweetheart. He's been there almost non-stop since your mother went in. He's only come home to shower and sleep briefly. He's begun living on hospital cafeteria food and McDonalds."

"Can you take me there?"

"Of course honey. I've made a big pot of vegetable soup. I was waiting for you to come with me to take some over. Would you like some?"

'Not now, I just want to see my mom."

"I understand. Do you want me to fix you a bowl for later?"

"No. I just want to see my mom."

"Okay. Lets get in the car. Your dad left your mom's keys so I can drive you over."

Sarah did not respond. She got in the car crying softly and the tears continued to flow for the entire trip.

She spent the next two weeks at the hospital at her mother's bedside. Her mother would wake up for brief periods each day. Each time Sarah would try to talk to her in a vain attempt to try to regain some of the innocence and youth stolen from her by this awful disease. However, her mother could barely speak, and by the end of the two weeks, she would barely even wake up each day.

Sarah would stay at the hospital around the clock. Her father, other family members and the hospital staff would try to convince her to go home and sleep, or go out and have some fun but she refused. She refused to leave her mother's side just as she had refused to leave hers. She sat there day in day out, night in night out, hoping, praying for a miracle. The miracle never came. Just two and a half weeks after she returned home, her mother passed away quietly in the night.

The worst part about it was that when her mother died Sarah had nodded off to sleep in a chair next to her mother's bed. When the nurse awoke Sarah to tell her the news, she erupted in tears. Not only tears of sadness, but there was a sinister tinge to these tears not present before. As she cried she started shouting out "I wasn't here," "I wasn't here." When the nurse asked her what she meant she said, "I fell asleep. I promised my mom I would be here to help her when she died, but I fell asleep. I broke the last promise I ever made to my mom, and she never broke a promise to me. I'm a failure. I'm worthless, I couldn't even stay awake for my mom." The nurse tried to reassure her that it was not her fault and that her mother would not be upset with her for falling asleep but to no avail. Sarah could not be consoled.

When her father arrived at the hospital he tried to console Sarah and tell her, it was all right that she had fallen asleep. "Honey, it's okay. You're mom won't be mad."

She just silently replied, "No."

"Nobody can stay awake twenty four seven."

"No."

"Even the disciples couldn't stay awake in the garden, remember?"

"No."

"I'm sure your mother is glad that you weren't awake. No parent wants their child to watch them die."

"No, I failed mom when she had never failed me."

"Come on honey, lets go home and try to get some sleep."

Sarah didn't respond, just melted in her dad's arms. A nurse helped Sarah's dad guide her to the car. Sarah sat in the passenger seat sobbing hysterically the whole drive home. When they returned home, Aunt Mary helped Sarah's dad walk her to her bedroom. Aunt Mary gave her some sleep medication to relax her. Finally, after crying in bed for an hour, Sarah fell asleep. Everybody assumed Sarah would slowly begin to feel better the next day. None of them had any idea what lay in store.

After Sarah fell asleep, her father called Steve and told him what had happened. Sarah had apparently not called Steve since she returned; she had been too busy at the hospital. Steve had left messages for Sarah never called him back. Steve began to grow concerned, and while Sarah's father's description of the events had been difficult for Steve to hear, he became somewhat relieved that Sarah was not sick, or injured. She had told her dad that she had called him back but that had been a lie. She only wanted to see her mom. She wanted to focus all her attention on her mom and Steve would have just taken attention from her mom.

Steve was to start his new internship in a week but drove down immediately, despite needing to get things in order for his new job. When Sarah woke up Steve was sitting in a chair next to her bed.

"What are you doing here?" She said when she woke and saw him sitting there.

"Your father called me and told me what happened. Why didn't you call and tell me? I would have spent the whole time at your side."

"You couldn't be here it just had to be my mom and me. Why can't anybody understand that?"

"Honey, I love you. I want to help you."

"You can't, nobody can."

"Don't say that. I'm here for you, your family is here, my family is here, and so are all your friends. We all want to help. Let us."

"You can't. Nobody had the relationship with her that I did. It was special. Now she's gone, and I'll never have that back, ever."

"I know it's hard for you right now. But just think, we are getting married in July, we're getting an apartment, and we're starting our life together. Now I know that I can't replace your mother but I do love you very much, and hope to have a similar deep relationship with you."

"No! No! I can't right now. My mom was planning that wedding with me. I don't think I can go through with it now, it will be too painful, I'm sorry."

"That's ok we can push it back until you are ready. I'll wait for you."

"Thank you. I will warn you it could be a while."

Steve feeling very confident said "I understand, I'm sure once you get back to school, start working towards medical school again, and start having fun with friends again you'll be all right."

"No I'm not going back, I can't, it's too hard."

"I understand "You've got other things to work through right now. Get yourself together and then you can start to move on. I'm going to go help your dad with some arrangements. Aunt Mary is here if you need anything." Steve assumed it was just the grief talking and that by the fall Sarah would be at least close to normal. However, he had no idea of the pit of agony that had formed and continued to deepen quickly inside his fiancée.

The summer continued, without a wedding for Sarah and Steve. Because of her mother's death, Sarah could barely leave her bedroom let alone go to a wedding. Periodically Steve and some other of Sarah's friends would stop by to console her. However, nobody could take the pain of losing her mother away.

As time went by people expected Sarah to get better however, she seemed to only get worse. Eventually she started keeping her curtains closed all day as to let no sunlight in. She locked her bedroom door and went through long periods of time in which she would not see anyone. She ate very little; her father would catch her occasionally nibbling on some dry cereal and would try to talk to her. However, Sarah would not respond, she just sat with her head sunk down seemingly shell-shocked.

The bright summer eventually faded into a cool fall. Everybody tried to get Sarah to return to school and finish her degree, but she just could not do it. The only excuse she would give was that she needed some time off. Everybody seemed to understand that her mother's passing had been difficult and she needed some time to recover. However, The University of Michigan removed her from the pre-med program when she did not enroll for fall. They told her that part of the requirements of staying in the program were that she had to maintain a full course load each semester which she had failed to do by not registering. Her family and friends begged her to attempt reinstatement but she refused. She did not have the energy anymore.

Her relationship with Steve became more distant as well. He worked long hours at his internship and met many new and interesting people. Steve began hanging out and having fun with them. Occasionally he thought of Sarah but for the most part, she moved to the back of his mind. Steve tried to get Sarah to go to various functions with him, plays, lectures, picnics, all things she had once enjoyed doing with Steve she would not do. He begged her to come to parties thrown by his company but she refused. He would beg her "Honey this is very important, all the bosses have their wives with them and all the interns their girlfriends. I end up out of the loop at the parties because of it. I know it's hurting my chances of getting hired full time, could you please just come to the one next Saturday?"

"Sorry Steve, but I can't." She responded and then hung up the phone.

For the next two weeks she heard nothing from Steve, then one day she received a letter in the mail, the letter read:

Dear Sarah,

Honey, I have tried and tried to help you through the death of your mother. However, the more I try the more you just push me away. You are no longer the girl that I fell in love with. The bright, energetic, goal oriented girl that I fell in love with has disappeared. I can no longer stay in this relationship; I have needs that you can no longer satisfy. I thought you would be an asset as my girlfriend during my internship, when instead you have been nothing but a liability. If I am not offered a permanent position, I will hold you responsible. I have met someone else. Someone who is goal oriented, happy, successful, and after the finer things in life like I am and you used to be. She goes with me to the parties now, and while I still feel bad about your mother's death, I don't understand why you can't just get over it and move on. That is what your mother would have wanted

Farewell Sarah, I hope you find what you're looking for. However, if what you want is to remain a useless vegetable for your whole life so be it. I cannot be a part of that; the world is too big for me

Good Luck,
Steve

At last came the rapid descent to the bottom ended with a resounding thud. Sarah had gone from the epitome of happiness to the lowest scurvy depths of despair and loneliness. Her mother whom she had loved more than anyone else was gone. The man who she loved had pretty much called her worthless. For the first time Sarah's life had become pointless.

Sarah lay in bed remembering the happiness of last Christmas, lost all control of her emotions, and decided to end her life. She went into her father's liquor cabinet, found a bottle of whiskey, drank half of it, and then took a half bottle of sleeping pills. She collapsed on the floor. Her father who had stepped out for a moment to go buy some groceries heard a loud crash as he unlocked the door. He rushed in and found Sarah unconscious on the floor. He saw the bottle of pills and the half empty liquor bottle and immediately called 911. Paramedics came, rushed Sarah to the hospital, and revived her.

At this point Sarah's family had two choices, they could take her home once the doctors cleaned her system out or put her under suicide watch. On Christmas Eve, Sarah's father along with her Aunt Mary and her cousin Amanda decided it was best to put her under suicide watch. At least that way she could get some counseling and recover. Her family knew that Sarah needed them more than ever. They knew they couldn't leave her alone in the hospital on Christmas. Therefore, her father arranged to have Christmas dinner, her presents, and her family come to the hospital and surprise her. They all snuck into her room early Christmas morning and surprised her.

Sarah was initially startled but somewhere deep inside her a warm feeling started to grow. A feeling that she had not had since her mother had been alive and while she was a long way from being back to normal it was a start. Even her father and a couple of her cousins caught a brief smile on Sarah's face as they had a Christmas feast. Even Sarah partook in the Turkey, stuffing, mashed potatoes with gravy, corn, cranberry sauce, and yes even a couple Christmas cookies. Sarah knew in her heart that this was the best day she had had since her mother died. Although it wasn't much it was a start on a long road to recovery, a road in which her family would be with her every step of the way.

Chapter 3
Family

It's funny how a person's family can influence their life. In the case of Mike, his mind lead him to believe that his family always told him he was not good enough and put him down. In Mike's mind, nothing he ever did was good enough for his family. His grades were never good enough in school, he was never good enough at baseball, he didn't go to college, he refused to stop chasing pipe dreams, when he did go to college, he didn't go to the right school, and his jobs were never up to his parents' standards. Mike just accepted these setbacks as part of life.

That kind of life had landed Mike at his current point. Twenty-four, living in his parent's basement, struggling his way through college, a failed baseball player, and stuck in a menial job which would never meet his or his parents' expectations.

Everything for Mike, throughout his whole life revolved around pleasing his parents. He would get a B in class; they would say why isn't it an A? Mike then would walk slowly back to his room rejected, not noticing the tone that suggested a B was good but you can do better. It just never occurred to Mike that his parents had different ways of expressing appreciation than Mike realized. His parents were not even happy for him when he pitched his shut out for the White Caps. Right after the game ended, he called home. "Dad, guess what?"

"I don't know."

"I pitched a shutout today."

"Why did you call to tell me that? Big deal, so you pitched a shut out. Get over yourself. I'm going back to watching TV, stop bothering us with useless stuff like that."

That phone crushed Mike's soul. He could not figure out what he had to do to get his parents to love him. It stayed in the back of his mind for a long time. In fact, it probably had something to do with him washing out in the minor leagues. Whenever he would pitch after that phone call he always heard his dad's voice in the back of his mind telling him that he wasn't good enough. Even if those were not his dad's exact words, Mike always interpreted them in that way.

Even after baseball, Mike's relationship with his parents remained strained. He went to college as they asked, but that did not improve anything. Mike did his best to avoid his parents, which was difficult because Mike's dad always stayed up late watching television. Therefore, Mike began staying out later and later most nights to avoid his dad. He mainly hung out in local bars. Which would have been a good thing had he frequented bars that attracted single women his own age. Perhaps he could have met a girl who would have built him up instead of tearing him down. However, Mike frequented small bars that attracted mainly middle-aged rednecks. Mike didn't mind though. Most of the men in there kept to themselves or their group, and Mike could easily sit quietly by himself in the corner and enjoy his drink of choice for the evening. When Mike first started going he mainly drank beer. Mike would sit at a table in the corner, nurse three or four beers over about four hours, and then head home. Stumbling in after midnight, sometimes his dad would be up, sometimes he would be asleep on the couch, and Mike could sneak quietly into his room. Mike did not want to stay out much later than that because he did have to get up for work in the morning. He took mainly night classes at college so he did not have to be home much during the day, which kept him away from his nagging parents. He'd get up at six o'clock in the morning, be out the door at 6:45, be at work by seven o'clock, work until four o'clock, come home shower, head to McDonald's or Burger King for dinner, go to class, then head to the bar, and finally head home around midnight.

After keeping this schedule for about six weeks, it really began to wear on Mike. There started to be mornings in which he could barely get up for work. For a while, he was able to manage but after about a month of barely making it he began to be five to ten minutes late on a very regular basis. After doing this for about a month, he got a notice with his paycheck, the notice read:

Dear Mr. Larson

You have been late three or more times within the last month. That counts as one unexcused absence. Should you have another unexcused tardy within the next ninety days your file will be reviewed, with one of the following actions taken, suspension for one week or termination. Here at Thompson Molding Inc. it is our policy to maintain a strict attendance policy. Our customers are our highest priority and poor attendance by our employees jeopardizes the outstanding service that we give to our clients. This is the only such warning that you will receive.

Thank You
Management

Mike knew he had to straighten up to keep his job. He started going to the bar less and spent more time at home. He tried his hardest but always felt uncomfortable around his parents. After a solid three weeks of staying home most nights and getting the necessary amount of sleep he started going back to the bar every night. Not that his parents really did anything to cause him to go back to the bar, Mike's lack of comfort at home eventually made staying home difficult to stand. About two weeks later on a Friday, Mike showed up five minutes late for work. At the end of his shift, the plant manager called him into his office.

"You wanted to see me, Jim?"

"Yes Mike, come in have a seat." Jim replied. "Mike, your tardiness is becoming a problem. Because you are often late we don't put you on a machine, then we start to shut machines down and you come in right in the middle of that process. The machines will break if restarted during the shut down process. This forces us to finish the shut down process, which can take fifteen to twenty minutes. Then we have to restart a machine for you, which can take up to another half hour. This means you are sitting and doing nothing for almost an hour while we are paying you for it. As a result of all of these factors, you have become a liability to this company and we are going to have to let you go."

Mike thought for a minute and spoke up. "Jim, I know I screwed up but I promise I won't be late again. I need this job to pay for college."

"We're way past that point now. You had your chance and you blew it."

"What if I come in late again I just sit and wait for a machine without punching in? Then I'm not costing the plant any money."

"Sorry, what's done is done. You can pick up your last check in a week."

Mike realized that he would be unable to change Jim's mind. He faked a smile, thanked Jim for the opportunity, apologized for being late, and walked out of the plant.

When Mike got to his car, he didn't know what he would do. He knew what his parents' reaction to him losing his job would be. He knew that they would never let him hear the end of it. Mike drove around for a while, and ended up stopping at a local mall. As he walked through he noticed a help wanted sign in the window of a sporting goods store. Mike thought to himself, wow that would be a cool job and they don't open until nine, so I could stay out late and not worry about being late for work. In addition, most of these places will work around a person's school schedule. Mike got excited; he went inside and asked for an application. The man behind the counter was tall, probably around 6 foot 2, had short brown hair and a medium complexion. The man's appearance worried Mike somewhat as he seemed like just the kind of person with which Mike usually did not relate well. Mike thought if this man was the manager, it might hinder his chances for getting the job. He hoped the man just worked as a sales representative at the store. Mike filled out the application. In the references section he decided not to put anyone from his old factory job because of his firing. Suddenly, he remembered that he still had Coach Cleary's phone number so he put Coach Cleary down as a reference.

When he completed the application, he handed it to the man behind the counter. His previous hope about the man behind the counter not being the manager were dashed when the man said "Well right now I'm just taking applications, I'll be calling back for interviews next week." He then looked at the back of Mike's application and said "Hey, you know Dave Cleary?'

"Yes, he was my pitching coach for a year with the West Michigan White Caps." Mike replied.

"Really? What's he like? I remember watching him pitch when I was a kid."

"Great guy, helped me with a lot of things."

"Hey if you have a few minutes now come on back and we'll go over this application together."

"Sure."

"Great come on back. My name is Todd Hatch. I'm the manager of this store. Keith, watch the register while I'm in back."

Mike shook the man's hand and introduced himself.

"So you played ball?"

"Yes I played two seasons for the West Michigan White Caps,"

"How did you get to know Dave Cleary?"

"He was my pitching coach for the second year I played with the White Caps."

"How come you're not still playing? Injury?"

Now Mike thought for a minute, he didn't want to tell Todd that he had washed out, and he just began to hope that Todd would never call Coach Cleary and after a long pause Mike said, "I tore my rotator cuff at the end of my second season. After that I could never get good velocity on my fastball anymore."

"Wow that's too bad, man. It must have been nice having people cheer for you in the stands. I bet your parents enjoyed seeing you pitch."

"My parents never bothered to come watch me pitch. My dad didn't even care when I called home and told him that I pitched a shutout."

"Tough break. Sorry to hear that."

"Thank You."

"Well, I'd love to sit here and just talk baseball but I wouldn't be doing my job if I didn't ask you about your application and work history."

Mike felt a bit nervous. He had just been fired, but he remained calm and collected and replied, "Fire away sir."

"Well, it says here you've been working at Suburban Plastics. Why do you want to leave there?"

"Well, I don't like getting up at 6AM for work, it's dirty, and it can be very hot or cold in the plant depending on the weather. I just want a change, if possible."

"Well, here the earliest you'd have to start would be nine o'clock, would that be a problem?"

"No that would be great."

"I see you go to school as well. Will you need us to work around that schedule?"

"Yes." Will that be a problem?"

"No not at all. Most of my staff is in school right now. Just write down your school schedule on a sheet of paper and I'll work around it when I fill out the schedule."

"What are you majoring in?"

"Business management."

"That's good. Once you get your degree there will be many advancement opportunities for you."

"Good. I'd like to find a company that I can start out at the bottom and work my way up."

"You've picked a great company to apply for then. This company believes in promotion from within. I started out as a sales rep, and then became an assistant manager, and when I finished school, I became the manager of this store. I did all of this in five years."

"Did you start here in college?"

"No I started in high school."

"So do you think my path to advancement could be quicker than five years."

"That's up to you. If you work hard, the only roadblock would be how long it would take you to get your degree. The sooner you got it, the sooner you could advance to general manager."

"That's what I wanted to hear!"

Todd glanced up at Mike. I like your enthusiasm. “When can you start?”

Mike was shocked. Nothing had ever come this easy for him, especially something that seemed this good. He could hardly contain himself. Nevertheless, he collected himself and thought for a moment. He told Todd that he needed to give his factory job one week’s notice before he left. Todd understood that and said, “So, you can start one week from tomorrow?”

“Yes, that would be great.”

“All right we’ll see you next Saturday at nine o’clock; I see the potential for rapid advancement in your future.”

Mike was unbelievably excited. He couldn’t remember the last time he had been this excited. It was probably when he made the White Caps, but even this seemed better than that. It may have been because it was current--somehow excitement always seems stronger in the moment than in the past. Mike thought perhaps the excitement of a wedding day or the birth of a child was just as exciting in the future as in the past but he couldn’t be sure. Mike had not yet experienced any of those things so he had no measure of comparison.

When he got home, he didn’t tell his parents about his new job. The thought of it terrified him. He merely decided to hang around the college during the day for the next week during his shift to fool his parents. That way they would never suspect the factory fired him. The move worked for Mike as the worst thing to come out of it was that he got a little bored hanging around the college all day. Yet, before he knew it his first day at the sporting goods store had arrived. His mother was shocked that he was up so early on a Saturday morning but didn’t ask him any questions. Mike believed that he would pull off the lie. What he failed to realize would be just how difficult the lie would be to carry off. Mike soon discovered that if he woke up later than his regular time for his factory job his parents would get suspicious. Therefore, Mike began getting up early once again, which defeated the whole purpose of having a job that started later. He would drive to the mall early and try to catch some sleep in the car but this created a new set of problems.

The situation was much different for Sarah. Sarah had always had unconditional support from her family and had achieved great things up until the death of her mother. Sarah had hit rock bottom when she had attempted suicide. It just goes to show that even with a supportive family and every advantage available a person can still lose their way. The Christmas dinner arranged by her family did a great deal to help Sarah begin to turn the corner and realize that her life was not over just because her mother ha died. She knew how much her father had loved her mother and as she saw him happy, strong, and celebrating with the people he loved, and the people who loved him back, suddenly everything seemed possible again. Despite this realization, Sarah still had a long way to go. After everyone else had left the Christmas dinner, her dad stayed behind for a while to visit with his daughter.

"You know, I saw that smile come across your face earlier."

Sarah kind of smiled and put her head down.

"Ahh...there it is again. Look Sarah, we all miss your mother. She was a remarkable woman and there isn't a day that goes by that I don't think of her. Your mother was always a very happy person and was always very full of life. She wouldn't want any of us to be so sad about her death, especially you. She loved you so much and wanted so much for you in your life that I know it must be very sad for her to be looking down from heaven and seeing you like this."

"I know. Life just seems so empty now."

"Life is never empty. There is always something to live for. Eventually you'll see this."

"I want to believe you are right. Deep down I know you are. Still, nothing seems as it should right now."

"I know, it's hard on all of us, especially at this time of year because she loved Christmas so much. Remember how she used to always go all out decorating the house? Well why do you think I didn't this year? That was always one of her favorite things and I just didn't have the strength to do so. I was barely able to muster up the strength to put up the Christmas tree. We'll develop new family traditions. You'll get married, have a family, and start new traditions. While it will never be the same as what we remember with mom it will be special nonetheless."

"I hope you're right." Sarah said with a small smile running across her face.

"Caught you again." Sarah laughed at her dad's quick comment.

"Can't get anything past you can I?"

"Right now I'm just paying very close attention to everything you do. As you get better I will almost certainly notice less."

"I sure hope so."

Sarah's dad smiled. This conversation was the first real conversation he had with Sarah since her mother's death. It gave him a warm feeling inside. However, he knew that he needed to go and let Sarah get some rest.

"I need to go for now dear. But before I do I want to give you something. I found this passage highlighted in your mother's Bible. She dated it about a week after she started having those headaches. She wrote next to it 'for my family in my absence.' It's almost as though she knew her time was near and she wanted to leave us with something to help us after she died. I brought it here for you today. I'm going to read it once with you and then let you read it and reflect on it as much as you desire."

He handed Sarah her mother's Bible and then pulled out one he had just purchased recently. They opened to a passage and her father began to read.

"Don't let your hearts be troubled. Trust in God, and trust also in me. There is more than enough room in my Father's home. If this were not so, would I have told you that I am going to prepare a place for you? When everything is ready, I will come and get you, so that you will always be with me where I am. And you know the way to where I am going." "No, we don't know, Lord," Thomas said. "We have no idea where you are going, so how can we know the way?" Jesus told him, "I am the way, the truth, and the life. No one can come to the Father except through me."

John 14:1-6

After he finished reading he brushed his daughter's hair back, gave her a kiss on the forehead, and said "get some rest honey, I'll see you tomorrow."

"Thank you daddy, it's like mom's final Christmas gift to us."

A tear rolled down her father's cheek as he kissed her on the forehead and then left Sarah to sleep.

Sarah read the passage a few more times that night, and each time she thought about her mother, and each time she got a feeling that everything would be all right. Then shortly after midnight she drifted off to sleep.

Chapter 4
Hardship

Hardship is a concept that is difficult for anyone to understand, especially the person who happens to be experiencing a great deal of it. Mike was exactly that person. Mike had never really had anything go easily in his life; everything had come through much suffering and difficulty. Mike didn't know things could come easily because they never had. He had to try out for the West Michigan Whitecaps, he wasn't invited, he had to deal with coaches who belittled him, and even when the coaching staff changed and he had support, he seemed to lose his stuff and fail anyway. Mike had always had difficulty in school and struggled to pass all of his classes at times, and struggled to get along with his parents on a daily basis.

So when Mike seemingly got a great job, with a great boss right after losing his factory job he thought something must be wrong. He couldn't see how there was any possibility that he could have anything work out this well. On top of all of that, he managed to hide his firing from the factory from his parents who would have crucified him for losing his job. Mike did not understand how this all had worked out but also didn't care. He had what he wanted and nothing else mattered.

Humans have always been creatures of habit. Throughout history, they have tended to build themselves up a nice routine in work, school, family, social, love, and professional lives. It's sort of a comfort zone, which most people are terrified to leave, even if that area outside the comfort zone is better than the area inside the comfort zone. People from the beginning of time have struggled to believe that something that they do not know can be something better than they know. Perhaps it goes back to when Adam and Eve ate of the forbidden fruit. They partook of the tree they knew was forbidden by God and as a result lost Eden. Maybe that is why people stay in these comfort zones which often leaves things unsaid, jobs undone, loves unloved, and accomplishments unaccomplished. Only the biggest risk takers leave their comfort zones, and although sometimes they meet with disappointment, many times they meet with great happiness, success, love, careers, and satisfaction.

Mike did not have the risk taker gene. His experiences had removed all willingness to take risk from his personality. Anything that happened to him that he perceived as good was out of his comfort zone because good things didn't happen to him. When in reality good things could and did happen to him, he just was not allowing them to happen. He would unconsciously sabotage any good thing that ever happened to him. Without even realizing it every good thing that ever happened to him in his entire life, he found a way to turn it into a bad thing.

By lying to his parents about his new job, he continued the cycle. He discovered that if he didn't continue to get up at his regular time for his factory job they would get suspicious. So Mike would get up at factory time, leave drive to the empty mall parking lot and try to sleep. The problem arose when Mike would fall asleep in his car and oversleep. A few times, he woke up at 9:15 and had to run in and change clothes in a mall bathroom, which got him into work at about 9:25. After a few occurrences of this, Todd had no choice but to step in. Todd talked to Mike about his tardiness and for a while, Mike got it under control

However, other parts of his job began to suffer. Like many other good things that had happened to him, he began to subconsciously sabotage his job. He would put stock in the wrong places, charge people the wrong price at the register, give people the wrong change on purchases, and perhaps the worst of all he started showing up late again. Mike knew he needed to get to work on time he just couldn't make it happen. He also continued drinking heavily, not so much because he was unhappy now but because he wanted to be unhappy, and he saw drinking as kind of a means to an end. It had ruined countless lives in the past so why couldn't it ruin his?

Mike had a blueprint of what he thought would happen. He thought first Todd would bring him into his office to tell him to straighten up. Then Todd would write him up once or twice. Finally, Todd would tell him he had no choice but to let him go, and then he would rationalize that Todd never gave him a real chance, and thus the firing would be Todd's fault. Mike had this very vicious psychological cycle down to a science.

Finally, about a month after being hired Todd called Mike into his office. He knew how this conversation would go. He played it out in his head at least a hundred times. Todd would reprimand him, make threats, and tell him to get it going or he would be out. That is how it would work. Mike refused to believe there was any other way it could work.

Mike walked with Todd into his office in the stock room. Todd sat down at his desk and told Mike to sit in the chair across from him. Mike knew exactly where this was going and was ready, or so he thought.

"Mike, I want to talk to you about your performance so far. How do you think your performance has been so far?"

Mike thought about how to respond to this, no boss had ever asked him what he thought of his performance. They always *told* him how he was doing. Mike thought for a minute and then responded by saying "I think I'm doing pretty good, but there are still a few things I need to learn." Mike liked that answer it said that he was doing well but it left Todd an opportunity to cut Mike down. Mike clenched his teeth, ready for Todd to belittle him. Belittlement had become like a drug to Mike and he had actually come to like the feeling.

Todd thought for a second and then began "Mike, that's how I expected you to be doing at this point when I hired you."

Mike thought to himself "Yeah, bring it on Todd, prove to me you're just like all the others, just go ahead and prove it."

"However, that's not where I see you right now. What I see is an extremely smart and talented guy that lacks confidence in himself."

Mike definitely did not expect this, and he did not know how to respond. All he could get out was a "What?"

"Exactly, you don't know what, because I don't think you've ever had a positive situation in your life. Mike, on your first day I watched you work, much of the time without you even realizing it. What I saw was a very eager and excited kid walk into my store around nine o'clock in the morning. About three minutes later, I saw a kid who became scared, and unsure of himself, and his surroundings. It was a very odd thing and I couldn't really understand it. I hoped that you would grow out of it but that hasn't happened. So, I want to ask you what the problem is. I know it's not the job, you could do this job in your sleep."

Mike had not prepared for this kind of talk from Todd. He really had no idea how to even respond. He was drowning, searching for a life raft but there was none in sight. His face had grown deathly pale. Todd, as he was watching Mike, noticed this and spoke up "I can see you are unprepared to respond to this and I kind of expected that. Mike today is Friday. You are on the schedule both tomorrow and on Sunday. I want you to take those two days off, and I want you to come up north with me to my family's cottage on Lake Superior.

"But...but, my parents, how will I explain this to them, I mean they still think I'm working at the factory, they'll kill me, I can't possibly go."

Don't worry about your parents. Come on man, you're in your twenties; they should be the least of your worries. But if you want when I come to pick you up I'll tell them I'm a friend who works with you at the factory."

"But they'll know, they'll know it's a lie."

"Mike, don't worry, everything will be fine, just trust me. Go home tonight, pack some things, and get some sleep, I'll be by at eight o'clock, tomorrow morning to pick you up. Just be ready, this weekend is going to change your life."

Mike reluctantly agreed. He stumbled out of the store confused and unsure of everything. Why had Todd invited him up north? Why couldn't Todd just yell at him and tell him to get in gear like everyone else? Most importantly, what would he tell his parents, and what would they think?

Mike stumbled around the mall for a good hour then he took to the streets. Finally, he found his favorite watering hole, went in, and began drinking. He needed to forget, he needed to wash away the fear of what would happen tomorrow morning. He had one beer, and then another, and another, and then he finished his fourth beer within the first hour he was in the bar. He felt buzzed, but not buzzed enough; he needed something stronger, something not just to dull the fear but also to take it away entirely. He started with shots of Jack Daniels, did about five of those, and then he noticed he was getting low on cash. By now, he was completely drunk. In his haze, he decided to leave the bar and go just blow the rest of his money on a fifth of Bacardi 151. He thought, yes that will do me up good and take away all the pain. He got the bottle, also got a two-liter of Coke to chase it down with, and went home. He took two small glasses and filled one halfway with the rum and the other halfway with Coke. He would slam the rum and then the Coke. After finishing half of the bottle, he passed out on his parents' front porch. When his parents saw him, they started yelling at him but he would not wake up. Already disgusted, they left him lying passed out on the front porch.

Todd pulled up promptly at eight o'clock the next morning. He saw Mike lying passed out on the porch, but wasn't surprised. Todd woke up Mike. Mike said half asleep, "What, where am I? What am I doing out here? What are you doing here? Where's my bottle?"

"Easy Mike. Remember, I'm taking you up north this morning."

"No. My parents are going to kill me. I can't go anywhere."

"Don't worry it's all going to work out."

Mike and Todd walked in to find his parents sitting at the kitchen table having their morning coffee. "Well, well, well, look what the cat dragged in. How's your head?"

"And who is this? Thanks for waking our son up and bringing him in. What made you take pity on him?"

"Sir, I work with your son at the factory. Your son is a great worker and a great person."

"I hope you're not his boss. I'd hate to have you see him like this. He can do better if he just buckles down and starts working harder. No offense to you or your factory but he should be done with college and have a great job by now."

"Well maybe he's just a slow starter. Maybe he just needs more help and encouragement and he would be just fine. Some people do develop quicker than others you know."

"We have encouraged him plenty."

"Really? Then why didn't you ever go see him pitch when he was with the Whitecaps? Why did you tell him throwing a shutout was not a big deal?"

"Look sir, I don't know who you are but don't speak of things of which you don't know. We wanted to go see him. The problem was I couldn't miss work. We went through much of our savings when I was out of work and as much as I wanted to, I couldn't miss a day of work to see him pitch. The company would have fired me and we would have been in danger of losing our house. So that's why, that's why we never went to see him pitch. I've replayed that phone conversation we had after his shutout many times. I told him it wasn't a big deal because at the time for me it wasn't. I was late on our mortgage payment and afraid of losing this house. I didn't want my boy to think I was a failure. That's why I said what I said. I wish I could take it back but I can't."

"Well I had no idea, Mike never told me that. I apologize if I offended you in any way, but why do you put down his job at the factory, and other jobs he has had in the past?"

"Perhaps I should have, but I still think not telling him was best."

"Look, I don't have all morning to sit here and argue with you. I'm taking Mike up north with me for the weekend. He's going to start getting the help he needs up there. I'll bring him back Sunday night."

"Please, do all you can. I know it seems like we don't care about him but we do. We just know he could be doing so much better than he is."

"You know what, Mr. Larson? Mike asked me not to tell you this but I'm going to anyway. I don't work at the factory with Mike. I manage Johnson's Sporting Goods in the mall. Mike has been working there for me for a month. He's following a new dream and he was scared to tell you. He's going to make assistant manager soon."

"Does he like the job?"

"I think he loves it."

"Well if he's up for assistant manager he must be pretty good at it."

"He is."

"Thank you for helping him,"

"You're welcome. Maybe I'm out of line here but may I suggest telling him about your financial issues. It may help him understand your actions and feel better about them."

"I'll at least think about it."

"That's all I can ask."

Just then, Mike came into the kitchen with a bag, visibly hung-over. He looked like he had not slept or eaten in weeks and he smelled like a combination of whiskey, pretzels, and cigarette smoke. Mike and Todd left the house. Mike did not say a word to his parents. He just walked out the door and into the passenger seat of Todd's car. Mike had a terrible hangover. He had suffered through many hangovers before but never one like this. It felt like a hundred heavy metal bands were playing in his head at the same time. Todd had some coffee ready for him to help soothe the hangover. Todd tried to talk a little to Mike on the way up but saw how badly hung-over Mike was and just gave up and told Mike to rest, they had a big weekend in front of them.

Mike sat quietly in the passenger seat and thought about all that had gone on. Although not an active participant in the proceedings, he knew everything going on in his parents' kitchen. He thought "What are my parents gonna do to me? What did Todd mean by that assistant manager remark? Why did they just sit there quietly at the end?' Will they let me into the house when I get home?" All these questions weighed on Mike's mind. Finally, he drifted off to sleep for most of the drive north. A sleep he badly needed, for it would be along weekend that would begin to change his life.

Hardship had been a completely different thing for Sarah. She had never really experienced hardship. Everything had been perfect for her. That is why when her mother died things unraveled so drastically for her. She did not know how to deal with hardship because she had never had any. She always had supportive parents, school came easy to her, she got a scholarship to college, had a great fiancé and the promise of the perfect life and the American dream. Therefore, when her mother died so suddenly she had no clue on how to handle it and in the end she just wanted out because life was not supposed to be like this.

Nevertheless, through the whole ordeal, after her suicide attempt, she saw the loving support of her family and she knew that eventually everything would be all right. She kept the Bible verse her father had given her bookmarked in her Bible. She looked at it whenever she felt depressed and needed strength. Eventually she wrote it on several pieces of paper and put it all over her room in the clinic so she could draw strength and inspiration from it constantly. She began praying her rosary every night, which was something she had done as a child but had forgotten in later years, as life got too hectic.

She went to counseling sessions with her counselor Tony every day. Sometimes she laughed with him, sometimes she cried with him, sometimes she just talked without showing much emotion, and Tony listened.

Tony was a thirty-one-year-old African American man who had grown up in the ghettos of Detroit. Tony had been involved with drugs and gangs as a teenager. One day, while going to buy drugs, shots rang out. Tony tried to run but a bullet hit him in his spine. The wound completely paralyzed Tony from the waist down. Tony didn't know what to do with his life at that point, however, a grief counselor from the very same center that Tony worked at heard Tony's story and took an interest. She came and talked to Tony everyday. Upon release from the hospital, she got him into the clinic for no charge. Tony finished school, got straight A's, and even won a scholarship to Wayne State University. Tony knew that he wanted to go into counseling as well. After 4 years, he graduated with a degree in social work. He then went back quickly and got his masters degree in counseling 2 years later. After finishing college Tony received a full time job offer at the counseling center, bought a house, met a girl, got married, and had a family. Tony did all of this while confined to a wheelchair. Even though he had to rely on others to help him get around, he never wavered in his resolve. Tony would always say how lucky he was that great people took an interest in him and always gave of themselves to help Tony if he needed to get somewhere. Tony had very short black hair that was receding in the front, a mustache, and a perfect smile. He had a muscular build and could probably play any sport if not paralyzed. He always wore either a sweater or a polo shirt with a pair of khaki pants.

Sarah saw hope in Tony's story. If he could do all of this while confined to a wheelchair, she could come back from her problems as well. She began to think that although losing her mother was very painful and that even though she still regrets not being there when her mother died that her life was not as bad as Tony's once was. Day by day, week-by-week she gained strength from that. Tony and Sarah talked about everything, her mother, her suicide attempt, her father, religion, school, her ex fiancé, and everything.

Finally, on Memorial Day Weekend it was determined that Sarah had improved enough to earn a weekend pass. She took it and her entire family went up north to their family's cottage on Lake Superior's Whitefish Bay. Sarah was doing substantially better but was still depressed at times. Most people believed she was no longer a suicide threat but they were still concerned about her. Her father had visited her every day at the center and had seen a big improvement. Despite the improvement, he had seen he was still very concerned about her. He was probably more concerned than anybody was; after all, she was Daddy's little girl. He hoped this trip would really kick start a rapid recovery. This had been such a long ordeal for him losing his wife whom he had loved and cherished for many years and then almost losing his daughter less then a year later. This horrific combination of events took almost everything that he had inside him to give. He had lost weight and had trouble sleeping. He had nightmares that he awoke from drenched in sweat. The nightmares were always the same. It always began on a happy family fourth of July. He is sitting at a picnic table with his wife, daughter, and the rest of his family. Suddenly the weather turns stormy; the rest of the family runs in the house. He, his wife, and daughter remain outside. Suddenly a tornado touches down, they all run for cover, his wife is sucked up by the twister immediately, his daughter then goes after her mom, he lunges to grab his daughter and pull her back. He gets a hold of her by the hand and hangs on for dear life. He struggles and struggles against the twister for what seems like an eternity but in the end each time he loses his grip and the tornado takes her away. Then, he returns to a house he has never seen, sits by a black fireplace, and cries.

He hoped that getting his daughter better would end those dreams. He tried several different counselors and different sleep medications but none could erase the dreams. The dream has returned every night since his daughter's suicide attempt.

Sarah could not wait for the weekend. However, she remained a bit nervous about being away from the center for the first time in months. Tony helped her develop exercises to help her if she feels like she losing control. Mainly breathing and repetition exercises designed to calm her down. She made sure to bring her Bible and her favorite quote as well. She prayed her rosary and repeated the quote several times on the way up north. Both seemed to have a calming effect on her. However, the upcoming weekend would be difficult. The potential existed for many setbacks. What Sarah did not know would ultimately change her life in a profoundly positive way.

Mike on the other hand, was not aware of very much as he headed up north. Mike continued to nurse a major hangover from the night before. As Todd drove up north Mike sat in the passenger seat, his head throbbing, and his stomach churning. The bumps in the road increased the nauseous feeling in Mike's stomach and seemed to add about four or five more bands to the ones already playing in his head. He hoped that Todd would not talk to him until his hangover went away. At that moment, he felt rather displeased with Todd. He wondered if Todd had any idea what his parents would say to him when her returned home, the name-calling, the screaming, and the belittling comments, and would be his punishment if he were lucky. Mike expected much worse from his parents when he gets home.

After riding for about an hour, Mike fell asleep. He slept for about two hours and then woke up. Todd turned to Mike and asked, "Feeling any better?"

At first, Mike didn't respond. He still felt groggy, his headache remained but it was somewhat better, he had that dry feeling in his mouth, that feeling of intense thirst that accompanies a bad hangover.

"You got anything to drink?"

"I've got a couple cans of Coke in the cooler down by your feet."

Mike reached into the cooler, grabbed one of the Cokes, and drank about half the can in one gulp. "Thanks."

"Well Mike, it looks like you had yourself quite a night last night."

Mike did not respond, just sat there quietly hoping Todd would leave him alone. After all, he thought Todd had just messed up his whole life with what he did back it his house. His parents would never stand for that and he knew he would take their entire wrath when he got home. So he thought *screw you Todd, you have no idea what you just did, you better not talk to me, I don't even know where you're taking me.* Of course, that is what he thought, but he would not actually say it. Mike often did not say what he wanted to. Mike was scared of rejection, humiliation, and ridicule. However, unfortunately for Mike today Todd would not just stop and leave things where they stood, he just had to keep picking.

"Hello Mike, you there?"

Mike eked out a very shallow halfhearted "Yeah."

"Well good, I'm glad to hear that you are with me. You had me worried there for a minute." Mike didn't respond just sat there slumped over in the seat with his half empty can of Coke in his hand.

"Not in a talkative mood? The whole point of this trip is to help you. I've seen you at work, you are intelligent and an excellent worker, however there's something that holds you back and keeps you from being consistent in your work."

Mike jumped right in at that statement. "What are you going to blame my parents? You gonna tell me to stand up to them? Well save your breath you don't know anything, just leave me alone."

"Easy there Mike, don't get hostile..."

Mike interrupts again, "Well you're just dragging me up here on this trip, making me come with you. Do you know how much crap my parents will give me when I get home?"

"So what if they do?"

"Are you kidding me? You saw how they talked to you and me back there. You saw what kind of people they are. Maybe you think taking me away from them for a few days is a good thing. Well for a few days it may be a good thing but in a few days I have to go back there and listen to them yell at me for hours."

"Mike, that's where you're wrong, you don't have to listen to any of that. You're an adult, you can do what you please."

"Oh yeah? What if they kick me out? Then I don't have any place to live. Then what? I guess then I'll just be Mike the bum and everybody in the world will be able to laugh at me." Right then Mike felt something welling up inside of him, he knew this feeling, Todd was about to say something when Mike yelled "Stop the car!"

"What? Why?"

"I'm gonna barf. Now pull this damn car over!"

Todd did pull the car over and Mike jumped out and threw up all over the side of northbound I75. Mike got back in the car and said "Just leave me alone man, just leave me alone, I don't feel good."

"All right, for now I'll leave you alone but I promise you we're going to work on this some more this weekend."

Mike did not care about the weekend at this point. All he cared about was that Todd finally stopped talking. Mike then tried to fall asleep, however this time he couldn't, his stomach was in knots, and his head throbbed, sweat poured out of him yet he still shivered. Mike knew this feeling, he had experienced it before, and he knew in time that it would pass. Actually, Mike had kind of come to enjoy the hangover pain. While unpleasant, it dulled the pain of the rest of his life and gave him something else to focus on. As unpleasant as hangovers were, they were more pleasant than dealing with the everyday problems of his life.

Chapter 5
Healing

Healing has always been a difficult concept to understand. Man has sought to heal every malady that has come about since the beginning of time with limited success. Society has always looked on its' healers with respect and reverence. After all, they make us better at our worst moments. We all have understood the physical process for a long time. We cut ourselves, we bleed, we put some antibacterial ointment on the cut, put a bandage on the cut, and in a week, it is just a bad memory and life moves on. Sure many physical problems require a longer healing time but we all know in the end the majority of them will pass, until that final physical ailment that takes our life. However, emotional healing has always been much more complicated and in most cases drawn out. That cut on your finger most times does not leave a lasting impression, however the loss of a parent, especially one you were close to never really fades away. It sticks with you in the back of your mind and can pop back into your consciousness when you least expect it to. Sarah struggled with this concept concept on a daily basis since her mother passed away.

Sarah became an emotional wreck after her mother died. It seemed in her mind that she had lost everything, her fiancé left, her college kicked her out of the pre med program, her chance to be the well respected doctor had gone, her innocence had been stolen, and most importantly the best friend she had ever had was gone.

Sarah could not shake her nervousness as she headed up to Whitefish Bay in Michigan's Upper Peninsula for the long Memorial Day weekend. She had fond memories of her childhood being on the beach with her mother. She remembered her mother helping her learn to swim in the shallow bay when she was just five years old. She was terrified that this would bring back memories that would make her revert back to wanting to kill herself, and that terrified her. The whole trip up she kept her bible clutched in her arm and her rosary clutched in her hand. She prayed for strength, her dad had his brother drove them up to the cottage so he could sit in the back seat with Sarah and comfort her. On the way up, he took time to pray with her hoping that would help. It did help Sarah somewhat but she continued to have conflicting feelings about her father. She loved her father and he had always been there for her but she began to think to herself, *why is he doing all this? Does he think he can replace mom? He knows he can't replace mom. Why is he trying to?*

Sarah felt guilty about these feelings and thoughts for a couple reasons. First, she knew her dad was only trying to help; yet, she was getting mad at him for something that she knew any good parent would do. Second, she knew her mother not want her to feel this way. She knew her mother would never allow her to have these kinds of feelings. Therefore, she could not understand why her dad let these feelings go inside her. She would sometimes think that there was no way he could know she was having these feelings and therefore should not be held responsible for making these feelings go away. However, a minute later she would begin to think that since her mother would have recognized the feelings and stopped them that her dad should have done the same thing and that began to breed resentment inside Sarah, a feeling she had also never really experienced before. However, Sarah stayed hopeful heading up to the Lake Superior shoreline.

The Upper Peninsula of Michigan is a unique place. Unless you have lived there or visited, there many times it is difficult to understand. To an outsider it seems like an unforgiving icebox with tons of bugs and mosquitoes. However, to those that live there and travel there frequently the place takes on an entirely different meaning. Those that know it well know that one dark night spent sitting on the shores of Lake Superior can heal a person's psyche, change a person's outlook on life, and relax a person like nothing else on earth. The scenery that you see by day is breath taking and awe inspiring, whether it is a tree lined forest decked out in green, a lake as blue as the sky, or a snow drift as high as the roof on a two story house. The sheer isolation from the fast paced get-it-done-yesterday-world of American society allows one to relax like nothing else. Sarah knew all of this going in and could not wait to be out on the beach alone at night. She knew they would not knowingly allow her to be out there by herself, but she knew she had to find a way to sneak out to feel the healing power of a northern night.

Sarah and her family arrived at the family's cottage on Whitefish Bay around 2PM. Memorial Day Weekend is not often a time of brilliant sunshine and warmth in Michigan's Upper Peninsula. Often times snow remains on the ground and temperatures can feel down right like winter. It's not often a balmy seventy, eighty, or ninety degrees. This year was no different. When they arrived at the family cottage, it was a mainly cloudy sky. There were a few breaks of sunshine but temperatures hung in the high fifties all afternoon.

Sara walked into the cottage with a bit of trepidation. She knew many painful memories would immediately come storming back. In fact, as soon as she walked in they all came rushing back right on cue. She looked across the loving room, across the sofa, easy chair, love seat, throw rug, hardwood floor, past the fireplace and stairway into the kitchen where she could just picture her mother at the stove putting the finishing touches on a hot meal on a cool summer night in which Lake Superior ushered in a chilling fog. That was tough for her to take, but she clutched her father's arm and slowly pressed on. She went into the bedroom she used to sleep in as a little girl in the cottage's upstairs. She then was flooded with memories of her and her mother watching fireworks outside the window when she was a little girl. The loud explosions of the fireworks scared her until the age of seven. So all the years before that her mother would bring her inside right before the fireworks started, she would then make a big bowl of buttery popcorn and then they would sit, look out the window and watch the fireworks. Because they were high off the ground they could see all the fireworks for miles, and the closed window lessened the loudness of the explosions and gave Sarah a view of nothing but beautiful plumes of reds, blues, greens, whites, oranges, and yellows outside the window. Then she was flooded with more memories of being outside at about age 10 and how her mother would make roasted marshmallows over the campfire and then after the fireworks had ended her mother, father, uncles, and aunts would tell her and her cousins ghost stories about the lake into the wee hours of the morning. Then they would all go to bed and the kids would be up just a while longer than normal stewing in their beds swearing every noise must be a ghost.

All of this began to overwhelm Sarah. She turned around, her dad stood in the hallway behind her.

"Daddy" she cried weakly, "I…I…I just can't sleep up here in this room yet, I'm just not ready.

"I understand honey. It will be ok, we can put you in the living room on the pull out sofa"

"Thanks. It's just so hard. I mean, I thought I could handle sleeping in here but I just can't. I miss mom so much. I really loved her y, I really really loved her, and I'll never see her again. One-day, I promise I will sleep in that room again. I'm going to get better, and I'm going to be a counselor, just like Tony."

Sara's dad just held her tight. It broke his heart to see his daughter crying in his arms, he wished there was some magical way he could make it all better but he knew there wasn't. He thought to himself that this must be the hardest trial a father can face, trying to take away the loss of a loved mother. Nevertheless, through all of this sadness he found a silver lining. This had been the first time Sarah had spoken about getting better and doing something with her life. He also sensed the determination in her voice when she told him that she would be able to sleep in that room again. He didn't quite know what to say but after a couple minutes of his daughter crying in his arms he said, "I know you will honey, you're a tough girl, and when you do sleep in that room again, I'll be right there to tuck you in. I promise."

Her father shut the door of Sara's old bedroom. Sarah decided that instead of making another family member switch and sleep in her room that she would sleep downstairs in the living room and out of respect for her mother nobody would sleep in her old bedroom on this trip.

Sarah unpacked her belongings and slowly began to relax. All of the memories of childhood that were haunting her in a way and causing her a great deal of tension began to subside just a bit. They subsided so much that she began to relax enough to begin having a good time. Sarah passed most of that first day relaxing in the living room of the cottage. Family members popped in and out and talk with her, joke with her, and laugh with her. It was a return of relative normalcy for Sarah and her family. While Sara was not her once high-spirited jovial self, she no longer resembled the completely sad, depressed, and despondent young woman either. Healing had begun, Sarah started hiking a long slow road to recovery, and while she was not where she wanted to be, or where anyone else wanted to be, for the first time in a long time everybody, including Sarah knew she would get there.

Sarah went outside about five o'clock to have dinner with her family. Despite the cool fall like temperatures, it was important for Sarah and the rest of the family to eat outside. Sarah's mother had started the tradition of the family always eating outside on Memorial Weekend despite the weather. Her mother's reasoning had always been that even if the weather did not feel or act like summer, it was the unofficial start of summer and as such the family should eat outside and welcome in the new season; albeit slightly premature.

Sarah's father asked her before they went up north if Sarah still wanted to continue that tradition. Sarah thought for a few minutes, she thought if she could handle it, she wasn't sure. Then, a new thought crept into her mind. She thought about her family and all that she had put them through in the recent past. She knew her family would love to carry on the tradition of eating outside, and that she would do her best to give her family this gift, so everyone could have a happy start to the summer.

In the end, Sarah was happy that she made that decision. Everybody including Sarah had a great time at dinner. The family barbecued, the men laughed and had drinks, the women prepared side dishes for dinner, and it became almost like old times. Even in her fragile state, Sarah couldn't help but smile. Everything felt good. She hadn't felt this good since her mom died. Sarah's father stayed abnormally quiet during the barbecue. His worry caused him to watch more than talk. It reassured to him that she smiled more than she had in months. His love, and concern for his daughter is what kept him quiet and he didn't mind that, he wanted his little girl to be happy again even if it was at his own expense.

Evening turned into night. Slowly family members filed off to bed until just Sarah and her father remained awake. Her father asked, "Do you want me to tuck you in before I go to bed honey?" Sarah really wasn't ready to sleep but knew tucking her in would be important to her father so she replied "Yes daddy, I think I'm getting a bit tired."

Her father tucked her in and said, "Good night honey."

Sarah replied "Good night daddy."

As he began, walking up the stairs Sarah called him back. "Dad."

"Yes honey."

"Thank you for everything, this weekend is turning out great. I haven't had this much fun in a long time."

Her father smiled and replied, "It's my pleasure honey. I just want to see you happy again sweetheart."

Her father climbed the stairs slowly, with a smile on his face. He walked in a way so that Sarah would not see the few tears that filled his eyes as he walked upstairs. These were not tears of sadness but tears of joy. Her father finally began to feel that he had not lost both a wife and a daughter, as he really believed his daughter was coming back to him. Her father said two rosaries that night, one for the continued recovery of his daughter, and a second thanking God for the progress he had seen in his daughter's recovery. As he drifted off to sleep, he still had a couple of tears in his eyes.

Sarah lay awake on the couch for about two hours. At about 1AM she saw that the clouds had broken, and then the moon began to shine over the lake and into the house. She found it very beautiful and decided to walk outside. She waited an extra half hour as to not disturb, wake, or scare anybody. She threw on a favorite sweatshirt and a flannel on top of that and walked out into the cool crisp night air. She walked up to the lake and watched the waves run in for about fifteen minutes. She marveled at the beauty in nature. She wondered if there were many grief counselors up in this area. She thought if there were not many that this would be a great place for her to come and start a career after she finished college. She wondered how many people that live up here may be struggling with grief and lack the resources needed to get healthy. Sarah felt she could do a lot of good up here. Suddenly, off in the distance she heard some shouting. She walked over in the direction of the shouting to see where it was coming from. These were not shouts of joy but shouts of anger, angst, depression, and fear. She could hear all these things in these shouts without even talking to the men. She could recognize them because she heard in the very recent past in her own sobs.

Sarah finally came across a young man shouting into the air, at the lake, and seemingly at everything. She thought for a second if she should talk to the young man. The young man didn't notice her. Finally, after about five minute she decided to speak to the young man.

"Hey, Hey, are you all right?"

The young man turned around and looked at her with a puzzled look.

Chapter 6
Chance

Mike and Todd finally arrived up north around two in the afternoon. They first drove through the town of Paradise Michigan about three miles south of Todd's cottage. Mike marveled at the utter smallness of the town. He had never seen a town that small. The town only had one traffic light and it constantly blinked yellow or red depending on which side of the light you were on.

"Does this light ever change colors?"

"No. There's no need for it to. There is so little traffic up here that it is never a problem. Mike looked around the town. There were two small hotels, two gas stations, a grocery store, a bar, and not much else. The entire length of the town seemed shorter than the street where he lived. They passed through the town of Paradise in about two minutes and drove back into a canopy of trees.

Todd pulled up in front of a medium sized cabin and said "Mike we're here." Mike slowly pulled himself out of the car. His stomach felt somewhat better by now. The worst effects of his hangover had subsided however, his head and stomach still did not feel right if he moved too quickly, but the danger of vomiting had ended. Therefore, Mike moved very slowly and deliberately when he got out of the car. Had he moved to abruptly or quickly, his head would throb horribly.

Todd opened the door to the cabin and they walked in. The door opened up right into the living room. There was a couch with a television across from it. There were windows around the entire living room that looked out onto the lake. The door they came in at was in the middle of all of the windows. A stairway on the right led to a small loft. The loft was not a huge room but it was just big enough for a queen sized bed, dresser, nightstand, and a lamp.

As they continued walking, straight back through the living room they walked into the kitchen. The kitchen was quite typical for what Mike would expect in a kitchen. It had a refrigerator on the far wall; on the wall to the left of the refrigerator were a sink and a counter. There was a window over the sink that looked out to the side of the house. Todd's car was visible through this window parked directly next to the cabin. There were two wooden cabinets on each side of the window. The cabinets housed plates, glasses, non-perishable foods, and a few liquor bottles. The entire kitchen and most of the cabin had a wood finish mostly in shades of light brown and tan. The wood floors were a deeper brown but not what one would consider dark brown. Mike saw a half finished bottle of whiskey in the cabinet and thought that was just what he needed to feel better. Todd happened to see that Mike noticed that and immediately grabbed the liquor bottles and dumped them down the drain. Mike was horrified.

"What did you do that for?"

"You're not here to drink this weekend Mike. This stuff will not help you. You think it will but all it will do is hurt you. This weekend is about getting better, not getting worse."

"I just wanted a shot. I've never tried that brand of whiskey before." Mike had tried to fool Todd, truth was he had drank that brand of whiskey several times before but he thought if he told Todd he just wanted a sip Todd would leave him alone.

Todd saw right through this. However, Todd also knew the timing was not right yet to really help Mike. He knew Mike needed to relax for a little while and so Todd just said to Mike "Come on and I'll show you the rest of the cabin."

There was a stove standing by itself on the wall directly across from the counter. There was a shelf over the stove with spices and a jar with cooking utensils on it. The bathroom was right next to the refrigerator. Mike found that weird, yet still a little funny, and let out a short chuckle. Todd saw this and said "I see you find a bathroom next to the refrigerator funny too. When

I was a kid I used to tell my dad that all we needed in there was a TV and we would have the refrigerator, toilet, and TV within five steps of each other. My dad always said that would defeat the whole purpose of being up here. We weren't here to watch TV we were here to relax and enjoy nature. At the time it made me pretty mad, but looking back on it I see he was right."

Mike thought to himself that Todd was crazy. He was not entirely sure why Todd had brought him here. He wondered why Todd just didn't fire him. Mike thought Todd firing him would have been much easier. He could have just continued fooling his parents and found another menial job.

Right in the middle of his thought, Todd interrupted him. "Hey Mike what you thinking about?"

""Nothing." What else do you have to show me?"

"Let me show you the back bedroom, backyard, then I'll show you the loft."

There was a back bedroom on the way to the back door. It was a small room with a single twin bed, a dresser, nightstand, and a lamp.

"This is where you'll be sleeping tonight."

Mike liked the idea of sleeping in the room. He thought this would be an easy place to sneak out of in the night to recapture some sanity. All he would have to do is slip out of the back door and walk around the cabin to get to the lake or walk out and start walking up the road. Mike noticed that there was a party store connected to one of the gas stations that sold beer a few miles back and he wondered if in the night he could walk there and grab a six-pack. He had it all figured out he could just hide it under the bed, drink it at night over the weekend when everybody was asleep, and Todd would never know. Mike got a bit of a rush out of this idea. He felt like a kid sneaking alcohol behind his parents back. The prospect of doing that this weekend made Mike feel cool. Mike did not feel cool too often anymore so it made him feel extra good.

Todd and Mike finally reached the end of the cabin. Behind the cabin, a walkway surrounded by trees lead to a road. Mike looked at it and thought to himself that escape would be very easy tonight. He would simply get up, walk to the back door, open, and close it quietly, and there was no view from the house back here so Mike had an easy escape.

Todd interrupted Mike's thinking again. "So what do you think?" Mike really did like the cabin but he was not overly excited about being there. He thought since it was a holiday weekend that he should be spending extra time at the bar and drinking twice as much to celebrate the holiday. However, Mike wanted to be polite and he responded by saying "It's very nice. I can see why you like it up here. The scenery is beautiful and it's very quiet."

"Do you like the quiet?"

Mike had varied ideas about this topic but felt uncomfortable sharing them. Nobody ever cared about his ideas, so he did what came naturally to him. He tried to joke his way around the question by saying, "Yeah I love the quiet, beats my nagging parents and the loud punk kids at the mall." Todd saw right through this and knew exactly what Mike was doing. Todd said to Mike "I know you're messing around, I can hear it in your voice. I understand. Why don't you tell me what you really think?"

Mike thought for a moment, and then began to speak, "You're right man, I do love places like this. They are relaxing. I really don't get to go anywhere much because my parents don't travel much and I don't have the money to. One day though I would like to have a place like this of my own."

Mike couldn't believe he had just said all of that to Todd. It kind of made him mad inside that Todd was able to suck him in and trick him into saying something real. Mike felt that he needed to save face after saying that by saying something funny and off color but before he could think of anything to say Todd said, "I understand. I can see how that would suck. Everybody needs to get away sometimes. My parents had this place from the time I was four years old. We would up here every Memorial and Labor Day weekend. We would also come up here on the 4th of July. Although in July, we would have stayed up here for the rest of the month. My mom would stay up here with us during the week and my dad would come up on the weekends. He would also always take a week or two off work, come up, and stay with us. I can't imagine a childhood without it, but I guess you can very easily. I sometimes forget not everybody had the same opportunities as me."

Mike felt encouraged by that comment. It made Mike think that Todd was not talking down to him and giving him an excuse for the way he behaved. Mike liked Todd, and didn't want to be a jerk to him so he continued the conversation by asking, "What was your favorite thing about being up here as a kid?"

"Wow I loved so many things up here but I would have to say the swimming was my favorite thing. I got to swim all summer, and for free. My friends used to have to pay for a membership at the local pool and go there. There were times I was a little jealous of them because I didn't get to see my friends for most of the summer but, at the same time I had a blast with my brothers and my parents."

"Were you able to play baseball or other sports in the summer? That was my favorite thing as a kid was playing baseball in the summer."

"My brothers and I played in a league for a couple of years." However, none of us really took to it. My oldest brother Randy really enjoyed football but that never started up until after we were back from the cabin. There were a couple of years in high school where he didn't come up with us for Labor Day because he had a game on Friday night, but he always drove my dad's old truck up on Saturday afternoon and met us up here. I'll never forget his senior year when we came back late on Monday night and the house was trashed. Randy had thrown a party right after the game and didn't clean up. He also wasn't smart enough to get rid of the beer cans before he left either. My parents grounded him for the entire fall semester of his senior year. My parents would wait for him outside the locker room after every game and march him home. Although that did help him study and probably helped him get accepted and succeed at Michigan State."

"Man how bad did your parents yell at him for that one? My parents would have killed me if I had pulled something like that."

"Well that's what my brother and I were hoping for, but my parents never yelled. We couldn't believe it. Here were my brother and I all primed and ready to see Randy get the beating of a lifetime and it was over like that. My parents told him his behavior was unacceptable, that he would be cleaning the entire house, and not just that night but every Saturday for three months, that he would not be allowed to go out, and that they were very disappointed in him."

"Damn. He got off easy if you really think about it." Mike said. "I mean no yelling, sure the punishments suck but no yelling, damn."

"I used to think that too but the more I thought about it the more I think he would have gotten off easier if my parents had yelled at him."

"Really? How could that even be possible?"

Mike was very curious about that as his parents' favorite pastime was finding reasons to yell, and then yelling at him.

"Think about it, how do you feel after your parents yell at you?"

Mike thought for a second and then responded. "Well I guess it makes me mad, I feel like garbage, and really just think that I'd better not get caught doing the same thing again."

"Exactly. All you are concerned about is how not to be caught again. You are still more likely to do the thing that caused them to yell at you in the first place but the point is you will still do it."

"Yeah, probably. Most of what my parents yell about I still do. They've been yelling about my drinking for years and I still do. They think I have a problem but they don't understand."

"What don't they understand?"

"You know damn well what they don't understand."

"Really I don't. I'm not trying to be difficult but I really don't understand."

"Think about it Todd, you have a bad day, you're stressed, and you feel like gum on the bottom of a shoe. You have to drink. You have to make yourself feel better. You see I don't have a problem, I only drink to make myself happy."

"You know Mike feeling happy is why many alcoholics drink."

"No way! That's the kind of stuff my parents tell me. They don't understand. I don't get hammered every night. I only do it when I need to relieve some stress."

"How often do you get drunk?"

"Usually only about three or four times a week. I mean that's no big deal."

"So what's your favorite drink?"

"Well I love my seven and sevens, my Long Island iced teas, and my Captain Morgan and Cokes. And of course sometimes you're a little low on funds so you end up drinking beer all night, which is fine too, it still gets the job done just a little slower."

"Do you like your job at the store?"

"Yeah it's pretty cool, I've always loved sports so it's a natural fit for me. I just wish you weren't such a dictator when it came to being late."

"Well I'm just doing my job. If an employee is repeatedly late, they are not fulfilling their responsibility. So to fulfill my responsibility I have to write them up."

"See Todd you seem pretty cool most of the time but then you start saying stuff like that. Why can't you just help me out once in a while? I mean I'm trying my best and you can't cut me the smallest break."

"I wasn't going to tell you this until the way back but to respond to what you just said I'm going to tell it to you now. I have given you breaks Mike, if I didn't you would currently be unemployed. I don't want to fire you though. You know more about sports than any employee in the store. If you could just become a little more reliable and cut down on the drinking just somewhat you would be almost the perfect employee. My bosses wanted me to fire you but I have stuck my neck out for you on this and as a result, I have convinced them that you deserve a promotion to assistant manager. It's up to you if you want to take the job but I really think you should. You would be great at it if you were on time and cut down on the drinking."

Mike was shocked. Nobody had ever gone out on a limb for him like this. Before he could even reply, Todd jumped in again. "You may not think you can do this Mike but you can. I want you to think about this until Monday and give me your answer on the way back. If you accept you'll start manager training Tuesday morning, if not you'll report for your regular shift as a salesperson. Can I tell you one more story before we drop this subject Mike?

"Yeah."

"Remember when you asked me about my brothers and I playing sports?"

"Yeah and your brother played football and trashed the house his senior year."

"Yeah well when I was a kid I played hockey."

"Sweet, I love hockey but I don't know how to skate. I wouldn't last thirty seconds on the ice. What position did you play?"

"I played defenseman, I was a grinder, lead my high school team in penalty minutes three years in a row."

"That's awesome man! When I was a kid watching the Red Wings, I used to love Bob Probert just because he used to get into fights with everybody. How many fights did you get into?"

"Lets just say I got in my fair share of fights. But that's not the point of my story. Right at the end of my junior year in high school my dad lost his job. His unemployment compensation did not pay enough for us to maintain our lifestyle. My older brother Randy was already in college at Michigan State. I wanted to follow him to Michigan State and major in business. However, when my dad lost his job my parents told me the only way they could afford to send me to Michigan State would be if I got a scholarship. My grades were good but not good enough for an academic scholarship; my last hope was to earn a hockey scholarship. I asked my high school coach what he thought my chances would be of getting a scholarship for hockey. He said that unless my game really improved during my senior year I didn't have much of a chance. At first, I was very upset. I didn't want to go to community college and figured that when I got out of high school I would get a full time job and work rather than go to community college. That lasted for about a week. I felt like crap that entire week. Finally after seeing me mope around for a week like a spoiled little girl my parents suggested that I go talk to the coach and see what exactly I needed to improve in my game to have a chance at a scholarship. I took their advice that Monday asked the coach what I would have to do. The coach said that I needed to work on my puck handling, needed to become a better skater, and lastly play tougher in the defensive zone and put a couple more pucks in the net. I asked him if he would be willing to work with me over the summer, he said he would. I got a part time job at the store so I could pay him, he said I didn't need to pay him but I felt bad if I didn't. Therefore, that summer I got up early every morning, met the coach down at the rink, and practiced for 4 hours every day except weekends. I gave up a lot of my summer up north and just worked and practiced my game. The following season I doubled my goal and assist totals, I also increased my plus minus rating from a minus two to a plus four. By the end of the season, I was skating with the first line and got that scholarship to play hockey at Michigan State. Before that summer after my junior year I would have thought that it was impossible for me to get that scholarship but in the end I did, I went to Michigan State, played hockey for four years, worked at the store every summer, and got my degree in business management. Then when I was done I became store manager, and I've been there ever since. The reason I want to make you assistant manager is that I want another sports guy to take over for me when I move on. Next year I will probably be moving to the corporate offices, so I would like to groom you for the position."

Mike was speechless after hearing that story. The silence was soon broken as the rest of Todd's family arrived at the house for Memorial Day. Todd's family came in, they all hugged, and laughed and then Todd introduced everybody to Mike.

"Everybody, this is Mike, the guy I was telling you about. The one that used to pitch for The Whitecaps."

Todd's dad jumped right in and said "Hey Mike how's it going?" Great to meet you.

"I'm doing fine sir."

"Ahh we've got a stiff one here I see. Well we'll loosen him up this weekend and get him laughing" his dad said. "Lets throw him in that ice cold water, that will get him moving."

"Now James" interrupted Todd's mother, "Leave the poor boy alone. He doesn't know anybody here and you come in acting crazier than an escaped mental patient. Don't mind him son, nobody ever does."

Laughter filled the house after Todd's mom jumped in. "Hey man I'm Randy, Todd's older brother."

Mike thought he would join in with the jokes now and replied, "Yeah Todd told me about you, you're the one who trashed the house and then got grounded for his senior year. Smooth move ex-lax."

"Todd you punk! I'm going to kill you for telling him that. You don't tell that story man."

Randy immediately tackled Todd onto a couch and got him in a bear hug and started hitting him saying "You like that? You like that you little hockey wuss. You can't hang with a football player you hockey wuss."

Randy finally let Todd up and Mike expected Todd to be crying and Randy to be gloating but they just came up laughing. Mike was a bit confused. He had never seen anything like that in his life. He didn't understand how Randy could go from mad to laughing just like that, and how Todd could laugh about being punked out like that.

Mike waited a minute but finally his curiosity got the better of him and he had to ask Todd how he could just take that and laugh. Todd said "We're brothers man that's what we do. Like Randy is going to be mad initially when I run up from behind him and cross check him into the couch."

Randy then turned around just in time to see his younger brother coming right at him and deliver a wicked cross check sending Randy flying through the air onto the couch. "See Mike he got me but I just got him back. That's what we've done our whole lives. It's taught us that when life gets us to get life back by busting your butt and getting what you want. You may get it in a different way than you thought you would but you still get it and so you still win."

Finally, Todd's mom broke in again saying, "All right boys that will be just about enough of that garbage, get yourselves unpacked. It is after three so we're going to fire up the grill in just a minute and have some steaks and some baked potatoes. "

Mike went to his room and unpacked. He looked around the room. He was in a much better mood now than when he arrived. The effects of his hangover had worn off and that steak and baked potato were sounding quite good. Mike was still in shock that Todd wanted him to be an assistant manager. Mike knew he had to take the job. The raise would give him enough money to get his own apartment in a couple of months and probably get his parents off his back. As he looked out the window of his bedroom Todd poked his head in the door and said "come on Mike we're going to play some football down by the water. Mike got up and went with Todd.

Todd and Mike teamed to face Todd's older brother Randy, and his younger brother Steve. Therefore, the next hour consisted of a lot of tackling, a lot of swearing, a little blood, and a lot of scoring. Mike had never played much football but he was having a blast. With the score 42-35 in favor of Randy and Steve Todd's dad came out and yelled "two minute warning men" and then set a timer on the side. Mike and Todd had to drive the length of the beach for the game-tying touchdown. Finally, they scored the tying touchdown with six seconds left.

"Yeah you got the touchdown but I bet you two chickens don't have the grapes to go for two and win this thing and not settle for a tie like wusses." Randy said.

"What do you say Mike want to go for two and take these girls out once and for all?"

Mike had never been a risk taker. However, a fire suddenly began to burn inside of Mike. He had never felt a fire like this in his life. So what's it going to be Mike want to go for it?"

"Lets do it. Just give me the ball Todd."

Todd's jaw dropped when he heard Mike's response; he had never seen this side of Mike before. "What should we run Mike?"

"Just hit me with a screen block Steve and I'll do the rest."

"You think you can get by Randy? He's a big guy."

"Just give me the stinking ball and don't worry."

"All right, you've got it." Todd couldn't believe what he was seeing in Mike. It was like twenty plus years of frustration were all coming out of Mike at one time. Todd was actually excited because he knew this was helping Mike get better.

Mike and Todd came to the line. Mike hiked the ball to Todd and ran sideways. Todd flipped the screen pass out to him. Todd then went and blocked out Steve leaving Mike one on one with Randy. Mike was easily giving up forty pounds to Randy. Randy smiled assuming he would make the stop and the game would be over, but suddenly Mike's face turned blood red and he ran full speed directly at Randy and that twenty plus years of frustration was unleashed on Randy. When Mike and Randy collided, Randy was not prepared for the force and hit the ground like a pound of lead into the sea. Meanwhile Mike ran into the end zone, scored the winning touchdown, spiked the ball on top of Randy, and said "Game over loser." Then Mike went to the table to eat dinner.

Todd, Randy, and Steve were all in shock at what they had just seen. Todd quickly regained himself, ran after Mike, and said, "That was awesome man how did you run him over?" Really Todd knew how Mike had done it but didn't want to just say it, he knew Mike had to work through his issues in his own way.

"I just ran at him and knocked him over. I knew he wouldn't be expecting it. I knew he would expect me to try and juke my way passed him so I knew his feet wouldn't be set and I could just run right through him."

"Well Mike that will definitely be the high point of the weekend." Todd's parents put the steaks and potatoes on the table and they all ate dinner. Randy was uncharacteristically silent during dinner.

After dinner, Mike sat quietly while Todd's family sat and told stories about the past and talked about the present and the future. Mike didn't know what to make of everything that had happened today but he did know that it turned out to be a good day when he was expecting it to be completely horrible.

About midnight the family went to bed. Mike went to bed to still with his plan to walk to the liquor store. Mike had never been to Paradise or The Upper Peninsula of Michigan before so he had no idea the stores were already all closed when he left the house at one o'clock in the morning. He quietly slipped out the back door, walked down the road into paradise, and got to the store at about one thirty.

"Damn! What kind of town is this? It's not even two in the morning and everything is closed. Dammit!" Mike turned around dejected and walked back to the cabin. When he got back he was too mad to sleep, so he walked down to the lake. Mike was very upset at this point. The lack of alcohol combined with his trouble grasping the meaning of everything that had happened during the day sent him into a torrent of obscenities and shouting. Mike was screaming at the lake, at the sky, at the sand, and at the trees. Then Mike heard a voice off in the distance.

"Hey." The voice said.

Mike stopped shouting and started looking around.

"Hey." The voice said again.

Mike could tell that the voice was getting closer now. He continued looking around and then saw the figure of a young woman coming towards him.

"Hey is everything ok?" The woman said.

Mike stared at her for a minute. He didn't know what to make of this woman. He then concluded that she wasn't real; she was just a ghost. Mike had read stories about all the people who had died on Lake Superior, and how many of their ghosts haunted the shoreline around Whitefish Bay.

"You're a ghost."

"No I'm not a ghost, I'm just a girl. Why are you yelling?"

"No! No! You're definitely a ghost. You can't be real. This doesn't make sense."

"Of course I'm real. Here give me your hand." The woman grabbed Mike's hand and touched it to her shoulder. "See I'm all flesh and blood just like you. I'm not a ghost."

Mike didn't know quite how to react. First, he wondered why this girl was walking around the beach at two in the morning. Second, Mike wondered why she would take the time to talk to him. Girls usually didn't talk to Mike. It's not that Mike was ugly. But all of the negative energy tension, and low self esteem Mike carried around shown on his face so girls would see him and realize without a word that he was not what they were looking for. However, this time Mike knew he would have to make conversation, he didn't really want to tell this woman what was wrong but she was asking and he knew he couldn't avoid her, and he also knew that he didn't have a good lie to tell her so he started talking. "All the liquor stores in town are already closed and I really need a drink."

"Don't you have any alcohol in your cabin?"

"It's not my cabin, it's my boss'."

"Doesn't your boss drink?"

"I think he drinks but he dumped out all the alcohol this morning."

"Why would he do that?"

"He thinks that I am an alcoholic which is ridiculous because I only drink to feel happy."

"You have to drink to feel happy?"

"Not all of the time just sometimes. Sometimes I just feel a bit overwhelmed and I feel I need some drinks in order to settle down. It's not a big deal."

"How often is sometimes?"

"Three or four nights a week. Boy, you sure ask a lot of questions. Here's a question for you toots, how come you ask so many questions?" Mike felt good about what he just said. He thought his toots comment would offend the woman enough to get her to leave him alone.

Sarah thought about Mike for a moment. She began thinking about what could be wrong with the guy. Why is the so defensive? What is he hiding from me? However, she was astute enough to realize what Mike was trying to do and she wasn't going to fall for it.

"First of all don't call me toots. I have a name it's Sarah. Second, I can't understand why you are so angry, did you lose a parent or something?"

"Lose a parent? I should be so lucky. My parents treat me like garbage. I wish they would die."

Sarah was horrified. She couldn't believe that someone would think that poorly of their living parents while her mother was dead. She thought he deserved to lose his mother not me. Why had God taken my mother and not his? Sarah couldn't get out anything intelligible to respond to Mike. She muttered a few things but couldn't get out words. Then Sarah became full of rage at this young man and his sick hate for his parents. She unconsciously raised her hand and slapped him right in the face.

"What the? Why did you slap me?"

"I'm sorry." Sarah couldn't believe she had actually hit somebody. She had never hit another person in her life, she hadn't even her sister when they were kids and they got into an argument. "I'm sorry I hit you. She said again. "I just lost control when you started talking so negatively about your parents. I just lost my mother last year and it has killed me. I was so close to her, she was my best friend. Then after my mom died I had such I hard time dealing with it that my fiancée left me and then I attempted suicide." Sarah couldn't believe she was telling her whole life story to some stranger. Somehow, though it made her feel a little better. She had told it to her father and her counselor but never to a complete stranger. Somehow it made her feel just a little better, maybe because this stranger didn't have the same reaction as everybody else. She could tell he wasn't having the same reaction by the look of utter terror on the young man's face. She felt she needed to say something but she didn't know what.

When Mike heard what the woman said he didn't know what to say. The situation got very uncomfortable for Mike. He felt bad for the girl because he knew that she had a worse situation than he did. Mike knew that other people had good relationships with their parents but sometimes in his hate for his parents, he forgot that. Mike really didn't hate his parents he just didn't know how to relate to his parents and they didn't know how to relate to him. He knew there was some love there on both ends but neither one knew how to express it to the other. Mike also noticed that while he was immersed so deeply in his own thoughts that the woman was about to say something to him.

"I'm sorry." I don't even know you and here I am telling you very personal things about myself and my family that you probably don't want to know. I'm sorry to burden you with my problems."

"No it's fine," I should be apologizing to you talking so negatively about parents when you just lost a parent that you obviously loved."

"Thank you," I'm sorry this has been an extremely difficult year for me and the death of my mother has penetrated every aspect of my life. I know it shouldn't but it just has. I've been working very hard at getting better that's why I'm up here this weekend. Why are you up here this weekend?" Sarah asked trying to change the subject.

Suddenly Mike felt very comfortable talking to this woman. He didn't know why he didn't usually feel this comfortable talking to anybody. "Well I guess I'm kind of in the same boat you are I work at a sporting goods store in a mall downstate. I've been drinking a lot because I just know I'm going to mess things up somehow and lose the job. I don't know why I think that; I'm good at the job. In fact, my boss just asked me today if I'd like to be assistant manager. But even though I plan on taking the job I just know that I'm going to find a way to mess it up."

"Why do you think you are going to mess it up?"

"I've messed up just about everything that I've ever done. I used to play baseball. I was a pitcher. My coach in high school used to blame everything on me and tell me how bad I was. So, when I graduated I wanted to show everybody that I really was good and that I could pitch so I tried out for The West Michigan Whitecaps. I made the team and pitched there for two seasons but I couldn't cut it. I never made it past A ball. My coach was right I was good for nothing. Then I tried to get into business but I failed at that, I couldn't get a job so I had to work in a factory. Then, I got fired from the job at the factory and got the job I have now."

Sarah thought for a moment and then spoke. "You know I'm not to familiar with baseball but it seems to me, even making a minor league team is an accomplishment. I think you should be proud that you managed to make it for two years. I bet there are many of people who never make it at all."

"I know there are, there are many of them, but I just wanted to prove that I was better than my old coach. I just wanted to pitch in the majors one time, and stick it down everybody's throat. My coaches, my teammates, and my parents all said I couldn't do it. When I washed out after two years, I had to face the reality that they were right. It was the worst feeling of my life."

"I'm sorry to hear that. But you can't let little setbacks like that ruin your life. I'm just now learning that in therapy. I'm learning that my mother is gone and that she would want me to move on and have a good life."

"I know. I try to tell myself that but it just doesn't work, and then things go wrong and it just reinforces that."

Just then, Sarah saw a light go on in her cabin. "My dad is awake and probably wondering where I am. I should go back so he doesn't worry about me. I really enjoyed talking to you...."

"Mike, my name is Mike."

"Mike, ok. Will you be out here tomorrow night? I would really like to talk to you again."

Mike was surprised that she wanted to talk to him again. "Yeah I'll probably be out here again tomorrow night."

Sarah said good-bye to Mike and ran back to her family's cabin. Her dad was waiting at the door.

"Are you all right?"

"Yes, I'm fine." I just met the most interesting boy down by the lake. We both have similar problems we're trying to overcome in our lives. It helped a little to talk to him."

"Well that's good. I just want you to get better."

"I know you do."

Sarah laid down on the couch. Her dad sat there with her. Sarah fell right to sleep. Her dad sat there next to her a little bit longer praying that his daughter continued to heal, and wondering whom this mysterious boy was whom she suddenly had a desire to help. He got up and went outside to look and see if the boy was still out there but he wasn't. Then he walked inside, shut the door, kissed his daughter's head, went upstairs, and went to sleep.

Mike lingered outside for a few minutes after the girl left. He didn't know what to make of the encounter he had just had. Mike had many thoughts in his head now about the girl, the store, the job, his parents, and of course Todd and his family. He waited about ten minutes after the girl left and decided to go in. He felt his plan of slipping out unnoticed would backfire if he stayed out much longer. He went inside, shut the door quietly, slipped back into his room, and slipped into bed. He laid there a while longer until the first hints of daylight were streaking over the sky. Then his mind shut off for a little while and he was able to drift off to sleep.

Chapter 7
The Weekend Continues

Sarah woke up around nine-thirty on Sunday morning. Her dad and the rest of her family were already awake.

"Good morning, I was just about to wake you up for church," her dad said. Sarah had not been to a real church in quite some time. She used to love going to church with her family on Sunday mornings. Sarah had not been in church since her mother's funeral. After the funeral, she refused to leave the house and then when Steve left her she attempted suicide and ended up first in the hospital and then in counseling.

However, church was not the first thing on Sarah's mind this morning. She kept thinking about her encounter with the young man on the beach last night. The conversation she had with him was unlike any other conversation that she could recall having in her life. She must have had a puzzled look on her face because all of a sudden her dad rushed over to her and said, "Honey, is everything all right? You look like something is wrong and you have been very quiet since waking up."

"No, everything is fine, I was just thinking about the young man I saw on the beach last night."

Sarah's aunt immediately jumped in, "Ooooh Sarah's getting over her depression all right, she's already looking to sink her claws into a new guy."

"Very poor taste Aunt Mary. That's not the situation at all. I just can't figure out why he hates his parents so much."

Her Aunt Mary apologized for her comment and went into the kitchen. "Dad, how do you think a person can hate their parents so much? I know that there are many horrible people out there who are abusive both physically and emotionally, but I am just having all kinds of trouble understanding how even those children can hate their parents that much."

"Well honey, for some people it is just impossible for them to forgive."

"But the Bible, it teaches forgiveness, right?"

"Well, yes it does, honey, but you also have to remember that not everybody is religious. Not only that, but not everybody who is religious reads the Bible. People like you and I take solace in reading the Bible and its' messages, while other people have never even seen a Bible. I would bet that any child whose parents are that abusive hasn't been exposed to religion much at all, so turning to God or the Bible is not a viable option for them."

"I understand what you are saying. I wonder if that man has ever read the Bible. Do we have an extra Bible here I could give to him if I see him again?"

"I have one I keep in the room your mom and I used to sleep in up here. If it would help you feel better, I could let you give it to him and then just pick up a new one to leave up here. I have wanted a new Bible for the cottage anyway. A real nice hard cover copy with a nice binding like the one we have at home."

"Are you sure that would be all right, dad?"

"Yeah it will be fine. After all, God wants us to spread his message to those who have not heard. I also believe that it will help you in your healing process if you can turn someone on to God."

Sarah hugged her father and went to the bathroom to get ready for church. She took a quick shower. The warm water felt good on her body especially given the chilly Lake Superior air of the morning. As she showered, she thought about the young man on the beach from last night. She wondered if he had even ever been to church. This was also a large breakthrough for Sarah. She was thinking about somebody else's life instead of her own and all the problems she had faced since her mother died. She was very excited at the thought of giving the young man the Bible. She thought it could really help him find peace. While she showered, she also debated whether she should put her phone number in the Bible. She would love to take the young man to her church. She thought that she could introduce him to all the people she cared about so much at church and that he could make some new friends. New friends, she thought, always make people happier.

Sarah turned off the shower, wrapped a towel around her, and got out of the shower. She saw the sun shining brightly outside through the small window that was in the bathroom. Even though she knew it was cold outside she opened the window to let in some fresh spring air. When she opened the window, she took a deep breath of the fresh, cool northern air. The air ran deep into her lungs and filled her with a sense of life and renewal. She had always loved the smell of the fresh air in the Upper Peninsula in the spring. It was always so fresh, clean, and new. The winters are so hard and cold up in the Upper Peninsula that when spring finally does arrive, the air has a newness to it that has the power to renew both mind and body. Sarah then looked at herself in the mirror. She smiled a weak smile, brushed her hair, put her clothes on, and went downstairs to meet her family for church.

Her family was already waiting for her when she got down there.

"Well there she is, you finally made it down to us, huh? We were starting to wonder if you were going to make it. I can tell you're feeling at least a little better, you haven't taken that long in the bathroom since before your mother died."

"I was just enjoying the shower," I was thinking about the boy from the beach again and was debating putting my phone number in the Bible. I would really like to take him to church. I think if I could get him there to experience the peace of the church and meet some of the people and make some new friends that it may do wonders for him."

"Well, don't push too hard, if you do, you may scare him off and turn him off of religion forever. Also, you don't know if he is already religious. Just offer him the book as a gift and go from there."

Sarah and her family then piled into the car and headed for church. When they got to the church, the sanctuary with its' radiant colors inspired them all. Sarah had almost forgotten just how beautiful a church could be. Soon after the family arrived and sat down the opening hymn began and the priest came in. Sarah sang softly to the song. She used to sing much louder before her mother had died but she was still facing some demons inside and wasn't quite ready to burst out in loud song, even though she was happy to be back at church she was still nervous and unsure of a great deal.

The mass continued and they went through the readings, the intentions, and the offertory. Finally, it came time for the passing of the peace. Sarah had been a little nervous about this part. She could not figure out why until she shook hands with her entire family and some other people in neighboring pews. Then she remembered, how her mother used to always give her, and the rest of her family a hug and a kiss during the passing of the peace and then give an enthusiastic peace be with you. There were even a few times Sarah could remember that her mother got so into it that she gave a hug and a kiss to people who weren't in their family and she didn't really know. She can still picture the look of shock on some of the people's faces that were only expecting a handshake and a "peace be with you" but received so much more than they bargained for. Sarah then thought back to when she was in high school and how embarrassed she would get when her mother would do that to other people. She can remember wanting to disappear and go somewhere far far away where nobody knew her so she wouldn't face any social embarrassment. When it came time for communion Sarah went up for the first time since before her mother died. Her father was not sure if she was going to go up for communion but was very pleased that she did. When the priest put the communion wafer in Sara's mouth, the Eucharistic Minister gave her the cup of wine, and she drank it she felt a warm feeling down in her stomach and she knew that it was God working inside her to help her heal.

When the mass ended, she went outside with her family. She had a great feeling of peace and contentment after the mass and wanted to kick herself for missing church for so long. She thought to herself how much church could have helped her if she had just gone after her mother died. She wanted to ask her dad why he let her stop going to church after her mom died but she wanted to do it in private. She was not comfortable talking about it in front of the rest of her family yet, but at that exact moment she knew that one day she would be.

When they returned home from church, her aunts and uncles began preparing a huge lunch. The post church lunch was a family tradition after the entire family went to mass. When she was a child and she went to church with only her parents they would always go out to eat after church. Going out to eat with her parents after church was fun, they would talk, laugh, enjoy some good food, and talk about the message in the sermon. While those lunches with her parents were fun, they paled in comparison to the ones with the entire family gathered together after church. There would be homemade sandwiches, homemade potato salad, homemade macaroni salad, fresh vegetables, tossed salad, fresh fruit, scrambled eggs, bacon, hash browns, sausage, toast, Aunt Mary's homemade preserves, and fresh baked pie. The family never finished all of the food. But each family member always got a little bit of their own to take home to make sure that none of it went to waste. Sarah loved when she was a kid and she would be able to take her leftover post church brunch to school for lunch on Monday. Somehow, the food tasted extra good the next day. In addition, her friends would stare at the massive amount of food she brought with her to school and get jealous of their own bag or school lunches. Moreover, sometimes Sarah's mother would give Sarah her share of the leftovers and Sarah would be able to take post church brunch leftovers two days in a row and really make her friends jealous. Because that did not happen, all that often the food tasted even better on the second day and Sarah loved seeing the look of jealousy on her friends' faces. Every time she saw that look in their eyes, she laughed a little bit to herself. Sometimes she wondered if her laughter was a sin, but always rationalized that God wanted her to have some fun and by laughing silently inside at her friends' jealousy, she really was not hurting anybody so it really was not a sin. Once she learned that jealousy was one of the seven deadly sins, she was able to rationalize that her friends were the sinners and not her.

The post church brunch was set up on the table. Everything looked so good to Sarah. She wanted to try to have a little bit of everything but she did not think she could eat that much and she had to save room for pie. The pies were the only things that were never leftover. If you ate too much and did not save room for pie you would not get any, so every member of the family paced themselves so they would each get their piece of the pie. Sarah's family, sat, talked, ate, and laughed. After the brunch the leftovers were packed and portioned, everybody helped clear the table and wash the dishes. When the cleanup was complete, Sarah went out, sat on the porch, and read her Bible a little. She thought about highlighting her favorite passages for the young man but she remembered what her father had said to her earlier and decided that may be a bit much.

As Sarah sat on the porch, the cool morning air faded into a warm sunny spring afternoon. At about three o'clock, the temperature reached the upper sixties, which is downright balmy for this part of Michigan in May. Sarah put her Bible down and began looking out over the lake. The repetition of the waves, the sun glistening of the top of the water and the warm spring breeze had a very calming effect on Sarah. She was more relaxed than she had been in a long time and that was the most important thing. She looked down the beach and happened to notice the young man from last night playing volleyball with three other guys. She thought about going over there and talking to him but she wanted to wait until later that night when they could talk in private about issues that are more personal. She thought if she went and talked to him now he would not talk to her about anything important, so she decided that her best course of action was to wait. She was glad she saw him playing though because now if he didn't show up on the beach tonight then she knew which cabin he was staying in and could drop it off on Memorial Day.

Suddenly her dad came out of the house. "Hi honey, gorgeous day isn't it?"

"Absolutely," she replied. "I'm so glad that we came up here. This is so relaxing and it's making me feel better."

"That's the best news I've heard in a while, honey," her dad said.

"Dad?"

"Yes, honey?"

"Can I ask you a question?"

"Of course you can, what's on your mind?"

"Well, I felt really good inside after church. I hadn't realized how much I missed going to church. Then I started to think of how much church could have helped me in the time right after mom died, and I started wondering why you let me stop going to church? You had to know that it could be helpful for me, so why did you let me stop going?"

"Well, I don't know if I can fully answer that question. I don't know if I'm quite sure what the answer is. Believe me, every week that you weren't at church with me, I silently wished that you were. However, I thought if I forced you to come to church with me that you may get upset and we would have to leave. It was extremely hard for me to go to church without you and your mother. There were times that I wanted to cry, there were a couple of times I even started to leave church with the intention of coming home to get you, but I just couldn't do it."

"I understand dad. But I've also got some great news for you."

"What's that honey?"

"I'm going to go with you every week from now on. I realized today how much I missed being in church. I felt the warmth of the Lord once again when I took communion. It made me feel whole again."

"That is great news honey! Sometimes I felt the same warmth you did today in the pew and I like to think that your mother is there in a spiritual way. I believe she is there with me every week in spirit, and having you back with me will make our family whole again."

"Dad, do you think that mom is in heaven?"

"I don't think that she's in heaven, honey." Sarah's face suddenly turned ghostly pale with that statement. "Let me finish honey, I *know* your mother is in heaven." The color came rushing back to Sarah's face. "Your mother had such a caring and giving soul I don't see how she couldn't be in heaven. If your mother isn't in heaven than I guess there is no such thing as heaven."

Sarah jumped right in and yelled at her dad. "You jerk! You said it like that just to mess with me and freak me out. Very nice dad."

Sarah's dad laughed. "Nice to see you getting your sense of humor back." Sarah's dad then smiled and went back into the house leaving Sarah alone on the porch again. She looked down the beach to where the young man had been playing volleyball just in time to see him and the three other guys go into the house. It looked like the young man was having fun and that made her happy, maybe he would be in a better mood tonight.

Sarah fell asleep on the porch for a couple of hours. It was a very restful sleep, the kind of sleep she really had not had in a while. Up until this trip, she had been having a nervous sleep, which she woke up from still tired. However, all of her sleep on this trip had been restful sleep and she was feeling one hundred percent better for it. When she woke up it was time for dinner. Just some barbecued hamburgers, some beans, and some fruit...nothing too special.

After dinner, she relaxed with her family for a while. About eleven o'clock her family went to bed. She got up and went outside with the Bible to wait for the young man. Her father was secretly watching her from the window to try to catch a glimpse of this mysterious young man. Sarah waited until three o'clock in the morning but the young man never came. She was very disappointed but remembered she had seen where he was staying and she would go there tomorrow and give him the Bible. Sarah's dad was very upset with the young man for not showing up. If he could find him and grab him, he would have wrung the young man's neck

Mike woke up in the morning very tired. He had only slept for a few hours. Todd came in and got Mike out of bed. "Rise and shine Mike, we have a busy day ahead."

"What? What are we doing today?" Mike asked.

"Well I thought you and I would go through a morning hike through the woods, then come back and maybe play some volleyball with my brothers afterwards."

"You go ahead, I'm tired." After walking into town and not finding any liquor last night and then walking, back the last thing Mike wanted to do was more walking.

"Come on man, the fresh air will do you good."

"If you only knew the fresh air I got last night," Mike murmured.

"What's that?"

"Oh nothing, nothing at all."

"Good. Get up, get some clothes on, and meet me out front in fifteen minutes. You don't have a choice in this Mike. There are some things I want to talk to you about."

"Are you kidding me?" Mike said quietly.

Mike grudgingly got up, put some clothes on and met Todd out front.

"So where we walking? Lets get this over with."

"We're just going to hike through the forest a bit. Here put some bug spray on, you're going to need it. "

"A few mosquitos and flies don't scare me."

Todd knew that Mike had never been to the Upper Peninsula so he also knew that Mike had no idea just how bad the bugs were up there.

"Trust me. I'm not talking about a few mosquitos and flies, I'm talking about a few thousand mosquitos and flies."

"You're just yanking my chain."

"Really I'm not, man. Put some on you'll be glad you did."

"Nah, man, let's just go. I told you I don't need any of that sissy stuff."

Todd could see that this conversation was going nowhere so rather than waste time he grudgingly said, "suit yourself, but you'll be sorry." Todd slipped the can of bug spray into his backpack knowing that eventually Mike would see its usefulness.

The morning was nice and cool. The temperatures were still around fifty when they left. Mike started complaining about the cold. "Don't worry, it will warm up quickly, and the cold will be the last thing on your mind."

Todd and Mike started walking. They had not gone more than one hundred feet into the woods when Mike starting trying to swat the bugs away from him left and right. Then the profanity started. "Stupid mosquito. Damn fly." Mike repeated over and over again. After about five minutes of that Todd asked Mike, "Hey I have some of that bug spray in my bag. You want me to pull it out for you?"

Admitting that he was uncomfortable would show weakness and Mike liked to believe that he was a man's man. Instead, he decided to show his toughness by making a joke, "I don't want you to pull nothing out, you sick freak."

Todd laughed. "All right man but just remember its there if you need it." The two men hiked for about another fifteen minutes. It seemed that the temperature had risen substantially the morning and the morning chill had vanished. Mike began to feel more comfortable temperature wise but much more uncomfortable bug and feet wise. His feet were getting sore from the walking Mike did last night combined with the walking that he was doing now with Todd. Finally, Mike broke down. "Hey Todd can I see that bug spray for a minute?" He knew Todd had put the spray on and noticed that the bugs weren't bothering him. In addition, he knew that he would be able to stop and rest his feet for a few minutes while he put on the bug spray.

Todd stopped walking, pulled his backpack off his back, opened it up, and found the bug spray. "Here you go."

"Thanks."

"See I told you that you would need it."

Mike remained silent not wanting to admit defeat.

Todd saw an opening for some good conversation so he went for it. "You don't like asking for help do you?"

"No. I prefer to do things on my own."

"Why?"

"Well I've always had to. My parents have never been that much help to me. Even when they try to help we usually end up arguing. They just can't understand that I need to do things my way."

Todd and Mike had continued walking at this point but Todd wanted to continue the conversation.

"Do you think that maybe your parents think they know a better way and are just trying to help?"

"Sometimes. I like doing things my own way though. I also like doing things at my own speed. My parents could never understand why I always put my chores off as a kid. I still finished them, just on my time. I don't get why they had to yell at me and constantly nag me about them."

"Well maybe they were just trying to get you ready for adulthood. Think about it. You almost lost your job for coming into work on your own time. You can't do that in the real world."

"I'm sorry about that, Todd. I know you're talking about the store. I'll take responsibility for that. But it still doesn't excuse my parents for treating me like a second class citizen just because I like doing things my own way."

"Your parents just probably think that your way of doing things will hurt you in life. I'm sure they want you to succeed. I don't know of any parents who wants their kids to live at home forever."

This conversation started to annoy Mike. He had no interest in continuing this conversation with Todd. Todd didn't know his family. Todd also didn't understand Mike's situation. So he finally said to Todd "Hey man can we just drop this conversation, I don't want to talk about this."

Todd saw that his current line of conversation was not helping Mike so he decided to try another angle. He knew Mike liked him and even respected him so he decided to try to use those two things to his advantage. "All right I'll drop this conversation, but you have to promise me something."

"What's that?"

"Well I'm sticking my neck out for you recommending you for assistant manager. If you take the job, which I hope you will, you have to promise me a few things. First, you promise me that you will be on time every day. You can't be late. Second, you promise me that you will never come to work drunk, or hung-over. Third, you promise me to finish your associate's degree in business, and at least consider going for a bachelor's degree. Lastly, you promise me that you will work your hardest every day. If you can't agree to those terms then I don't want you to take the job."

Todd had guessed right, Mike didn't want to let him down. He did like Todd and he did respect Todd. Mike knew he could do all of the things Todd wanted he just had to set his mind to doing them.

"All right Todd, I'll do what you ask."

"Does that mean that you will take the job? Remember my four conditions, they are non negotiable."

"I can do it. I promise I won't let you down.

"That's the kind of attitude I've been wanting to see Mike. We'll have to celebrate tonight. Without alcohol of course."

"Well I don't know how we'll celebrate without alcohol but I'll trust you to find a way. I've always been open to trying new things."

Mike started feeling very comfortable talking to Todd. Mike had never had any real close friends but he could see Todd becoming that kind of friend, the type friend who was more than just an acquaintance as most of Mike's current friends were. He knew Todd believed in him so he wanted to ask him something. Mike had never achieved his dream of becoming a professional baseball player, but he thought he still had a chance at becoming a coach. He wanted to see what Todd thought of the idea.

"Hey Todd."

"What?"

"Do you think I could ever be a good baseball coach?"

"I don't see why not. You seem to know a lot about the game. I'm sure you'd do well."

"Well I never got to play professional baseball but I think I could be a great coach if given the opportunity."

"I watch all the local sports talk shows and your opinion usually coincides with theirs so that bodes well for you."

"I just don't know how to get into it."

"Call some of your old coaches from the Whitecaps. I bet they could help you. I might know someone who could help you too. I'll talk to my old hockey coach and see if he can talk to one of the baseball coaches at the school. Maybe you could catch on as an assistant. But you call your old coaches."

Mike was excited that Todd might know somebody who could help him. He did not intend to call his former coaches from the Whitecaps. He knew there would be no job with The Whitecaps for him; he didn't have the type of experience needed for that kind of coaching job. But maybe if he could catch on with a high school team he could develop a reputation as a good assistant and move on from there. He felt very confident in that prospect.

Todd and Mike finally got back to the cottage about one o'clock. They had some sandwiches for lunch and then Steve and Randy challenged Todd and Mike to a game of volleyball. Steve and Randy had gone so far as to set up the net on the beach before they got home. Mike would have liked to sit and relax, he was tired, and his feet throbbed with pain from the walk. However, Mike also knew they could not back down from the challenge.

Mike was two steps slow the entire game. Randy also took every chance possible to spike it down Mike's throat as revenge for the football game. After the game, Randy was gloating heavily about how he has exacted his revenge on Mike. This went on well after dinner. Finally, Todd got tired of it.

"Hey Randy, shut up. Stop being a poor loser and winner. Give the guy a break. We are going to celebrate him becoming assistant manager at the store, and me becoming general manager." Todd also hit Randy upside the head to hammer home his point.

Randy stood up. "You wanna go little man?"

"Really?" Todd said. Todd didn't even wait for Randy to reply before he gave him a leg sweep and then slapped on a figure four leg lock reminiscent of Greg "The Hammer" Valentine. Randy moaned in pain.

"You going to be cool Randy?"

"Yeah you win this one."

Todd released the hold and Randy swallowed his pride, walked gingerly over to Mike, held out his hand, and said, "Truce?"

Sure man." Mike said as he shook Randy's hand. The four men then proceeded to crank up some old classic rock, Van Halen and Aerosmith mostly, grill some burgers and rock out until Todd's parents came home from visiting friends in the area. Todd's parents came home about ten-thirty and everybody was in bed by eleven o'clock. Mike wanted to sneak out again and go see Sarah, but he was so tired that he fell asleep as soon as he laid down and didn't wake up until about eight o'clock the next morning. He was upset that he missed seeing her but thought he could walk up the beach and try to find her today before everybody left to head home.

Ch. 8
Memorial Day

Memorial Day dawned bright and sunny. It was going to be the warmest day of the holiday weekend. Unfortunately for both Sarah and Mike, they would be unable to spend the entire day and night in Paradise once again. Both would be returning home later that afternoon. Mike would be starting his new job on Tuesday and Sarah had to report to Tony so he could monitor her progress.

Sarah got up around nine-thirty once again. The rest of her family was again awake before her. She got up and headed for the shower. It was a little warmer outside this morning so the shower did not posses quite the same invigorating power that it had yesterday but it still felt very good and helped Sarah relax. Once again Sarah's thoughts turned to the young man she met on the beach early Sunday morning. She was debating when she should go over and see him. Her first thought was to go right away in the morning in case he was leaving Paradise early. She thought that was her best course of action but then she started to think that he might lose the Bible if she took it over too early. She didn't want to wait too late because then he may be gone by the time she got over there and she would never be able to give him the Bible and invite him to church. This was a new situation for Sarah. She usually did not have this kind of a debate in her head before making a decision. Usually she weighed her options quickly and came to a decision.

This situation was different however. She had never approached a boy and given him her phone number. She never had to; boys usually came up to her. Also, she was not trying to date this young man; she just wanted to help him feel better about life. She also did not know how to explain to the young man what she wanted to do without offending him. She was quite certain from her one meeting with him that he was not a person who accepted help very willingly.

Before her mother died, she would have never understood why someone would not accept help. However, after her mother died she knew that she would not accept help from anyone. Therefore, she thought she understood what the young man was going through and that she could help him.

Finally, right before the end of her shower Sarah made a decision. She decided she would take the Bible over to the young man the first chance that she got. She also decided that she would put her phone number into the Bible along with a note explaining that she wanted to take him to church and why she wanted to take him to church. Therefore, she decided that right after she got out of the shower that she would begin working on the note. It was not going to be a long note, as she didn't want to overwhelm the man.

When Sarah got out of the bathroom, her dad was waiting for her. Sure, he tried to disguise that he was waiting by making a bed in a room across from the bathroom but it was obvious to Sarah that he was waiting for her hoping to find out what happened on the beach last night. Sarah still did not know is that her father had been watching her the entire time she was out there. He was lurking outside of the bathroom was to see if he needed to do damage control because his daughter was stood up on the beach.

Sarah came out of the bathroom and before her dad could even get a word in edgewise, Sarah started talking. "Good morning dad. Boy, it sure is a beautiful day. What are you up to?" She said all of this with a hint of sarcasm in her voice. She wondered if her father would notice her sarcasm.

Her father, completely not expecting sarcasm from his daughter, did not notice it at all. "Good morning honey. How did your meeting go with the young man on the beach last night?" Rage at the young man built up inside him. He wanted to find the young man and strangle every ounce of life out of him for standing up his daughter.

However, Sarah surprised her father by not acting sad at all. "He didn't show up last night."

"Are you all right honey? Are you feeling ok?' Her father asked.

"Yes I'm quite fine," she said. "I saw him yesterday playing volleyball in front of a cottage so I know which cottage that he is staying at. I'm just going to go drop it off this afternoon."

Sarah's father was shocked that she was handling it so well. Still he was not convinced that she was fine with the man not showing up last night. Nevertheless, to placate his daughter and not seem like he was spying on her he told her, "Well that sounds like a good idea Maybe you can go over there before dinner." Really, he didn't want her going over there. He didn't want her to have any contact with that man now as he got it stuck in his head that contact with him would only disappoint her and hinder her recovery.

"I'm going to go write a note to the young man to put in the Bible." Sarah said.

"Sounds like a plan." Her father replied.

While Sarah went to write, her father quickly hatched a plan and then rushed to put that plan to work. He told the entire family about the situation and devised a family reminiscing session that would last until dinner, then they would all leave right after dinner and she would never have the chance to see the boy again.

When Sarah came downstairs, the family was sitting together talking. "Come join us," said her dad. "We are talking about our favorite memories up here." Sarah came over and sat down. She figured that she could share a couple stories and then run the Bible over to the young man. However, she lost track of time while they were talking about all sorts of things by this point. She had not uncovered her father's plan to prevent her from going to see the young man.

After a few hours, Aunt Mary went to start dinner. "Sarah can you please help me with something in the kitchen?"

"No problem, Aunt Mary," Sarah replied.

Sarah and her Aunt Mary walked into the kitchen. Before Sarah could ask her aunt what she needed her aunt spoke. "Run next door and give that Bible to that boy now. Your father devised this whole family togetherness thing in an effort to keep you from giving the Bible to that boy."

Sarah still not understanding the real reason that her father did not want her to give the man the Bible said, "Well, if he really wants the Bible, I don't have to give it away."

"It's not the Bible," replied her Aunt. "Your dad was spying on you while you were on the beach last night. He saw that the boy didn't show up and now he has got it stuck in his head that the man not showing up is going to hinder your recovery. He arranged this family time quickly while you were writing the note to the young man to keep you from seeing him again. If you don't go now we'll eat dinner, and leave before you ever have a chance to talk to him."

"That's ridiculous! I'm going to go have a talk with dad then go give the boy the Bible."

Aunt Mary grabbed her and said. "Take it now! Then talk to your dad."

Sarah did as her Aunt said and took the Bible out the back door and went to give it to the young man. Helping Aunt Mary was the perfect cover; her dad would not suspect that she was really going to give the man the Bible.

When she got to the cottage the man was staying, people were packing up cars to leave. She saw Mike standing by the water by himself so she walked up to him. "Mike."

Mike turned around, saw Sarah, and walked over to her. "Hi. Sorry I didn't come down to the beach last night. I was very tired after everyone else went to bed and I just fell right to sleep. My friend Todd made me do this long hike yesterday, then we played volleyball, and I was just dog tired."

"It's fine. I was really looking forward to talking to you again but I understand. Really, I just wanted to give you this Bible. The Bible has always helped me and judging by you last night, I think it could bring you some peace."

Mike didn't know how to react to this act of kindness. Nobody had ever given him something like that before. Mike had been to church before but he had never read the Bible. All he could come up with for a response was "thanks."

"You're welcome." Sarah said enthusiastically. "So how was the rest of your weekend?"

"It was pretty good, I got a promotion at work to assistant manager at the sporting goods store in the mall." Mike could not understand why he just didn't say the sporting goods store. It was unlike him to add that much language to something should be short. Really, it was just Mike's subconscious hoping that the girl would remember that and come see him at the store sometime. Mike didn't have much experience with girls other than knowing that most girls didn't care for him. This girl was also quite attractive and Mike would not mind getting to know her better.

"Congratulations." Sarah said. Her comment took Mike by surprise,

"What?"

"Congratulations on your new job. It sounds exciting."

"Thank you." Mike said sheepishly.

Suddenly a voice called out to Mike, "Hey Mike, we're all packed up. We need to go if we are going to beat the traffic heading back to Detroit. Traffic on I75 south towards Detroit always backs up at the end of a holiday weekend. I've sat motionless in it for hours too many times, I don't feel like repeating the experience tonight."

Mike wanted to give the girl his phone number but did not know how. Finally, Sarah said, "It was nice meeting you. I hope to see you again sometime. In fact, I'd like you to come to church with me. I left my phone number in there, don't be afraid to call."

That was a huge weight off Mike's shoulders for now at least. He would be able to call her. Although that would be easier said then done, as Mike was always very shy about calling new people on the phone. He was always afraid that somebody would yell at him.

"Wait a minute! Let me give you my digits," Mike said, striving, and failing to be cool.

Sarah looked at Mike out of the corner of her eye and slid the paper with his number into her back pocket.

"Bye." Mike finally said to Sarah. It was all he could get out. Sarah said good-bye to Mike and walked back to her cabin.

Aunt Mary was waiting in the kitchen when Sarah came back. "Perfect timing," she said, "I just finished dinner. How did it go?"

"Really good, I think that he will go to church with me at some point."

"Good. Do you like him?"

"I don't think so. Maybe I do but I really don't know him that well. I'd have to say that I don't. I just want to help him find contentment in life. I'm thinking that whenever I go back to school I want to go into counseling so I can help people feel better. It has really begun to interest me this weekend."

"Well that sounds great. I'm sure you'll make an excellent counselor after all that you have been through."

"Has dad noticed I'm gone?"

"No. He is clueless. I even called your name a few times while I was cooking to make it seem like you were here. Are you going to talk to your dad now?"

"No I'm going to wait until sometime this week. I think he'll be in a better frame of mind about the situation by then and he'll be more understanding."

"Good idea," said Aunt Mary.

Sarah and Aunt Mary carried dinner out to the family. Sarah's father was glad that Sarah helped her aunt even though her dad had no clue where she had really been. The dinner for the last night was Salisbury steak with gravy, mashed potatoes, peas, and rolls.

During dinner Sarah's dad nudged her and whispered, "I can tell you had a hand in creating this fine meal. Great job." All Sarah could do was laugh to herself knowing that she hadn't touched this meal and accept the compliment from her father.

After dinner, the family cleaned up the kitchen, packed up their belongings, loaded up the car, and went home.

On the way home, Sarah's dad asked her if she had a good time.

"I had a great time. I really do feel a lot better." Sarah told her father.

"I'm glad to hear it. And hey, don't worry about that boy who stood you up last night."

"Oh don't worry dad. I'm not worried about him at all," Sarah said with a smile. Then she closed her eyes and fell asleep. Her dad was confident that the weekend had been success for Sarah and that she would never see that jerk from the beach ever again.

Chapter 9
Going Home Again

Mike was in a daze. He had never had a girl offer to give him her phone number before. He decided to just sit back in the car and bask in the glow of his new accomplishment. In his mind he knew it was a good thing because getting a girl's phone number always meant you had a foot in the door when it came to possibly hooking up with her later on. Mike was trying to think to himself and analyze the situation but he didn't get much of a chance to before Todd and his brothers came and interrupted his quiet contemplation.

"You dog you." exclaimed Todd. "How did you manage to pull this off? She ain't bad looking either."

Mike had never been in a situation like this before in which other guys congratulated him for his success with women. He thought silently for a moment. He thought what comment would earn him the most praise and congratulations from his new friends and would not get him made fun of. He thought for a moment but couldn't answer before Todd interrupted again, "Well come on Romeo, let us in on your secret. I want to hook up with a girl like that too."

In all reality, Todd had dated a number of girls like that in his life. Todd wasn't a love them and leave them kind of guy but he was smart, athletic, funny and wasn't ugly so he always had a number of girls who were interested in him and he dated regularly. At the current time, he was single but he had a few options on the line already. His goal was to try to make Mike feel better about himself and try to build some confidence.

Todd's comment gave Mike an idea for an opening in the conversation that he felt he could say something that would not only get him congratulated for getting the girl's number but also for putting a nice burn on Todd.

"Hey Todd, some guys have it and some guys don't. And you my friend don't have what the great lovers like myself call 'it.'"

Todd's brothers had to laugh at Mike's comment. Actually, they couldn't stop laughing. They enjoyed seeing their brother taken down a peg or two. They didn't enjoy it in an evil way but in a you're-my-brother-and-it's-funny-to-see-you-get-ripped on kind of way.

"Shut up!" Todd said to his brothers.

"Hey when you've got it you might as well use it."

"So just what exactly is it that you have Mike? Go on; explain. I want to know what you have."

Mike thought for a moment. He thought about all of his heavy metal heroes and the stories they related in their songs about their conquests. They lent him little help however. Finally, he just said, "If you don't know what "it" is I can't teach it to you. You either know it, or you don't."

"You are so full of it, maybe it was bad idea to bring you up here. Now you're all full of yourself. Maybe this is a good thing. Mike I can get as good as I give, but even though you got me good tonight I will not hold a grudge, as long as you take this fire and energy to your new job next week, we're cool. If you do any job with that kind of fire, you will succeed at it. It may be difficult but that kind of fire will allow you to succeed in any job."

Mike thought for a second and said, "Sure, I'll take this fire to work if you promise me one thing."

"Look at this guy making demands now. Well Mike or should I call you Charlie Bronson? Just what are your demands?"

Mike found it cool to be referred to in the same sentence as Charlie Bronson, but quickly regained his thoughts "Promise me you won't say anything that lame again."

"You jerk. Shut up and get in the car and lets get out of here."

Todd and Mike got in the said goodbye to Steve and Randy. Steve and Randy drove off. Todd and Mike climbed into Todd's car and drove off shortly behind Steve and Randy. It would be a much longer ride home for Mike than it was on the way up there. Mike had of course been hung over on the way up and slept much of the way. However, today he was wide-awake and would be for the entire ride home. Todd and Mike made small talk for a while and then both just sat silently for a little while. Todd and Mike got about half way down state and Mike began to get impatient.

"Good Lord! How long is this ride? I want to get home." Mike said this without thinking about the fight he had with his parents before he left and the fallout that he would face when he got home.

"Boy didn't think you'd be in such a hurry to get home after the exchange you had with your parents before we left."

Mike suddenly remembered part of the argument he had with his parents before left and how mad he was at Todd for causing it to happen.

"Thanks man thanks a lot. Now I'm going to have to listen to their complaining all night."

"Hey Mike it may not be my place to suggest this but why don't you talk to your parents about the good things that are happening in your life now. Tell them you're going to be starting a job as assistant manager tomorrow and tell them about the girl that you just met. Maybe if they can see you doing some good things in your life then they won't be so upset with you."

"Yeah right. That isn't going to happen. They'll just tell me how much of a failure I am and tell me that I'll fail at this job like I fail at every other job and that I will never amount to anything. Then there will be a big argument and we'll just stop talking to each other again."

"Why don't you just break down and tell them about your new job at the store?"

"They still don't know that I'm not working at the factory. If I tell them what happened there they're liable to kick me out for good."

"How can you expect your parents to ever take you seriously if you don't even tell them where you are working at? Just tell them look this is what I'm doing with the confidence you've had this weekend and I bet they will respect that."

"No they'll just yell at me."

"Hey just try it. The worst that can happen is what you already expect to happen. So, what is the harm in trying something different? Obviously, what you all have been doing hasn't worked to well. I'm not saying that this approach will work but it's worth a try. Then no matter what happens you know that you have tried your best to resolve the situation and then you have grounds to complain about how your parents treat you. If that's the case, don't use it as a crutch; use it as a motivator to get out on your own so you don't have to be in that environment anymore. Does this make sense to you Mike?"

"Let me think about it for a few minutes." Mike was trying to process everything Todd said. He didn't completely agree with anything Todd had just said but he needed to work it all out in his head.

"That's fair, but when you make your decision I want you to tell me. You need to have a decision made before you get to your house so you can go in with a game plan.

"Agreed" Mike said and began to sit back and think. He thought about all of the arguments he had with his parents, however this was the first time he really thought about them with a clear and sober mind. He thought about all of the arguments and yelling and screaming back and forth over the years. He tried to put himself in his parent's shoes and after a while, he was able to somewhat.

Mike's parents were blue-collar people. His dad had worked as an electrician ever since he had gotten out of high school. He worked for few companies going out and making house calls and saved up some money to start his own business. His dad had a friend who also wanted to start an electrician business and, because neither one of them were rich, they decided to start a partnership and run the business together. They did well for a couple of years but eventually the company started losing money. A year after that, his dad's partner took everything he had from the business and left his dad with a very large amount of debt. The debt from the business put a big financial strain on Mike's parents for the next few years. His dad's business failed and it took his dad a while to find another job with a company where he again made house calls. Even though the money was decent with the job he remembers over hearing his dad talking to his mom one night and saying that he hated making house calls at this point in his life and that he thought he would be in a management position by that point. The failure of his business and his dream had zapped some of the life out of him. Mike began to think how his dad was much angrier and much less happy after his business failed. That's when it hit Mike that maybe his dad wasn't trying to hurt him by bashing his decisions but maybe that his dad didn't want him to go through the same hardships that he went through. Mike began formulating a plan to talk to his dad about how much he loved working at the sporting goods store and that since he was unable to succeed in baseball that working in a sporting goods store and doing sports related work made him happy. He thought if his dad still gave him crap after that explanation then that would be his dad's problem and he would just do what Todd said and use it as motivation to work hard and get out as soon as possible

Todd and Mike had just passed the city of Flint when Mike made his decision about what he would do when he got home. He started talking to Todd and told him what he had just been thinking about and Todd listened and told him he thought his strategy for talking to his dad was a good one. Todd then began to tell Mike about something else that he could add to his ammunition for talking to his dad. Todd told Mike that because of all of his involvement with hockey at his former high school that he was a good friend with the coach. He went on to explain that there was an opening for a pitching coach on the varsity baseball team and that his hockey coach was a good friend with the baseball coach that he could get him to put in a good word for Mike.

Mike did not know what to say to this. He was literally speechless. Being a pitching coach would be an ultimate dream for him. Mike had no idea how to thank Todd for this but he knew he wanted to do something special for him. As they got close to Mike's parents house Mike was wracking his brain about what he could do for Todd. Finally, shortly before they arrived at Mike's house, Mike asked Todd "Todd is there anything that I can do to repay you for all that you have done?"

Todd chuckled slightly and said, "No, I didn't do any of this to get anything in return. My father always brought me up to help people and do the right thing. When I saw you in the store that first time I knew that you had problems but I also knew that you had potential, that's why I hired you. You may not know this but I called Coach Cleary that night. I asked him about what kind of person you were. He told me you were a great person and recommended to me that I hire you but you had some confidence issues that you needed to work out. He also told me there was not anything you could not do if you tried and that I would never have a worker that would work as hard. He also said he wishes you would call him once and a while to check in. He really meant it when he told you to call him any time."

Mike was shocked when he heard this. He had been certain that Todd hadn't called Coach Cleary. A million thoughts raced through Mike's head. Suddenly Mike felt a firm slap across the back of his head, before he could even respond Todd jumped in.

"Hey take it easy man, I can see the wheels of your mind turning on your face. What I told you the coach said is what he actually said. Don't get your panties in a bunch over it. Just settle down, relax, and enjoy the rest of the ride home. If you spend your whole life worrying about what others say and think you will be miserable."

Mike was stunned even more by Todd's comment; the comment was somewhat mean but not meant to be particularly hurtful to him. He felt unsure about how to respond so he just decided to smack Todd upside the head and say "Payback butthole."

When Mike hit him Todd swerved trying to pretend that Mike's hit was going to cause him to lose control and crash the car. Todd screamed. Mike could tell the scream was forced and faked and told him to stop acting like an idiot and just drive the rest of the way home.

Todd's car pulled up in front of Mike's house at about eight thirty in the evening. Todd asked Mike if he wanted him to come in for support while talking to his parents. Mike told him that this was a battle he had to fight on his own, said goodbye, and told Todd he would see him in the morning ready to start management training. Todd waited in front of the house until he saw Mike walk in the house.

As he was walking from the street to the house, he noticed the smell of barbecue in the air and he knew that his parents had just eaten dinner not too long ago. Mike was nervous as he walked towards the house, he didn't know what quite to expect from his parents, if they would yell at him, or if they would even talk to him. However, the weekend had given Mike a new confidence that he didn't have before, he knew in his head that what happened when he went into the house would probably be a difficult situation but he had a feeling that everything would work out and that everything would be all right in the end. Mike knew that Todd was waiting for him to go in the house, and he knew that Todd would linger a few minutes to make sure everything went smoothly. This did not make Mike mad like it would have in the past. Mike understood that Todd was truly his friend and truly had his best interest in mind. Nobody had ever done as much for him in his entire life as Todd had done in a couple short months. He also knew instinctively that Todd would be his friend for the rest of his life regardless of what paths each of them chose in their lives. He knew that even if he ended up in California and Todd ended up in New York that they would still talk on the phone on at least a semi regular basis. As Mike continued thinking, he finally stopped for a second and realized that he had walked into his house, walked right past his parents and into his bedroom. Mike stopped for a second and laughed at the sheer irony of the fact that he was nervous about what his parents would do when he came home and that he had probably just pulled the ultimate power move by completely ignoring them when he came in the house. Mike regained his composure, put his bag down, and walked out to talk to his parents.

Mike's parents were in the kitchen talking in hushed tones almost certainly about Mike. Mike took a deep breath, walked into the kitchen, sat down at the table next to his father, and across from his mother and spoke before his parents even got a chance to speak "Mom, Dad I need to talk to you both. I know I haven't exactly been a model citizen or son lately and that you are both probably furious with me but before you say anything to me there are a lot of things I need to tell you both. Can you both at least just hear me out and then you can say whatever you want to me. If you want to yell, feel free to yell, if you want to kick me out, feel free to kick me out, but I hope you will hear me out and I hope we will have a calm and rational conversation about some things that have been going on. What do you say? Can you do that for me?"

Mike's parents were flabbergasted. Unsure of what to think they agreed to hear what Mike had to say. His mother looked at his father and his father said "Ok son, you have our attention, what's on your mind?"

"Well that guy who came here and got me on Saturday morning was Todd, he is my boss, not at the factory, but at a sporting goods store at the mall."

"We know! He told us! Why did we have to hear it from a stranger? Why did you lie to us?" His dad yelled.

"Remember dad you said you'd let me speak. Let me finish and then you can yell if you want to."

"Sorry, I forgot, but what happened to the factory job? It just sounds better than working in some store in the mall."

"Well dad I'll be honest with you. I got fired from the factory for showing up late too many times." Mike could read his dad's face at this point and Mike knew his father wanted to kill him at this point."

Mike responded immediately to the look in his dad's face. "Yeah I know it was a dumb, stupid, irresponsible thing to do." This statement by Mike seemed to take his dad's anger level down a notch or two.

Mike noticed this and continued talking. "You see when I lost the factory job I refused to take responsibility for my own actions. I knew I needed to find a job, but I was scared to tell you both what had happened at the factory. I was scared because I knew you both would just yell at me and criticize my decision making, and before you jump in, I'll say it for you; you would have been right in doing so. I was acting immature and stupid, I thought the whole world was against me and that made me scared, scared that I would never amount to anything. So, I got this job at the sporting goods store but after the first few weeks, I began to fall into old patterns and I almost lost another job. However, Todd, the guy that came and got me Saturday morning, saw potential in me and refused to fire me. Actually what he told me this weekend was that he wanted to promote me to assistant manager as long as I clean my act up. Todd and his family showed me that there was so much more to life than drinking, bars, and self-pity. So tomorrow morning I start training to be an assistant manager. It will be full time and I will get a nice raise, and I can keep going to school because they will work around my school schedule. I really feel good about this and finally feel like I belong somewhere and that I finally have a job I can grow in and a job that I enjoy. I know dad you had a dream of owning your own business and that your dream came crashing down, but the point is you followed your dreams that is what I want to do as well. I never made it to the Major Leagues as a player but Todd knows a hockey coach at a local high school that has an opening for an assistant junior varsity baseball coach. I am very excited about that opportunity. I may have never been good enough to play baseball for a living but I know enough about the game to have a chance to be a great coach. I have a passion for the game and even being a coach will fulfill a dream of mine. Well I said just give me a chance to speak and you have done that, now you can yell at me, beat me, throw me out of the house whatever you want, you've heard my piece."

Mike's parents were not quite sure how to respond. They were shocked at what seemed to be a complete transformation in their son. Finally, his mom jumped in and asked a question that she had worried about ever since Mike had turned twenty-one and could legally drink alcohol. "What about your drinking? Are you going to quit? You can't drink like a fish and expect to do your job well when you are a manager of a store and if you're going to be coaching high school students what kind of an example would it be setting if their coach was an alcoholic and showing up to practice or games drunk?"

"That's a fair question mom. I'm going to try. Drinking had become such a crutch, I now know that I have a problem and I need to fix it. And I know you probably think that I won't be able to do that but I've got so much riding on not being an alcoholic that I can't in good conscience do that again. I couldn't let Todd down like that after all he has done for me. I know it won't be easy but I know I can do it."

"You darn well better." His mom said as tears tracked down her cheeks.

"I will. I promise, you don't have to worry about me. I know it's hard to believe but I really have changed."

Mike's dad was still silent, finally, he sat up in his chair where he had been slouching, and he spoke. "Son, when my business failed and I lost everything it hurt me, it hurt me a lot. It hurt me to have to take a menial job for young guys as a middle-aged man to support my family. I didn't want you to have to go through the same thing, that's why I've been so critical of the baseball. You knew as well as I did that the odds were against you making the majors and that's why I pushed you away from it. I want you to have a better life than me and now you're doing it again thinking coaching is the way to go. Son, when will you learn to just get grounded in reality and work hard and make a good living?"

"I understand what you're saying, dad, but I have to do this. I mean you had to know before you opened your business that there was risk involved but you followed your dream, and while your business didn't succeed, you can say you did it. You tried your best, gave it 100%, and even though you didn't succeed you tried something few would dare to try and for that you should be commended."

Mike's dad felt all of those same feelings come back that he had right before he opened the business, the excitement, of trying something new that is a dream for you and he knew instantly no matter how hard he tried he would not be able to talk his son out of his decision. At the same time he wanted to make sure, his son had something to fall back on if coaching didn't work so he started pressing about his new job as an assistant manager. "So what does being an assistant manager pay?"

"I'll be starting out at thirty thousand dollars a year and I'll get full benefits in ninety days."

"What kind of advancement is there in this job?"

"Well once I finish my degree I can move up to a general manager, and then up to corporate. General manager start at forty five thousand dollars a year and corporate is fifty thousand a year and up. So there is advancement and I do like the job so far."

Mike's dad knew that his son's plan was solid. After thinking for a moment he spoke. "Well it seems like you know what you're doing here. You have our support. Good luck in your new endeavors."

"Thanks dad. That really means a lot coming from you and mom."

Mike and his parents sat at the table a little bit longer about Mike's new job and about some of the things that had happened in the past. They agreed to put the past behind them. Mike seemed like he was on the right track so they forgave his past indiscretions and hoped he really truly had changed. They were still skeptical but they were more trusting of their son than they had been in years.

Mike finally stood up and said, "I'm going to go get some fresh air and then I'm going to hit the bed. I've got a big day tomorrow."

Mike going out for air on a warm night was nothing new to his parents. Ever since he was a child, Mike enjoyed sitting outside in the evening and smelling the air and listening to the sounds.

"What time do you start?" His dad asked.

"Nine AM, bright and early. I'm going to try and get there about ten minutes early just to make a good impression and show that I am serious bout this job."

"Sounds like a good plan," replied his dad. "Why don't you make it fifteen minutes early just in case there's traffic and then you will still be there early."

"Not a bad idea dad."

Mike walked outside not so much to get air but as a chance to find Todd and tell him everything went well. Mike had noticed Todd driving by more than once through the corner of his eye and wanted to let him know he knew Todd was driving by. He got a feeling of smugness from catching Todd spying on him. He noticed Todd slowing down so the car did not make as much noise as he drove by. Mike stood on the sidewalk outside his parents' house waiting for Todd. He knew Todd would be back before too long. Finally, after about five minutes of waiting, Mike saw a pair of headlights at the end of the street heading his way. He knew it was Todd and started pretending to hitchhike. Todd pulled up in front of Mike and rolled down his window. Before Todd could say anything Mike said "Hey babe, you going my way?"

"Shut up Mike. Judging by your jocularity I am guessing that everything went well with your parents."

Mike looked down and got a very sad look on his face. “No man, I got kicked me out. They refused to even listen to me. They won’t even let me get my stuff. I don’t know where I’ll go tonight.”

Todd’s jaw dropped as he listened to Mike. “You need to stay with me for a while? I’ll help you get your stuff to.”

“No I’d rather sleep in a box than under the same roof with you.”

Suddenly Todd realized Mike was joking. “Touché. Everything went well, didn’t it?”

“Yeah it was a little tense but it worked out ok. I think we came to an understanding.”

“Well that’s great considering you’re a punk.”

“Maybe but you have to admit I got you.”

“Yeah you got me, this time. See you in the morning for training.”

“See you tomorrow.”

Todd drove away and Mike went in and went to bed. It took him a couple hours to fall asleep but he finally drifted off thinking about starting about his new job in the morning.

Chapter 10
Redemption

On Tuesday morning, Sarah met with Tony. Sarah was looking forward to the meeting. She wanted to talk to him about the young man she had met up in Whitefish Point. She knew that Mike had some issues that he needed to work out and she thought if she told Tony the story about him that he could give her some good ideas on how to talk to him. She had not called him yet. She had decided to wait until she talked to Tony, not just about Mike, but also with the angry reaction that her father was sure to have when he found out that she was still talking to him after he had stood her up that last night up north. She knew her father didn't mean to be angry and that he just had her best interest at heart and wanted to see her get better, but still she was kind of mad at him, after all she was an adult and could make her own decisions. Certainly, she had just had some major problems in her life but she knew and she knew that her father knew that the worst was behind her and that she was on her way to recovery.

Sarah walked into Tony's office around ten o'clock in the morning. Tony's office was small. It had a desk, a big plant in the corner, some pictures of The Simpsons on one wall, his degrees from both Wayne State University and Michigan State University on another, a picture of Tony with his wife and young son on his desk, a filing cabinet in the corner, and a television mounted on the wall with a DVD/VCR at the bottom.

When Sarah entered the room, Tony was at his desk writing something down. This was slightly odd as every other time she had walked into Tony's office he was already in front of the desk. When Sarah walked in Tony greeted her immediately "Good morning Sarah, how are you on this warm sunny late spring morning?" Whenever Tony said hi to anybody, he always added something about the weather in the greeting. Sarah was not quite sure why Tony did this but she assumed that it was something that he learned in college to help put people at ease.

"Good morning." Sarah said back to Tony. "I am feeling pretty good this morning. I had a great weekend up north and there are some things that happened this weekend that I would really like to talk to you about."

Tony figured that there would be quite a bit that she wanted to talk to him about. Tony assumed that Sarah would talk to him about all of the great memories of her mother that returned while she went up north. Tony had no idea that the memories of her mother were the furthest thing from Sarah's mind this morning. Tony was encouraged that Sarah came to see him in a good mood. He knew this was progress and that she was on her way to getting better. Finally, Tony replied to Sarah, "Sorry Sarah, I'm just finishing up this application to teach up at Michigan State University part time. Do you mind waiting here while I take this down to the mail?"

"No not at all, do what you need to do."

"Thanks, do you want something to drink?"

Tony kept a small mini refrigerator under the desk in his office and always had it stocked with Coca Cola, Diet Coke, Sprite, bottled water, and small orange juice cartons. Tony believed that giving his patients a choice of a beverage made them more comfortable and helped them in discussing personal issues. At least that's what Tony claimed. Most of the time Tony had an open partially full can of Coke on his desk that he would drink from as he worked with his patients. Tony enjoyed Coca Cola greatly, it was almost an obsession of his, and he would not drink any other type of cola. One time as a joke a co-worker dumped out his Coke and replaced it with another cola while he was out of the room. When Tony came back, he took one sip from what he thought was his can of Coke and instantly spit it out all over his desk. The spray of cola coming from his mouth left a sticky film all over the top of his desk, which made the prank all the more funny to his co-workers. Tony who can usually take a joke very well barely spoke to any of his co-workers for the next three days while he cooled down from the prank. The prank went down in legend at the center and Tony still sours a little bit when someone reminds him of the story.

Sarah replied that she would like water. Tony grabbed the water from his refrigerator handed it to Sarah and left the room. Sarah sat down in one of the chairs across from Tony's desk. The chairs in Tony's office were very large and the cushions were soft. A person could easily fall asleep in those chairs, especially if Tony was doing more of the talking than they were. Nevertheless, because Tony tried to make his patients do most of the talking very few patients ever fell asleep in the chairs. Sarah opened her water, took a sip, and then began looking around the office. She looked at the pictures of The Simpson characters on the wall. Sarah was familiar with the show but never watched it very much. It came out on television when she was in elementary school and she remembered a big buzz about it in her sixth grade class as well as her middle school classes. Many of her classmates loved the show, watched it every week, and then talked about the previous night's episode with each other the following day. Sarah did not see what the big deal was about the show. She watched a few episodes each of the first two seasons and tried to like it so she could fit in and join in the very intellectually stimulating middle school level discussions of the events the next day but she never could get very into the show. By the time high school, came around most of the other students had stopped talking about the show and it seemed to lose some of its' luster. While she didn't care for the show she could appreciate why Tony had them in the room, not just because he was a big fan of the show but also because it created kind of a light hearted atmosphere in the office.

Tony meanwhile hurried down to send out his application. Teaching a college level class had always been a dream of his and having a chance to do it at Michigan State, a school he went to and grew up loving made him even more excited. He had planned to have the application mailed before Sarah came in; he hated to keep patients waiting. He always felt that by keeping them waiting he was making them even unhappier than they already were and thus making their problems worse. He was behind schedule because of a big traffic tie up on the freeway that morning. Of course, this would be the morning that there would be a problem making him late. Tony was a full hour late because of the back up. That is why he was not done with the application. Since the application deadline was this week and the fact that he procrastinated and put off mailing it in until the very last minute he had to get it out in the mail that morning so his application made the deadline. He dropped the application packet and the mailbox and headed back to his office. By the time, he got back to his office he was slightly out of breath. He apologized to Sarah for starting the session late and then took his usual spot in front of his desk, grabbed a Coke from the refrigerator, grabbed his notepad and paper and was ready to begin talking to Sarah. He was all ready to talk about how the memories of her mom made it a difficult weekend.

"So Sarah, how did your weekend go?

Here it came thought Tony, she is going to talk about her mom and I'm going to help her deal with the difficult issues.

"Well Tony, I met this guy on the beach late Saturday night or actually early Sunday morning."

Tony's jaw dropped, which was hilarious because he had his pen in his mouth and when his jaw dropped the pen fell directly into the opening in his can of Coke. Tony struggled frantically to come up with a response. The only thing he could come up with at first was "You met a what on the what now?"

Sarah laughed aloud at Tony's botched question.

Slowly Tony regained his composure. He took a deep breath and took a long drink from his can of Coke.

"You're still going to drink that after your pen fell in it? That's kind of nasty."

"Oh it's fine, it wasn't in there very long, and the Coke still tastes fine, I'm not going to waste it. But you met a guy? I was not expecting that at all. What about your mom?"

"You know that was tough especially when I first got there. But that night, I met this guy, so angry, for seemingly no reason. I couldn't understand it, both of his parents were still alive and he talked so negatively about them. I just couldn't understand why. And in that moment my focus shifted from my mom to helping him."

"Well I'm not trying to be mean, or put you down here but how do you expect to help someone so soon after such a long traumatic period?"

"I know, I thought of that too. But it just feels right. I feel like I need to help Mike."

"Well how do you plan to help him?"

"Well I asked him about his faith and he said that he really didn't care much about religion. The Lord has been so instrumental in my recovery that I thought I could take him to church and open his mind to the Lord and that would help him."

"What if he refuses to go to church? You can't just force your religious views on someone. It's not right and it usually doesn't work."

"I know that. He did give me his phone number and he did agree to come to church with me.

Tony thought for a moment. He could tell that this experience had helped Sarah psychologically quite a bit, however he also knew that if the situation didn't work as she hoped, it could be potentially devastating. He knew she had to see this through regardless of the outcome but he also knew that he had to make sure there would be no regression if her desired outcome failed to materialize. After careful calculation he said, "What if this man is unreceptive and this situation doesn't work out the way you want it too?"

"Honestly, that will be tough to take. But at the same time, I feel at peace with the situation. I really want to help people who are going through rough times because of how good both you and my dad have been to me."

"Speaking of your dad, how has he reacted to this young man? Has he met him? Does he even know about him?"

"He knows the situation somewhat but not completely."

"Explain."

"Well he knows that I met the man on the beach. However, he was supposed to meet me Sunday night and talk to me again but he didn't show."

That made Tony nervous but he reserved judgment and just motioned Sarah to go on.

Sarah continued, "My dad forbade me to see him at that point. I still felt strongly moved to go see him. He was staying in the cottage next to ours with some guys. So on Monday before we left my aunt helped me sneak away and go see him for a few minutes."

"And what happened when you saw him? Why didn't he show up Sunday night?

"He said that he had fallen asleep and never made it outside. He said that he planned to come out and talk but he just couldn't stay awake. He said he would be willing to go to church with me and he gave me his phone number. I also gave him mine."

"So what's your plan? Are you going to call him or wait for him to call you?"

"My plan is to wait until the weekend and then invite him to church next weekend. If he calls me sooner that's fine but I don't think he will."

"Why not?"

"Well he told me he is starting a new job this week. He told me he received a promoted to assistant manager of a sporting goods store. I assume this will take a good deal of his time this week and that he won't have time to call me."

"What if he doesn't answer or return any of your calls?"

"I'll be disappointed but not deterred. I really think I may have found a new calling."

"And what might that calling be?"

"I think I would like to be a social worker or a psychiatrist. I think being a child psychiatrist would be a rewarding job. The way it sounds Mike had a very rough childhood, and I have been wondering if someone had talked to him sooner what he would be like now. Also, I thought about how much you have helped me and I would love the opportunity to help someone else the way you have helped me."

"Those are very admirable goals. Plus with all that you have been through you could draw on a wealth of personally experience."

"I thought the exact same thing. It would make me so happy of something that amazing and positive could come out of all this."

"So Mike works in a sporting goods store as an assistant manager you said."

"Yes, I guess he is just starting management training this week."

"Do you know if this is a lifelong dream for him?"

"I don't. But he sounded very excited about the job."

"What did he say that made you think that he had a poor relationship with his parents?"

"Well when I first met him on the beach he was yelling and screaming out at the water and most of it was directed towards his parents. Then when I talked to him he told me how he hated his parents and wished they were dead."

"How did that make you feel having lost your mom and having such a problem with it?"

"Well at first it made me very mad."

"That's understandable."

"I couldn't believe how someone who had not lost either of his parents could talk so badly about them."

"Well you have to remember to that not everybody on this planet has had parents as loving as yours."

"I know. I thought of that and that helped me calm down and have a conversation with this guy instead of just taking his head off."

"That's good that you were able to show that kind of restraint. It shows that you are really making some progress."

"Thank you."

Tony sat back and thought for a moment. This was not the conversation he had expected to have this morning. He was astounded at how much better she seemed this morning. He was actually considering letting her go home and releasing her from inpatient care. He decided to dig a little more though. After all, he had never seen such a turnaround in a person so fast. He did not want to make a mistake and send her home too soon.

He finally said to her, "Have you had any more thoughts about suicide since you met this man?"

"Why would you even ask me that?" Sarah said with a hint of anger.

"It's my job, I have to ask you that. I have to know that you are not a danger to yourself or anyone else if I am going to let you go home and strictly come and see me on an outpatient basis."

"You mean you would let me go back home and live with my dad?"

"With the change that I have seen in you there is no reason to keep you here full time. But you still haven't answered my question. Have you had any suicidal thoughts?"

"No."

"Are you sure?"

"Yes I am one hundred percent sure. I really feel I have a purpose again. I need to help people who are in similar situations as I was. I can't kill myself, there are too many people to help."

"That's good. I'm glad you are doing so much better. That Upper Peninsula really must have done something to you."

"Have you ever been there?"

"No, I have never been up that way."

"You definitely should take your wife and son up there. It is so beautiful and so peaceful and it just centers you in a way that nothing else can."

"Well judging by the changes that I have seen in you today, I would have to agree. Maybe this summer I can get some time off and take the family up there for a few days.

"Trust me you will be glad that you did."

"It sounds like I would."

"We still have to talk to your dad and tell him everything from this morning's session and make sure he agrees with this decision."

"I understand. He is waiting down the street at the diner. He has his cell phone if you want to call him and bring him in now."

"Boy you really are in a hurry to get out of here aren't you?"

"I sure am."

Tony was now confident that Sarah would be fine. Tony called Sarah's dad and he was in Tony's office in ten minutes.

Sarah had been thinking about Tony teaching a class of college kids from a wheelchair. She knew how horrible young kids could be and she was afraid that college students would make fun of him. Finally, she couldn't stay silent on the subject and saw the time spent waiting for her dad as a great opportunity to ask him about it.

"Tony?"

"Yes."

"Are you nervous that the students will make fun of the fact that you are in a wheelchair? I know how cruel young people can be and it makes me nervous for you."

"Don't worry about me. I will be fine. Even young people, when they hear my story, usually end up tripping over themselves to try and not say anything that I could construe as the least bit offensive. In fact, more often than not they annoy me by not treating me like a normal person and attempting to bend over backwards to make me feel better. Besides, I pity any person who would make fun of my situation. Making fun of something like that shows that a person is full of nothing but fear and anger, and I can't imagine the sadness of a life like that."

"Wow, how profound." In that moment, Sarah gained even more respect for Tony. She almost saw him as a modern day hero. At that point, Sarah's father walked into the room. Tony invited him to sit down and began explaining the results of the morning's session to him.

"Well, it seems we have some good news this morning sir."

"I'm always ready to here some good news."

"I have determined that Sarah no longer needs inpatient care. She can return home and live at your house but she still has to come in and see me for an hour a day five times a week."

"How long will she have to come see you for?"

"For the foreseeable future. As she continues to get better, we can lessen the amount of visits until she no longer has to come in."

"Well that sounds great. What brought this on?"

"Well Sarah told me about her weekend and about some future plans that she has and I do not think she poses a threat to herself or anyone else. Now Sarah, why don't you tell your dad about the plans you have for your future?"

"I want to be a counselor or child psychiatrist so I can help people who are in similar situations as me."

"Well I think that's a very noble aspiration."

"Sarah," Tony jumped in, "tell him why you want to do this."

"It's because of that boy I met up north."

"Him!" Her dad exclaimed, his face turned red, and he yelled, "I'll murder him. He's hurting you. I knew your aunt let you sneak out, damn it!"

"No it's not like that. I did talk to him before we left and we exchanged numbers."

"Damn it Sarah the boy probably just wants to get in your pants."

"No just listen, I want to help him. He had so much anger towards his parents that I want him to find something he can be a part of that is positive. I want to take him to church."

At this point Tony jumped in and spoke to Sarah's dad. "Sir, this is something your daughter has to do. I can understand why you think this boy is bad for your daughter, but ultimately helping him will help her. You have to let Sarah do this for her own health."

"But what if he refuses her help? What if she tries her hardest and he doesn't change? What if that causes more depression? What then? We're right back where we started."

"I am very confident that will not happen. I would not be releasing her if I thought there was any chance of a relapse. That was my first concern as well but talking to Sarah has assuaged my fears of such an event occurring."

"You really believe that she will be fine?"

"I do. She has made a miraculous recovery. And if there are any problems I will still be seeing her five times a week, and remember you can always bring her back in if there is a problem, but I don't think there will be, just talk to your daughter about it sir."

"Daddy," Sarah jumped in." I know you are scared. I know you don't want to lose me, but I promise you don't have to worry about that anymore. I may not be one hundred percent better, I know that but you have to believe me, everything is going to be all right from here on out."

Sarah's dad looked into his daughter's eyes. He suddenly noticed a little bit of a spark. The same spark he had always seen in her eyes before her mother got sick. Suddenly he knew that both Tony and his daughter were right and that everything would be fine from now on. A smile slowly came over her dad's face and a couple of tears slowly rolled down his cheek. These were not tears of sadness but tears of joy. He finally realized that he had his little girl back. He realized that the Lord had sent the young man to bring his daughter back and he was no longer mad at him. He knew that Sarah had to try to redeem the young man's soul; it was the right thing to do. Sarah and her dad hugged and Tony smiled and watched. Sarah's dad knew that Sarah's life and soul would achieve redemption through helping this young man and others like him. He knew there was a chance of failure but he also knew that succeed or fail, Sarah, his precious little Sarah, was back.

"I love you honey."

"I love you too daddy."

Tony smiled. "Well I'll draw up the papers and then you two can be on your way."

Tony got the papers ready, signed them, and then gave them to Sarah and her dad to sign. They both signed them, and by twelve-thirty, Sarah was in her dad's car, heading home once again.

Chapter 11
A New Start

Mike woke up early on Tuesday morning. This was unlike Mike. Mike often had to wake up early for work; he usually had little difficulty with that unless he was hung over. However, Mike had not just woken up early he had woken up early on a morning after he had trouble sleeping and that either never happened or almost never happened. Mike lay awake in bed until sometime shortly after 2AM. He was excited about starting his new job. He felt like a little kid on Christmas Eve lying awake in bed with insomnia waiting to see what new toys Santa Claus left under the Christmas tree. Mike knew that excitement well also, he had often been one of those kids who had a very difficult time sleeping on Christmas Eve; it drove his parents to the brink of insanity a couple of times in Mike's younger days.

Mike decided that since he was awake that he might as well get up. He thought maybe he would have a nice breakfast and take a shower. Mike usually showered only at night and not in the morning but this was no ordinary morning. He was starting a new job, a job that he knew he would actually like and do well at, and a job that offered Mike a chance for advancement. The jobs that Mike had held up until now had all been dead end menial jobs with absolutely no hope for advancement or as it was often called in, these times "career growth." Mike stood up next to his bed, stretched, let out a bit of yawn, even though he did not feel tired and walked into the kitchen. When his mother saw him, she almost spit out her coffee in surprise. Mike's parents had not seen Mike out of bed earlier than he had to be since he was ten. This was a monumental occurrence in their house. His parents had asked Mike before he went to bed what time he had planned to get up in the morning and he had told them eight o'clock, and here it was only seven fifteen and

Mike was strolling into the kitchen forty-five minutes before he had planned to get up.

Mike's mother regained herself from nearly sending a shower of coffee onto the kitchen wall across from her chair and asked Mike why he was up so early. "Just couldn't sleep. I woke up wide awake and decided I might as well get up, have breakfast, and maybe take a shower before work."

"Take a shower! You just took a shower last night, why do you need another one?"

This question wasn't meant to be a shot at Mike just a question more about money than showering. Mike's parents were not rich and lived much of their lives trying to stay just ahead of winding up in the poorhouse. His mother's main concern was about the water bill and not whether Mike was clean and smelled good or not.

"Hey this is my first day as management. I feel I need to project a certain aura. Two showers in less than twelve hours could help with that."

"Aura shmura, you'll be fine. You want to project an aura put on a suit."

"None of the assistant managers, or even the general managers for that matter wear suits. I don't know how smart of a career move it would be to upstage my boss by wearing a suit. Besides there is a required uniform I must wear."

"Excuses, excuses. You know what they say excuses are like don't you son?

"Yes mom, I am well aware. Very classy by the way."

"About as classy as passing out from drinking in various places around the house, I suppose."

"Low blow, mom."

Mike was not angry by his mom's comment. He knew that she said it in good fun. Actually, the jocular exchange with his mother filled Mike with confidence. He had not had such an exchange with either of his parents in a very long time. It signaled to Mike that his parents were behind him on his new venture and that he had their support. That had not happened between Mike and his parents since he could remember.

Mike ended up just having a bowl of Cheerios in milk for breakfast. His grand plans of making sausage, eggs, and pancakes, evaporated with the passing seconds as he stalled hoping his mom would volunteer to make that for him. By the time he gave up his quest of getting his mother to cook him breakfast he only had time for cereal. That was not any different than any other day however, cereal is what he usually ate for breakfast. Mike was not overly excited about the Cheerios either. He liked them but he liked the Honey Nut Cheerios better. However, those were not in the cabinet. Mike could have sworn there were some left still but he was wrong. His mom or dad must have finished them over the weekend and left Mike with just regular Cheerios for the week. He silently cursed Todd briefly for him getting shut out of the last of the Honey Nut Cheerios, ate his regular Cheerios, threw his bowl and spoon in the sink, and went in the bathroom to shave and wash his face. While washing his face, he heard a yell from the other room. "Mike you left your cereal and the milk out on the table come and put them away."

Mike knew right away that it was his mother yelling and while he thought to himself that, she was right there why couldn't she just put the stuff away but he knew it was a moot point in presenting that argument. Mike finished washing his face and before he went to put his uniform on, he walked into the kitchen and put the milk and cereal away.

Mike then went to his bedroom, got dressed. He then grabbed his car keys and walked out onto the front porch. It was a beautiful late May morning. The clouds that were hanging in last night must have broken up during the night and now there was nothing but clear skies and bright beautiful late spring sunshine. Mike stood feeling the light breeze on his face and smelling the morning air for a few minutes before getting into his car. After a few minutes he yelled back through the open screen door to his mother that he was leaving for work, climbed into his car, turned on some music and took off for work.

Mike was a bit nervous as he drove to work. Ever since childhood, new things had always made him at least somewhat nervous. Nervousness ranged from minimal to off the charts depending on his situation. This situation was no different. He was a bit nervous that somehow, someway things would not work out and he would be right back where he started, then what would he tell his parents, especially after the conversation, they had last night.

As Mike got closer to work his anxiety grew. He started to think what if I really didn't get the promotion. What if somehow it fell through at the last second and I didn't get it? What would he do then? How would he tell his parents? How would he survive the embarrassment?

Mike pulled into the mall parking lot and parked. Mike never parked right by the entrance for a couple of reasons. First, it was against the rules. The spots nearest the doors were supposed to be reserved for customers. Mike honored this request while many other co-workers; Todd included, ignored it, and parked close to the door. Mike didn't mind the longer walk to the store even when it was cold out. However the second reason Mike did not park close was simply he did not like to park by other cars. Mike didn't like having to back out from in between two cars. It was just more difficult than it needed to be so he preferred to park far away and have an easy out.

Mike sat silently listening to the end of a song and then shut the car off, got out and locked it up. He began what seemed to be a longer than normal walk to the store. It seemed longer than normal because he was walking slower with the anxiety of perhaps something falling through and him losing the promotion weighing on his mind. Finally, as he got close to the store, he was able to swallow his fear, realizing that he had to appear confident to Todd on his first day of training.

Mike entered the store and Todd was right there waiting for him. There was a man in a suit standing next to him that he had never seen before. Mike at first thought that the man was a customer but quickly realized by his posture and body language that he was someone of importance in the company and that he was undoubtedly here to begin his training. Mike saw this as a good thing seeing as though someone like that would not come all the way down just to tell Mike that the promotion had fallen through. Also by reading Todd's face he didn't see any disappointment in Todd's expression which also reassured Mike that everything was still the same as it had been last night. The man standing next to Todd was tall, overweight and wore a grey sport coat with a white shirt, a red tie, grey pants, and black shoes. Most of the man's original hair color had faded to grey. In his mind, Mike guessed that the man was in his fifties. He was a large enough operate that his stature combined with his rank in the company gave a somewhat intimidating vibe to Mike.

As Mike walked in Todd began to speak right away, "See, look at that, right on time. I told you this guy was trustworthy."

The man in the suit replied to Todd, "Well Todd, as I told you before, we trust your judgment. We would never have promoted you if we did not trust you."

Mike was getting a bit nervous that neither Todd or the man in the suit had spoken to him yet and he had been standing there for a couple of minutes. Finally, after what seemed like an eternity, Todd spoke to him "Mike, what's up man?"

Mike was relieved that Todd was talking to him in such a lighthearted way. His level of anxiety quickly plummeted and he was able to respond to Todd calmly. "Not too much."

"Ready to get started?"

"You know I am. Just tell me what to do."

"Look at this guy, can't even contain his excitement."

Mike could see that the man in the suit was starting to get impatient. He was about ready to ask Todd who the man was when Todd jumped in. "Mike, this is Phillip Lavello, the vice president of human resources and training for the state of Michigan."

Phillip extended a handshake to Mike and Mike quickly accepted the handshake. Mike was sure to use a strong grip yet not too strong. He wanted to show confidence with a firm handshake but he also wanted to be conscious not to hurt the man's hand. Mike was also sure to say, "Nice to meet you, Phillip." Mike wanted to be sure to be polite. He had always learned to be very polite when dealing with superiors in business no matter what the situation and how angry he may be, this way when it came time for promotions the people who make those decisions would remember your character and help you out as a result. Mike knew how business worked. Nepotism ruled and right now, he was at the bottom, so he had to be the world's best employee for everybody, especially Phillip.

"It's nice to meet you, Mike," Phillip began, "Todd has told us great things about you and we look forward to having you join our management team. I will be working with you today and tomorrow to go over the corporate side of your trainings. You will be learning many company policies, as well as techniques for managing a successful store. Todd will work with you the rest of the week on day-to-day operations of the store to complete your training. Do you have any questions so far?"

"No. Just anxious to get started"

"Excellent. Then we'll get started. We will start this morning by watching some videos on the company and what we do. This will also give you an in depths look at our product line. We'll have lunch about noon and we will continue this afternoon in our satellite Detroit area office in Novi this afternoon. Are you familiar with the Novi area Mike?"

Mike did not know the area well. He had been to the Twelve Oaks Mall off I96 a couple of times but that was the extent of his knowledge of the area. Mike however wanted Phillip to think that he was smart so he said, "I know it pretty well."

Phillip smiled and said, "Good, here's the address, we will meet there after lunch and tomorrow morning."

Mike then went with Phillip into Todd's office. When they got in his office Phillip shut the door and began telling Mike about his history with the company, "I started working for Rudy's sporting goods when I was 17 and a senior in high school. I started as a sales associate. I then attended Oakland University where I pursued a major in business administration with a minor in human resource management. During my second year of college, an assistant manager position opened at my store. Since Rudy's believes very heavily in promoting from within, I was offered the job and I accepted it. I worked as an assistant manager until I got my bachelor's degree and was then offered the chance to manage my own store down in Toledo. While I really didn't want to move out of Michigan, I took the job. I knew it would be a huge stepping-stone for me. The store was failing when I got there. I turned it into a money maker, and just as a side note, I lived in Dundee, Michigan so I wouldn't have to be a resident of Ohio and I could still commute to work."

Mike could tell that Phillip was looking for a laugh at his Ohio comment so he was sure to give it a small chuckle. Phillip smiled when Mike chuckled. Mike really didn't find it that funny but he knew charity chuckles were part of being the model employee.

Phillip continued "I managed that store for three years and then finally an entry level position in human resources opened up here in Novi. I applied, interviewed twice, and got the job. So on my way home that night I bought a ring for my girlfriend, took her to dinner, popped the question, she said yes, we got married a year later and now we've been married for ten years. We have a son named Jeremy who will turn six on June 30 and will start first grade this September, and we have a daughter named Elizabeth who just turned 3 two weeks ago. In the last ten years, I have applied for and received four promotions, right now there is only one position left for me, and that is to be president of human resources. That is my goal. There is room for great advancement in this company if you are willing to put in the time and the effort. Are you willing to do that Mike?"

"Definitely," Mike answered without hesitation. "I definitely want to find a company to advance in. I also love that this is a sporting goods company. I have played a great deal of baseball in my life and follow baseball, football, and hockey religiously. I even pitched for a couple of years in A ball over in West Michigan."

"Yeah, Todd mentioned that to me when he told me about you. That must have been a great experience So seeing as you follow sports religiously what did you think about our Lions last year?"

"Pretty pathetic. It's difficult to watch. I'm a huge fan and I follow them constantly but that can be pretty brutal at times"

"Brutal is putting it mildly." Just wait until you're thirty-eight like I am and you've really had some time to witness their futility. You don't know the meaning of the word brutal until you've suffered as long as I have."

Mike laughed and the two men got down to work. The morning was a rather boring one for Mike. He had to watch about two hours of videos on the company and its products. As Mike was walking out at noon to go to lunch Todd stopped him. "How is it going?"

"So far it seems to be going pretty well. We even laughed together a little bit."

"Yeah, Phil is a nice guy. You holding up all right?"

"Yeah, everything is fine. Just going to shoot out to Novi for the afternoon."

"Give me a call when you get home tonight."

"No problem. All right take it easy."

"Always do."

Mike headed out to the car. He did not intend to get lunch. He wanted to find the Novi office. Mike was not great at finding bland buildings while driving so he knew he wanted to get there early just in case he had trouble finding it. That turned out to be a great decision. Mike did have trouble finding it but because he had left early, he was able to find the building with ten minutes to spare. He chugged down some Coke, scarfed down a cereal bar that was in his car to tide him over, and went into training.

The afternoon was full of reading through manuals and talking with Phillip about products and company policy. He found the stuff boring but he knew he had to do it and that the job would be much more enjoyable than the training. Mike left at five o'clock and headed home. The freeway traffic was awful and he finally got home at about six-thirty.

His parents had saved some dinner for him and he sat down and ate it. It was meatloaf, mashed potatoes, and corn. Mike was starving so everything tasted awesome. However, Mike knew that by staying out in a common area of the house he would be subject to a million questions from his parents. The questions started right on cue.

"How was your first day?" his mother asked.

"Fine."

"What does fine mean? What did you do?"

"Watched some videos, read some manuals, had to go to Novi in the afternoon."

"Novi, what did you have to go all the way out there for?"

"That's where the corporate office is for the Detroit area. I have to go out there again tomorrow."

"Corporate office? Already?" his dad said with a smile and a laugh.

"Yep," Mike said trying to eat his dinner.

"Well, Novi is so far. You don't have to go out there all week do you?"

"No. Just tomorrow and then I'll be at the store for the rest of the week after that."

"Well that's good. You don't need to be wasting all of your extra money on gas. It wouldn't be worth it."

Mike agreed with a nod and finished his dinner. "So are you tired"? Mike's mom asked as he was putting his plate and glass in the sink.

"Yeah a little bit. Probably going to go to bed early tonight as I'll have to get up really early tomorrow to get to Novi by nine with traffic the way it is."

Mike called Todd as he said he would. He told Todd about the day, the boredom, and all of that. Todd knew exactly what Mike meant when he talked about the boredom. He had gone through the same training. He knew that it could get pretty mind numbing. "Hey just think you've only got one more day of this and then the rest of the week is easy stuff in store. It will seem like heaven compared to what you are doing right now."

"Heaven huh? Well thank God for that. I don't know how much more of this stuff I could take."

Mike got off the phone with Todd, took a shower, and went to bed. He slept very well until his alarm rudely jerked him awake at seven. Mike grudgingly got up and went back for day two of training. Todd was right. It was just as mind numbing if not more so than the first day. Mike made it through the day and came home again. Thursday, Friday, and Saturday were much better days for Mike. He was in the store, which he liked and working with Todd was not like working for a normal boss. Mike had never been a friend with any of his former bosses as he was with Todd. This made the three days of training seem to fly by. A few minutes before five on Saturday, Todd called Mike into his office and gave him a certificate of completion for having completed management training for Rudy's. The certificate had both Todd, and Philip's signature on it and it felt good to Todd that it was all finally official.

"Hey buddy congratulations! You up for going out to celebrate a little?"

"Yeah that sounds cool. What did you have in mind?"

"We were thinking about getting some tickets to the Tigers' game tonight down at Comerica Park."

"I would love to go but my parents want to go out to dinner to celebrate the end of training. But let me call and see if they are willing to push that up until tomorrow." Mike pulled out his cell phone and scrolled through the contacts for his home number. "Hi mom. It's Mike."

"How is your day going? Is there something wrong? You never call me during the day while at work?"

"No nothing is wrong but Todd just invited me out to the Tigers' game tonight and I was wondering if we could push our dinner up until tomorrow night?"

"That shouldn't be a problem. Actually, your father will probably prefer that. He had to work today too and you know how he feels about going out after work. It's not exactly his favorite thing in the world. You go ahead and go to the game. I'll tell your father and we'll just grill up some hamburgers and have some baked beans and potatoes on the side. Should we make a plate for you?"

"Let me ask Todd. Hey Todd what time do you want to leave for the game?"

"Well, the game starts at 7:05 and it would be nice to get some dinner before hand so I was thinking that you could go home, shower, and change while I picked up my brothers and we'd be over to get you by 5:15."

"That works. Mom, I'm just going to come home, shower, and change and probably be gone within a half hour so you don't need to fix me a plate. We're going to grab something before the game."

"That sounds fine, son. Enjoy the game."

"Well unfortunately that's not up to us. I hope that they give us a good game. They've had a rough year this year."

"That they have. It's pretty bad that I can tell that having not watched any games but just listening to your father swear at the television from the other room."

"I know what you mean. He has been very...animated. I should get going."

"No problem dear. See you when you get home."

"Right."

Mike hung up the phone and then turned to Todd, "we're all set, buddy."

"So you were able to reschedule dinner?"

"Yeah, we're going to go tomorrow. My dad hates going out after work anyway. He just likes to eat dinner, relax, and watch television. He'll be thrilled that we changed the dinner to tomorrow."

"Sounds a little bit like my dad some nights. What happens to people's energy, as they get older? My dad was always doing something after work when we were kids now he just relaxes and does nothing more often than not."

"I don't know but I hope that never happens to me. A life sitting in front of the television with no higher aspirations just seems so mind numbing, not that I'm criticizing my father. I mean we all have our own likes but there is just so much beauty out in nature and there can be so much excitement out on the town that it would seem to me that I would miss something by watching television all the time. Some nights I really enjoy it, but not every night."

"Wow, deep thoughts from Mike today. Could it be that our weekend helped you?"

"I'll be honest Todd, looking back on it after only a week, it has done wonders for me. I feel like I owe you something big."

"You don't owe me anything, just keep working hard and when the opportunity presents itself repay the favor for someone else."

"I definitely will. I should get home, shower, and get ready for the game."

"Yeah, you should, you smell like golf equipment. Not hot."

"What kind of insult is that?" Mike said with a rising anger in his voice.

"Obviously a pretty good one, it got you pretty worked up, looks like you are even turning red."

"Don't worry, I'll get you later, but for now I gotta go."

Mike ran into the house when he got home. It seemed like on his way home that he was driving behind every slow driver on the planet. He got frustrated many times and was complaining to himself the entire way that all of these slow drivers were making him late. Although in reality, they only added four minutes to his drive, in Mike's mind it seemed like they added fourteen minutes. Mike ran through the kitchen passing right by his mother then down to his bedroom and grabbed some clothes. He grabbed an old Detroit Tigers shirt that he had as he was going to the game and a pair of khaki shorts. Then he ran back upstairs into the bathroom and shut the door. On this night, Mike took what his father would call a military shower. That meaning he turned on the water got in, rinsed himself for thirty seconds, then soaped himself up, rinsed off for another thirty seconds, then rinsed his hair for thirty seconds, shampooed it up, rinsed for a minute then shut off the water. In and out in four and a half minutes, he said to himself when he was finished. Mike had been looking forward to a long hot shower after work today as that was one of his favorite ways to relieve the stress of a day of work but today he was more anxious to go to Comerica Park for the first time. He had been to a number of games at the old Tiger Stadium with his dad and his uncles but he had never been to the new ballpark yet. Mike had made his own silent protest against progress over the first couple of years that the stadium had been opened, but now he had felt it had been a long enough time that he wasn't doing anything wrong by going to the new park as long as he didn't like it better than the old Tiger Stadium.

When Mike came back out into the kitchen his mother was waiting for him. "Well hello to you too, son" she said sarcastically. "My son is so busy now that he doesn't even have time to say hello to his own mother."

"Sorry mom traffic was terrible on the way home and I was in a bit of a hurry so I would be ready when Todd got here."

"That's still no excuse for not saying hi to your mother. Promise me it won't happen again."

"All right I promise I'll say hi to you when I come in the house." Mike knew he could not back up the promise. He knew he would forget again at some point. Not because he did not notice his mom but just because he knew it was in his nature to forget and in her nature to remind him when he forgot. Actually, that characteristic is probably present in all mothers, not just Mike's

"Thank you son."

"You're welcome mom."

Mike grabbed a bottle of water out of the refrigerator and gulped down about half of it while waiting for Todd. When Todd got there, Mike said good-bye to his mom and left.

Mike began to open the door to Todd's back seat when Todd yelled out the open window, "Mike, don't go back there, we're celebrating you tonight, I called permanent shotgun for you for the entire night when I picked up my brothers so you're up front for the evening."

"You don't have to do that, let one of them sit up front, I feel bad, after all they're your blood."

"Don't be silly Mike it's your night." Suddenly Randy interrupted Todd from the back seat, "don't worry about it Mike you are doing us both a favor. We see him all the time and sit up in his front seat all the time; we are actually relishing the opportunity to not have to sit next to him. In fact we're not sitting next to him all night, that's all you all night Mike."

"I can just feel the brotherly love just oozing out of this car," Mike said while laughing. "I guess I'm riding shotgun all night." Mike walked over to the other side of the car and got in the passenger side of the front seat. They drove down and parked near Comerica Park. Mike could already tell that the parking was better at the new ballpark. He had memories of being at games with his dad and his uncles and parking at some seedy looking lots near the old Tiger Stadium. But that didn't phase Mike much as he realized the parking wasn't what counted, it was the experience of the ballgame that counted and that could only be had inside the stadium, and while Comerica

Park is a beautiful park, he thought in his mind that the atmosphere inside would never live up to what Tiger Stadium was.

The four men had dinner at Cheli's Chili Bar located right next to Comerica Park. Mike had always wanted to come here. The restaurant, owned by former Detroit Red Wings defenseman Chris Chelios had become a popular destination for all Detroit sports fans. They enjoyed their dinner then went into the ballpark and got to their seats about 6:55, ten minutes before the first pitch. They were sitting in the upper deck on the first base side of the field almost directly behind first base and about fifteen rows up. Mike sat down, and looked around and thought that they had done a good job in building the new ballpark. His seat was very comfortable as far as stadium seats go and the field was beautiful. At least in these seats, they had a great view of the field. Mike knew he would be able to see everything that happened perfectly. Todd turned to Mike, "So is this your first time here?"

"How could you tell?"

"The way you have looked around at everything the entire evening you're like a wide eyed kid going to Disneyland for the first time."

"That obvious?"

"Even more. So what do you think so far?"

"Well it's a beautiful park. I can't get over the openness of it. I love the statues of the hall of famers past the outfield seats and the retired numbers on the brick wall. That is very cool. The view from the upper deck here is awesome it looks like there is not a bad seat in the house. I remember seats at the old Tiger Stadium that were behind giant poles. Luckily for me I was never unfortunate enough to be sitting in one of those seats."

"Yeah this place is so much better than Tiger Stadium was."

"As nice as this place is, Todd, I have to disagree. Tiger Stadium just had a certain atmosphere to it that I don't feel here. This is a much more comfortable and aesthetically pleasing park but the atmosphere of a game at Tiger Stadium in my mind can never be matched."

"Well, we'll have to see if we can change your mind. I liked Tiger Stadium a lot too and I was even skeptical at coming to the new ballpark but I think I like it better."

"Well that's your opinion and you're entitled to it. I would love to go to one of the other old ballparks to see if they have the same atmosphere as Tiger Stadium did. I especially want to go to Wrigley Field in Chicago. The Cubs have always been my second favorite team behind the Tigers. I remember when The Cubs were playing the Padres in the 84 NLCS, I was hoping that the Cubs would win so I could see my two favorite teams play each other in the World Series."

"I've been to Wrigley and it really is one of the best places to go see a game. Definitely make your way out there, you won't regret it one bit."

"My cousin said the same thing. In fact, everybody who I've talked to that has ever been there has said the same thing. I will definitely get there while I have the chance."

The game began, as Mike and Todd were finishing up there conversation about Wrigley Field. They all watched intently as it was a rather exciting game. The Tigers were playing The Kansas City Royals and there was a great deal of offense in the game. However, in the end they all left the game disappointed as The Tigers blew an 8-6 lead in the top of the ninth when the Royals scored four times to take a 10-8 lead. The Tigers were able to make it interesting in the bottom of the ninth as they cut the lead to 10-9 on an RBI single but the last batter struck out with the bases loaded to end the game. While Mike, Todd, and Todd's brothers were, disappointed in the outcome of the game they all had a great time and Comerica Park's traditional Saturday night fireworks display took the sting out of the loss. Mike was very impressed with the fireworks. He was expecting a quick and cheap display but got what he thought may have been the best professionally done fireworks display that he had ever seen. They drove home, or rather, tried to drive home as they found themselves caught in the bumper-to-bumper traffic that ensues after every Tiger game. For the entire trip home they laughed, joked, and had a great time. Mike realized that this was the best night out that he had been on in a very long time and he was both amazed and satisfied that he was able to accomplish this without alcohol.

Mike pulled up in front of Todd's house around 11:30. "Hope you enjoyed the game."

"Awesome time! Thank you for taking me. It was great. The fireworks were unbelievable."

"They usually are. Comerica puts on a great show. What are you doing tomorrow?"

"I'll probably just relax. I have dinner with my parents around four-thirty but the rest of the day I'll probably just sleep in, listen to some music, sit outside, and watch some television. I'm not sure yet."

"Sounds like a good plan. I'll be around to the store periodically to check on you but I know you'll have it under control."

"I sure will. Take it easy."

"You too, get some rest and enjoy your day off." With that Todd pulled away and Mike went into the house."

Mike's dad was still awake watching television when Mike came in. "So they blew another one, eh?"

"Yeah, that team needs some relief pitching big time."

"You got that right, son. So how was the ballpark?"

"Really nice. It's very open and it doesn't look like there is a bad seat in the house."

"Well I doubt it's better than the old Tiger Stadium."

"In some ways it is. There are no obstructed views, the parking is better, and safer, and aesthetically Comerica Park is better than Tiger Stadium. But Comerica Park can't touch the atmosphere that Tiger Stadium had. There isn't a real organ, and the hot dogs aren't as good as they used to be, so overall, Tiger Stadium is better. For once we agree."

"Excellent. Hope you had fun and I'm glad we could agree on that." Mike's dad went back to watching television and Mike went to the bathroom, brushed his teeth, and then went to his room and went to bed.

Mike did exactly what he told Todd he would do on Sunday. He hung around the house, watched some television, listened to a couple CDs, and played some video games. At four-thirty, he went with his parents to an Italian restaurant called Louie's that was not far from his parents' house. Louie's was his dad's favorite restaurant and, although Mike wouldn't want to admit it at the risk of having something in common with his dad, it was his favorite restaurant as well. Louie's was a family owned restaurant and the food was excellent. They gave you large portions and the service was always top notch. Mike's favorite dish there was the lasagna and that is what he got that day. Mike could normally only eat half of it, as he would always fill up on minestrone soup, salad, and bread before his main course came. That did not bother Mike, as the leftovers would become his lunch on Monday at work. Mike and his parents sat and talked through the entire meal like they hadn't done since Mike was still in middle school. They talked about Mike's job, the Tigers, goals, and just made general small talk getting to know each other once again.

After dinner, Mike went and sat outside for the evening. It was a warm summer evening and Mike just sat at the picnic table in the yard. Mike watched as the sun slowly descended below the trees that were in the yard behind his house. He sat until the sun was gone and it was completely dark. As Mike sat outside, now looking at the moon instead of the sun, he knew a new chapter in his life was opening. He quietly thought that he could not wait to see where it took him.

Chapter 12
Moving on

Sarah walked into her bedroom. It was the first time she had been in this room in nearly five months. The room definitely brought back some painful memories that made her slightly uneasy. She looked around at the carpet, the walls, looked out the window, then looked at the bed where she had nearly died. The entire scene was almost too much to take in. Sarah's eyes flashed over to her dresser and mirror where there still hung pictures of her and Steve from happier times. She looked at the pictures for a moment and suddenly realized that the pictures of Steve brought something other than sadness. She continued to stare at the pictures and suddenly noticed that there was a bit of anger brewing inside her at Steve for abandoning her in her darkest hour. Sarah was unsure of how to interpret this feeling. She had never been an angry person and really could not remember a time when she was truly angry with a person. Sarah had been angry before in her life but she had always been angry for short periods over trivial things that worked themselves out quickly. This anger inside her did not seem like it would fade away quickly. The idea of lingering anger made scared Sarah. Having studied in the medical field, she had read many studies on how pent up stress and anger can make people sick. When she first started reading such studies she did not believe them and she dismissed the idea as pseudo science and thought little of it. However as she continued to read more and more studies with statistics showing that pent up stress causes chronic disease she began thinking that with so much data the theory can not be wrong. She immediately became concerned that the anger would not go away and it would lead to stress, which in turn would make her sick. She also saw herself as being at higher risk for such things because of what she had experienced.

Then just as suddenly as all of that negative energy hit her she noticed a positive. She began to think that since she was concerned about the stress and anger that she must really want to live. She surmised that if she still did not want to live that she would welcome the anger and stress as they would only hasten her exit from her own personal torment. This brought a smile to Sarah's face and while she knew there were still lingering feelings of ill will towards Steve, that she would be able to control them and not allow them to become a major issue. She even cracked a small smile as she reached up to the mirror and began to take the photos of her and Steve down and throw them into the trash basket beside her desk.

Meanwhile very quietly and without Sarah's knowledge, her father had been lurking in the hallway outside of Sarah's room out of her sight. While he trusted Tony's opinion, he remained skeptical as to whether his daughter was ready to return home. He thought it would be a good idea to hide in the shadows out of sight near his daughter just to make sure that she was not having any problems. The problem with his strategy was that he was not the most stealthy individual and further complicating the problem was the fact that he believed that he was quite stealthy so often times it was his own arrogance that ultimately lead to him being found out in situations in which he tried to eavesdrop. His wife had been especially good at catching him. He had never heard any part of a conversation that she did not want him to hear. She would find him out within seconds and was not shy about banishing him to another room in the house. Through the years, he always assumed that his wife was just a master detective and that his eavesdropping skills were actually quite good when in all reality they were not. While Sarah did not inherit quite all of her mother's keen observation skills she did inherit some and that combined with her dad's overall ineffectiveness at eavesdropping she eventually heard him breathe as she was tossing out old photos of Steve into the garbage. Sarah was not mad that her father was eavesdropping, she knew why he was doing it, but she decided to have a little fun with her dad in an attempt to show him that she was in fact doing much better.

Sarah pulled the last few pictures of Steve off the mirror but instead of throwing them away held them in her hand. Quickly she worked up some tears. Her father trying to remain in a state of cat like readiness heard the tears and was ready to spring into action to save his daughter. He was so eager in fact that he tripped over his own feet and landed sprawled out on the floor in front of Sarah's door. Sarah was not a skilled enough actress to continue the crying game after seeing her father stumble; try in a vain attempt to catch himself and then ultimately land with a thud on the hallway floor. Sarah immediately busted into laughter. Her father surging with adrenaline from the combination of his fall and his daughter's crying popped right up off the floor like a wrestler pretending to be injured and sprang to his daughter. "Honey, Honey, what's the matter? Are you all right? I heard crying. Why are you laughing? What's wrong?"

"I'm sorry dad. I heard you eavesdropping in the hallway and thought I would play a little prank. I had no idea it would turn out like that. Did you hurt yourself in the fall?"

Her father, realizing a he had been had and hearing the laughter that his daughter was trying to hide tried to maintain what little dignity he had left in the situation. He knew Sarah was fine, he had not heard her laugh like that since before her mother was sick. "That was a very lousy trick to play honey. Making me think you were in trouble." He said this in a very sad and sullen voice looking to draw sympathy from his daughter and make her feel a little bad for causing him to fall but Sarah was not going to buy it.

"Nice try dad, but I did find that funny. You know I can't resist physical comedy."

"Well don't think I'm going to take it easy on you forever. I will get my revenge. Yes I shall bide my time and when you least suspect it BAM I will have my revenge."

"That's nice dad. Good luck with that by the way."

"I'll get you. Just you wait. I know you don't believe me but I will get you."

"I'll be waiting."

Sarah's dad went downstairs slightly dejected, his plan had not gone quite as planned. Sarah threw the final remaining pictures of Steve into the trash basket and looked out the window. She decided she would go have some lunch as she was starving and then she wanted to sit out in the yard with the phone calling a couple of friends. She went downstairs where her dad was already heating up some left over chicken.

"Sarah are you hungry? Do you want some chicken? Just barbecued it last night, always tastes good reheated."

"You don't have to sell it dad. I love your barbecued chicken, sounds good."

"Good I'll fix you a plate."

Sarah grabbed the carton of orange juice out of the refrigerator and poured herself a glass while her father heated up the chicken. Her father meanwhile was looking for the most delicate way to broach the subject of Steve. He decided to wait until they were both sitting down to eat. He finished heating up the two plates of chicken and then sat down at the table with his daughter.

"This chicken is great dad."

"Glad you like it honey. It was always one of your mother's favorite's."

"I know. Mine too."

"So I saw you had some pictures of Steve in your hand upstairs. How are you doing with that?"

"Dad I have to ask...is it all right to be a little mad? I mean I've never really been mad at a person for a long time but I can sort of feel myself potentially being mad at him for a long time."

"I think that morally there is some basis for that sort of anger. Steve proclaimed to be the love of your life and that he would always be there and then when the going got tough he bailed out. I struggle sometimes with anger towards him. I sometimes sit and wonder if he had not left if your recovery might have been easier? Would you have gotten as bad as you did? Of course, I do not know the answer to either of those questions, and on the surface, it seems anger towards him is perfectly acceptable. However, anger is a funny thing, well maybe not funny maybe the word debilitating is more appropriate. You see what I have learned is that anger starts out small, in the beginning you even make yourself believe that the anger is making you feel better, when in reality it is slowly eating away at you inside. The longer that you stay angry the more it eats you up inside. It's much like the cancer that took your mother. If you allow it to anger will eat you up inside until there is, nothing left, just as the cancer did to your mother. After your mother died, I was very angry, with God for taking her. I wondered why she had to go. I wondered how God could do this especially when I saw your downward spiral. Going to church became extremely difficult for me to handle. I put on a brave face in an attempt to appear stoic and do what I thought would help you through this difficult time. However, what I found out was the irony I just shared with you about the anger and the cancer. If I had let it, the anger would have eventually taken me. The anger would have taken a different form like cancer, a heart attack, or a stroke but it would have conquered me and ultimately been my ruin. Once I realized that I resolved that I must put it behind me, I knew you couldn't stand to lose me too. Sure there are times I feel anger for God and for Steve for leaving when you needed him most, however, I then look around and put things into perspective and I know things could be much worse. I also know that God didn't take your mother away because I'm a bad person or even for his own personal entertainment so he could watch us suffer. I know that death is a part of life albeit an unpleasant part but it helps to know that your mom is in a better place she is no longer suffering. The headaches your mom had during her few months of life were excruciating. I can't imagine what they felt like as I saw them suck the life out of her face on a daily basis. But I've gotten off track, to really answer your question, yes I believe some anger is all right but you must not let it consume you, you must let it got quickly before it claims you as a victim as well."

Sarah thought for a moment. She had never heard her father speak so deeply. She wasn't quite sure what to make of it all, as it seemed like an awful lot to absorb. Her father must have noticed the puzzled look on her face because he interjected before Sarah could speak. "Honey, are you all right? I hope my speech hasn't caused any relapses."

"No it hasn't." Sarah quickly shouted not wanting her father to think he had sent her into another tailspin. "I'm just trying to process everything that you said. I've never heard you talk that way before. That speech is something

I would have expected from mom and not you so I'm just a little taken aback that's all."

"Well that's a relief, you had me pretty scared there for a second."

Sarah instantly searched her mind for a witty comeback to lighten the emotional load but all she could come up with was to say, "Good, I'm glad I can still put one over on my old man. Now that I'm back at home that will come in handy when I want to sneak out of the house."

Her father looked at her with a bewildered look on her face and finally she jumped in "Lighten up dad, I'm just messing with you. Take it easy."

The bewildered look left her father's face replaced by a look of relief. Sarah turned away, and as she was walking away told her father that she was going to sit outside for a while and think about what he said. Her father on the other hand decided that a nap was the best course of action after that deep exchange with his daughter. He had also discovered that worry makes one very tired much like anger. However, he knew he couldn't banish his worry as easily as his anger so he thought a good cure for that albeit temporary would be a nice nap. He went to his room and laid down in bed, after about a half hour his mind shut off and he fell asleep.

While her father slept, Sarah sat outside in the backyard on the patio. She always enjoyed sitting out on the patio, the flowers and bushes that surrounded the patio along with the trees along the back of the fence always made her backyard feel like a little piece of the country in the city and she enjoyed that. She always called the backyard her thinking place. In high school, she would come out, sit on the patio on many evenings, and think about the events of her day and her future. She thought back to those times and realized that of the many times she had thought about her future on this patio she had never imagined it like this. Sarah them remembered how often her mom would come out on the patio and sit with her. Her mom always knew somehow when her daughter had thought enough in solitude and was ready for company. Sarah found it odd that every time her mother came out to sit with her after one of her meditative sessions that she was never once upset that her mother interrupted her alone time Her mom instinctively knew when it was safe to come out. Sarah then surmised that this must have been a trait that she inherited from her mother and that is why her mother always knew when to come out and when not to. As she thought more she realized all of the times in high school or college when she had a date or went out with friends that she would come home and her mom would be on the patio if it were not raining. Sarah then found a little piece of her mom that she didn't know was in her and that made her smile. She knew that she had a lot of her mom inside her but she thought she knew what all of it was. This new revelation almost seemed like a surprise that Sarah's mom had intended her to receive after she was gone. It was like a birthday and a Christmas present all rolled into one, and who wouldn't enjoy getting one of each.

Sarah sat and continued to watch the sun continue to roll across the sky. She watched as the shadows fell, felt the breeze on her face, and listened to the leaves on the trees and bushes rustle in the breeze. She thought a great deal, about what her father had said about anger. After a while, she concluded that her father was right. She still was not quite over being angry with Steve, however she realized that anger like all other emotions created energy, in this case negative energy. But she thought that maybe she could harness that negative energy and use it to do some good and that would help her lose the anger and do something she could be proud of. Her thoughts again went to the young man on the beach and she thought maybe if she could harness his anger and help him, it would free her of her own. That seemed to feel right inside of her so she resolved to call him sooner rather than later.

She did not get a chance to call Mike until Saturday evening. She decided that she wanted to be alone when she called him. She did not want anyone to know what she was doing, she wanted this to be her battle, and she wanted to win it without the help of anyone else. So on Saturday when her dad was invited for golf and dinner by some of his friends she insisted that he go. He was going to refuse so he could stay with Sarah but she reasoned with him that he needed to get away and that she would be fine. Finally, he grudgingly agreed to go. "You're just like your mother," he said. "You know how to push my buttons and manipulate me to do what you want."

"I know," she said, with a sly smile across her face. "Mom taught me this one when I was very young and I'm glad she did."

"Well I am and I'm not all at the same time, but enough chatter, I'll be leaving shortly."

After her father, left Sarah microwaved some leftover chicken and mashed potatoes and ate it for dinner, and washed it down with a bottle of water. After she was finished, she cleaned up her mess and went upstairs to find Mike's phone number. After finding it, she went and grabbed the phone and took it outside so she could call him from the patio. She figured that she did her best thinking out there and that would be advantageous for this first conversation on the phone with Mike. She then sat down in the chair, dialed the number, and then the phone began to ring.

Chapter 13
Intersections

Mike woke up Monday morning ready for his next week of work. This week would be different from the last. This week he would be in store the whole week managing. Monday and Tuesday, his first two shifts, Todd would be at the store helping him and then Wednesday he would be on his own for the first time. Mike was both nervous and excited about this idea. He was nervous because he would be in charge and there would be nobody to ask for help but at the same time, he was excited because he would be in charge. Mike had never felt in charge before. Somebody was always telling him what to do, when to do it, and how to do it. Now he would be telling others what to do. He liked the idea; it rather made him feel like he was the president barking out orders to his cabinet, even though Mike knew that the president didn't always give the orders.

Mike went into work with the intent of studying everything Todd did then trying to replicate that on Wednesday when he was on his own. For about the first hour of work, Mike did exactly that. He followed Mike around noting how he handled everything from customers to schedules, to employees. After the first hour of this Todd must have noticed and he said to Mike, "Hey, are you following me around trying to memorize everything I do?"

Mike, not wanting Todd to know he was right, tried to lie. "No, I thought that this was still training so I was following you waiting for you to tell me what to do."

"Don't give me that garbage."

"What garbage?"

"Fine here's your training for the day. Find your own way to manage don't be like me. You'll be miserable, not because I am but because you are not me. You have to do this job your own way to do it well and enjoy it."

"But then why do we have training?"

"It's just a big waste of time. If you ever get into the corporate part of this business you'll find that ninety percent of what they do is a waste of time. You won't use any of it here. Do your best, do it your way and you'll be fine. By the way did you call my old coach?"

"I haven't had a chance to yet."

"Well make sure that you call this week. I told him you would call and he said he would talk to the head coach but he couldn't guarantee the position would be open for a long time so if you want it you'll need to jump on it."

"I'll call Thursday morning."

"Sounds like a plan, now get out there and manage."

Mike gave Todd a phony salute as Todd went into the back of the store. Mike began to think he needed a game plan for Wednesday. After all, if he was in charge he needed a plan of action. He decided he would work on that tonight and Tuesday night at home.

Mike finished his shift and left at five. After dinner, he sat in his room with his cd player on writing down ideas in a notebook for how he wanted things to go. He was very interested in treating all of the employees equally. He decided that he would rotate jobs like stock and cleanup duties among the employees. He would make it so that everyone did each job the same number of times throughout the week. He didn't want to play favorites on anything. In a couple of weeks when he started making the schedule he would give everyone equal time off on the weekends as he knew most of the employees coveted weekend days off. In his mind, Mike vowed everybody would get one per week. It was also important to Mike that he have a positive relationship with the employees below him. He wanted them to like working for him. He believed this would make them work harder for him and be less likely to call in when they knew he was managing. On Tuesday night, he even put it in outline form for easy reference, which was unlike him.

His first day of managing on his own went well. Being that it was Wednesday and not a particularly busy day, Mike had only two other employees with him. Jonathan was a college student studying business management and Carrie was still a senior in high school. Carrie didn't seem to have the same zest for business that Jonathan did. Carrie sometimes spent more time talking with friends that visited her at the store than selling sports equipment. He felt comfortable leaving both Jonathan and Carrie out on the floor unsupervised but when it came time for Jonathan's break he was not comfortable leaving Carrie by herself. Right before his break, Jonathan came up to Mike and asked him if it would be ok if he took an hour lunch.

Mike wondered if this was legitimate or if it were Jonathan attempting to take advantage of him because he was new. "Why?"

"I have to drop off this check for my summer class at school."

Jonathan showed him the check and Mike asked, "Why didn't you do it yesterday when you were off?"

Jonathan got a somewhat embarrassed look on his face and quietly said, "My dad just got paid yesterday and didn't have the money until last night and by the time he got home student accounts was closed. If I don't get the money there today they will drop me from my classes."

Mike could see in Jonathan's face that he was telling the truth so he allowed him to take the extra time. Jonathan thanked him and went out on break. As planned Mike stayed out and watched Carrie on the floor while Jonathan was gone. After Jonathan was gone, Carrie came over to Mike to talk to him. It was almost as if she was waiting for a chance to talk to him

"Mike, I know you're doing the schedule now and I was wondering if you could give me more hours?"

"Why should I give you more hours? You don't exactly work hard when you are here."

"I just really need the money. My dad lost his job and I am supposed to go to Northwestern in the fall but with my dad, losing his job my parents may not be able to afford it. So I was wondering if I could get more hours to help pay for college?"

"The only way that I can give you more hours is if you start selling more merchandise and start being nicer to the customers."

"But how do I do that? I walk around but nobody ever asks me for help"

"That's because you are supposed to ask them if they need help. Also, try walking around with more of a smile on your face. Usually you look like you don't want to be here. The long conversations you have with your friends don't help either"

"Well, honestly, I don't want to be here. My parents were supposed to be able to pay for my college without any problem. Last year the company, my dad worked for cut his salary. When his salary was cut, he told me I would have to get a part time job and good financial aid to pay for Northwestern. I applied at clothing and department stores but none of them even called me for an interview. Rudy's and Burger King were the only places that called me for an interview. Neither is a great fit for me but this beats fast food any day"

"I know. I've done that it's not pleasant. I'll tell you what, I'll watch you closely for the rest of your shift, and if you do well, I'll give you a few extra hours next week. If you keep doing well, I'll add more hours the next week. Remember you do get commission so the easiest way to make more money is to sell more products."

"How do I do that?"

"Just be friendly. Smile at all the customers, make small talk, like you would with friends."

"It's that easy?"

"Not all the time. But the majority of the time yes it is. People don't come in here unless they are at least a little bit interested in buying something. Truthfully most customers are just looking, a good salesperson can turn just looking into buying at least half of the time. Just try it with the next customer that comes in. Wait until they are looking at something and then go talk about what they are looking at. Don't say can I help you because if he says no you have nothing else to say but let me know if you need anything, and 90% of the time they never do."

"I'll try."

"That's all I can ask. I'll even sweeten the deal, if you make the sale I'll give you an hour lunch and only make you punch out for half of it."

"Really?

"Scouts' honor."

"What if I don't know anything about the product?

"You don't need to know anymore than what you can see with your eyes. Make a general comment or get the person talking about something else and they will sell themselves."

"Talking about what?"

"Anything. Weather, sports, politics, school, it doesn't matter, if you can get them talking you have increased your chances of making a sale quite a bit."

Carrie went back to the floor. About ten minutes later, a young man walked in. He couldn't have been more than twenty years old. He walked over to the football equipment and began looking at the footballs. Carrie went over to him. "Hey, how are you today?" She said

The young man turned to her and said, "fine."

"So do you play football? I see you looking at the balls."

This young man was clearly not a football player but suddenly his pride got the best of him. "Yeah I played a little bit on my high school team."

Mike tried not to laugh at this, as he knew the kid never had played.

"What position did you play?"

"A little receiver, a little safety too."

"That's cool. I was a cheerleader last fall for my school and next year when I'm at Northwestern I'd like to try out. Are you going to buy that football?"

"Yeah I guess I will."

"Don't forget pads. I wouldn't want you to get hurt."

"Well I wouldn't want that either--might negatively effect my time to spend with the ladies."

Carrie just smiled at that comment, as she wasn't quite sure how to handle it professionally.

Suddenly the man's eagerness to buy went down some. "I don't know if I should buy the pads. My friends and I just play touch football now and they might call me a wuss if I wore pads. I think I'll have to pass on those."

"Your friends would do that?"

"That's what guys do."

"Well that's not very nice. How about one of the jerseys over on the wall, they can't make fun of you for that. Then you'll look like a real football player in the jersey."

"Yeah, I think that is a good idea. I've always wanted a jersey. I think they look cool."

"They do. Which one do you want? I'll have my manager get it down for you."

"Well my little brother is a big Peyton Manning fan and it would make him jealous if I had a jersey and he didn't so I think I'll go with that one."

"Which color, the blue, or the white?

"I'll go with the blue, it's my favorite color."

"What size?"

"Large."

"Sure. Mike can you get a large blue Peyton Manning jersey down for this gentlemen?"

Mike came over; with the hook the store used for getting the jerseys down and got down a blue Peyton Manning jersey. Carrie rang up the sale. The young man paid with his Visa card. Before he left, the young man wrote something down on a piece of paper and said "hey here's my phone number. Give me a call and I'll wear this jersey for you."

Carrie was unsure of what to say. She had dated many boys before and didn't have a problem talking to them but because she was at work, she wasn't sure how to handle it. She meekly said "ok" and took the piece of paper with no real intention of calling him but wanting to get the awkward moment out of the way.

The young man left after putting more than one hundred dollars on his visa card. Carrie was extremely excited. She threw the number in the trash and then said, "Oh my God I can't believe that worked, that was so awesome. I can't wait to see the commission on my next check."

Mike walked over to her "And just think you work 4 days a week, if you just do that twice in each shift your income will probably double if not triple. Then you'll be able to take your new boyfriend out on a date."

"Gross no way! I can't believe he gave me his number. It felt weird. What should I do if that happens again?"

Mike thought for a moment, "Well it's never happened to me but I would say do what you just did. Politely decline the number. Just tell them you have a boyfriend. Most of our customers probably won't ask you though."

"I hope not."

Carrie's mind shifted gears quickly within a couple of seconds she said, "Just think of all of the money that I can save for college."

"You are well on your way to Northwestern. Keep doing this all summer and you will be fine."

"Yes!" Carrie yelled enthusiastically.

"All right settle down Carrie. I can't have you yelling in the store, I don't want to have to write you up."

"No worries, I'll be good."

From then on Carrie always worked twice as hard for Mike and was always very polite with him. The next spring when she graduated from high school, she even invited Mike to her graduation party.

On Thursday, Mike called the number that Todd had given him. An older sounding man answered the phone.

"Hello?"

"Hi my name is Mike Larson I am looking for Coach Stopac."

"You got him," said the voice

"I was given your number by Todd Hatch."

"Yeah, I hear you played some minor league ball."

"I played two seasons with the West Michigan Whitecaps."

"What position did you play?"

"Pitcher."

"Good, I need someone to work with my pitchers. What was your out pitch?"

"Split finger fastball."

"I would love if I had a guy with a split finger for next year. Why don't you come down and we can talk some more?"

"Sounds good" Mike replied.

"What's your schedule like?

"The only day I am free this week is today."

"Can you come about four-thirty?"

"Yeah that would be perfect."

"All right, I'll see you then good bye."

"Bye and thank you" Mike replied and then hung up the phone.

Mike arrived at the school at about four fifteen. He had to sign in at the main office and a secretary directed him to Coach Stopac's office. Mike walked down three different hallways to get to the coach's office. This school was much more modern than his high school. This school had skylights in the hallways and the lockers were freshly painted. The floor was much more modern looking than the fifty year old tile in his old high school. There were televisions and computers in every classroom Mike could see. His high school didn't have either. His high school had televisions on carts and computers in the library along with just two computer labs. The gym also looked more modern with a nice weight room with modern equipment rather than secondhand equipment. Mike felt a little out of place and uncomfortable. He wasn't used to such opulence but knew he could very easily get used to it. Mike saw that the coach's door was slightly opened but more closed than opened. He could tell someone was in there so he knocked on the door.

"Who is it?" a voice called out.

Mike immediately recognized the voice he had talked to on the phone and replied "It's Mike Larson. I'm here for my four thirty interview."

"Yeah come on in and have a seat." Mike walked in and sat down across from the coach. Coach Stopac was not a young man. He was probably in his fifties with mostly grey hair and slight remnants of brown that the coach sported in his younger days. He was slightly overweight and talked with a lightly grizzled voice. Coach Stopac continued when Mike sat down, "thanks for coming in today."

"No problem."

"It's rare I interview anybody with any experience in professional baseball."

"Well, I don't have much."

"You have more than anyone at this school. That's why I want to meet with you."

"Thank you."

"Do you think you could teach a couple of my pitchers a split finger fastball?"

"I'm sure I could."

"Well we came within one game of winning the state championship this year and it was pitching that did us in. We lost to East Side High School. The coach was horrible to our kids after the game too. He actually led his team in taunting our kids. We have good kids on this team, kids that deserve much better than that. Our old pitching coach, a science teacher here voluntarily stepped down so we could find someone to work with our pitchers. We return all but two players next year and we want revenge."

Mike suddenly said confidently "I'm your man." He said this more confidently than he had ever said anything in his life. Coach Stopac's eyes bulged at the sound of Mike's statement. The boldness of Mike's statement took him by surprise.

"Well how can you be so confident?"

Mike told Coach Stopac the entire story of his high school baseball experience at East Side High School. About everything, the coach had done and said to him and how the other players had treated him. Mike felt surprisingly comfortable telling this to Coach Stopac. He could tell Coach Stopac was a different kind of man than his high school coach. He could tell Coach Stopac would never do what his former coach had done to him. Finally, Mike wrapped up his story by saying that he wanted nothing more than to rub success in his former coach's face and since he didn't make the majors, this would be his best chance. Once Mike finished speaking, Coach Stopac did not hesitate, he hired Mike on the spot and told him anyone who hates East Side High that much would fit right in on the team. The only thing he wanted Mike to do was tell the team his story to get the pitchers to buy into what he was teaching. Mike agreed and that was it, he would be coaching baseball next year. He was more excited than he could ever remember being.

Mike met with the team before work on Friday. Mike was working that night so he went early. Coach Stopac pulled his team out of their classes that would end next week for summer vacation and they all came down and listened to Mike speak. As he spoke, he could tell he had the team's undivided attention. They seemed to marvel at his tale of high school woe. Finally, at the end Mike promised them they would return to the conference championship and beat East Side next year. The kids stood up and cheered, Mike had won them over.

Mike worked Friday night and again on Saturday morning. He got home from work on Saturday about six. Mike had a steak his dad had made for dinner along with some potatoes and some green beans, and washed it down with a Coke. Mike then showered and then settled in to watch some television. Just then, the phone rang. His mother answered and then came to the living room. "Mike you have a phone call, it's a girl."

Mike had no idea who it could be as he took the phone and said, "Hello."

Chapter 14
The Conversation

"Mike. This is Sarah."

Mike thought for a second. Since there was a pause on the other end of the phone Sarah added, "from Paradise? The beach that Saturday night?"

"Oh yeah. Sorry. I've been at work all day. I'm very tired. My mind just didn't work right away."

"That's okay. How are you doing? Any more yelling out loud in the open?"

"No, not lately. I've been too busy with my new job."

"That's right! You were going into manager training for a sporting goods store, right?"

"Yes, I did training last week and then Monday and Tuesday of this week. Since Wednesday I've been out of training and on my own."

"That's good to hear. How is it going so far?"

"I'd say it's going pretty well. I taught this high school girl, Carrie, how to be a better salesperson. She came to me asking for more hours but I told her I couldn't give her the hours unless she made more sales."

"You couldn't just give her more hours?"

"No. I would have to justify it to Todd and he would have to justify it to those above him and without an increase in her sales they would reprimand me."

"So did she make more sales?"

"Yes. She's the kind of girl who doesn't like the job and therefore doesn't put much into it and she walks around with a constant frown on her face. I told her to act cheerful, smile at the customers, and make conversation. So far, it has worked, she made a sale right away, and she's been making a few sales a day since. In fact, one customer tried to giver her his phone number. It was kind of funny actually."

"Are you sure that's wise? What if she gets hurt?"

"I wouldn't worry about it. The whole incident freaked her out just a bit. She does not intend to call the guy. I told her in the future just to tell them that she has a boyfriend."

"Why couldn't she just tell them the truth? She's not interested."

"Well that's pretty much what she's doing."

"I know but I just don't like lying. I guess you've done her a good service by helping her learn how to sell."

"Don't worry about it too much. I don't expect it to happen too often. Most of our customers are much older than the one that gave her his number. Actually, that incident happened about four days ago and it hasn't happened again since. I'm hopeful it will not be too much of a problem. But I will giver her your advice and tell her just to tell them the truth if you like."

"I would, it's just the right thing to do."

"All right I'll tell her when I see her on Monday."

Sarah saw an opening to bring religion into the conversation at this point. Since she wanted to ask Mike to church, she jumped at the chance. "Mike, have you ever been to church?"

"I went all the time with my mom when I was a kid. Now I maybe go once or twice a month when I'm awake early enough on a Sunday morning to do so."

"What religion are you?"

"Catholic."

"We are Catholic too. We go to St. Michael's. I like it because everyone there is very friendly and the priest is young and gives very interesting sermons that are relevant to life today. He is very interesting. May I ask why you do not make church a priority?"

"I don't know. It always seems boring. We have this old priest and his voice is so monotone, it puts me to sleep. Plus, the congregation is old. I sometimes liken the church to a morgue."

"That's a rather grotesque analogy. But I understand what you are saying. I've been to other churches where it just seems like the energy has been sucked out of the building with a vacuum. It's sad really because there is so much energy and excitement in God's Word."

As Sarah was talking Mike began to think here we go, that's what this is all about she is just keen on Jesus, but at the same time he had a feeling that this girl was genuine and not a part of some freaky cultish church. Mike didn't know exactly what to say so he responded with a standard "that's cool."

"Would you be willing to go to church with me tomorrow? I know it is short notice but I really think you would enjoy it."

Mike tried to think of a way out at first he said, "What time is mass?"

"It is at eleven o'clock."

Mike's plan backfired. He was expecting her to say something like eight o'clock or nine o'clock and he could just claim he was too tired and wouldn't go but now he was drowning, trying to think of an excuse when none would come to him, finally he grudgingly agreed to go.

"Great!" I'll meet you out in the parking lot at ten forty-five, how is that?"

Mike agreed, he didn't know what else to see. He felt like a master debater who had just lost the biggest debate of his life.

"Great! I'll be wearing a white dress and I'll put a yellow flower in my hair so you'll know it's me. Do you know where St. Michael's is?

Mike knew exactly where the church was, he had once worked at a factory down the street from there and now he welcomed the opportunity to save a little face by showing his mastery of where thing's were. "Yeah, I know right where that is. On Hiedelbeck Road, just past Fifteenth Street right?"

"That's it. I can't wait to see you tomorrow. Will you go to lunch with me after?"

"Lunch would be cool."

"Then it's settled. I'll see you for eleven o'clock mass tomorrow and then lunch. Well Mike, it's been fun chatting but I should let you go."

"Yeah, sounds like something exciting just happened in the Tiger game, I should go check it out."

"Are they winning?"

"No."

"Well maybe they are now. Have a good night."

"You too."

Mike hung up the phone and immediately his mother began grilling him about the girl on the phone. "So who was she?" His mother asked with an inquisitive tone.

"Just some girl I met up north."

"Does this girl have a name?"

"Sarah."

"Well how did you meet Sarah?"

"We started talking on the beach up north." Mike didn't want to answer any more questions so he announced he was going out for a drive.

"What about the ballgame?" His mother asked.

"They're losing. Besides, if I want I can turn it on in the car."

He planned to return after ten when he knew his mother would be in bed and would not ask him any more questions. Mike enjoyed his drive, it was a warm night, and he drove with the windows down and radio up all the way. He came home about eleven o'clock and both of his parents were asleep. Mike watched television until about midnight, then showered and went to bed.

Mike got up about quarter after nine, he had breakfast and left about ten. He drove around for a while before church. He was sure to dress up and sure that he wanted to be a few minutes late so Sarah would be there when he got there. She was. He parked and walked over to her.

"Hey Mike! You made it."

"Yep, here I am."

Sarah's dad was standing next to her. Mike could sense he was not too pleased with him. He stood, hands folded, with no discernible look on his face. His presence made Mike feel slightly awkward. However, it was almost time for church to start and they very quickly walked in ending the awkward moment. When they walked in Mike noticed that there were no pews similar to what he remembered but rather cushioned chairs. "Where are you supposed to kneel?" He asked Sarah.

"We don't kneel. We merely stand during the traditional kneeling parts of the mass."

Mike could tell this church was different. The sanctuary was very bright, the windows were not stained glass windows, the congregation was much younger than he would have expected and people were talking to one another inside the church. Mike had never seen this much talking in church. His mom taught him that talking inside church was disrespectful and often ended up in trouble for making noise in church as a child. Over the years, he had programmed himself to always be quiet in church no matter what.

Sarah and her father lead Mike to a row of chairs about halfway between the alter and the back of the church. After sitting down, Mike looked all around taking everything in. Sarah was sitting next to Mike and leaned over to him asking, "So what do you think?"

Mike struggled briefly for an answer. Truth was he did not know what to think yet but he wanted to offer an answer that would not offend Sarah or her father. Finally, he said, "It's good." He couldn't think of anything else to say but that answer seemed to make Sarah happy. She smiled and said, "Good, I'm glad. I think you will really like this church."

"Why are people talking? I always got in trouble for talking in church. In fact nobody talked in my church."

"That's because your church is old and dying. This one is young and vibrant. Just watch the service. I think you'll see many differences."

Mike did just that. The mass began as the first hymn played and the priest entered. The priest was a young man, probably mid thirties, with mostly brown hair starting to turn slightly grey. He was maybe about six feet tall with a medium build. When he spoke, he spoke with a voice that seemed booming. The volume was not too loud or obnoxious but rather filled with excitement. Mike could tell the pastor was very enthusiastic about what he preached and that actually made him feel comfortable. He didn't feel like the priest was trying to sell him something like he often felt like in church. The sermon for that day was especially appropriate for Mike and Sarah. The main idea of the speech was that God's ways are not our ways. The preacher went on to say, "God has his own ways. He works on his on pace and timing. Just because we pray for something doesn't mean that God will give it to us. Whether we all want to admit it or not, God knows each and everyone of us better than we know ourselves. He knows our strengths, weaknesses, wants, needs abilities, personalities, maturity, spirituality, and sins. Therefore, when we pray for something, God knows whether or not what we are praying for will truly benefit us and the others involved. God does not fail to answer our prayers because he dislikes us, rather God does not answer our prayers because he knows what we want is not best for us or everyone else that would be involved in the situation. In all reality, most of our prayers are answered at some point in time just not when we make those prayers. It could be ten days or ten years later depending on his timing. Remember the story from The Book of Daniel about Shadrach, Meshach, and Abednego. King Nebuchadnezzar was going to throw them into the furnace and yet the three men did not waver. They knew that even though God may not answer their prayers that they would eventually be in paradise with God. So they did not fear and God spared them. So the next time you pray just keep in mind that what you are praying for may not be in God's plans even though it is in ours. It is not a personal attack against you by a vengeful God but rather a loving and all knowing God doing what is best for you and the rest of humanity."

Mike was surprised that the sermon actually held his attention. Most sermons caused him to sleep but this sermon made him think, maybe everything that I prayed for I wasn't ready for. Mike knew that he had a large amount of anger inside him and he wondered if God had failed to answer his prayers, not because he hated Mike, but rather because Mike had some growing up to do before he could have those things. It was a crazy thought but it had the potential to have some truth to it. He was not sure yet but he knew that the idea would require more thinking from him.

Sarah, meanwhile, understood exactly what the priest was saying. She immediately related it to her mom's death. As much as she prayed for her mother to survive and live on, she realized her mother was in excruciating pain and living longer would have meant unbearable for her. Sarah was glad that she was in church to hear this sermon. It helped her quickly put some things in perspective, which she needed to do. It would not be a cure all but it would help. She then turned and looked at Mike and wondered what kind of impact the sermon was having on him.

After church Sarah informed Mike that they would be having lunch at the diner, two blocks up the road. Mike nodded saying that he had eaten there before and knew right where it was. Mike followed Sarah and her father in his car. On the way over Sarah told her dad she would like to sit with her new friend by herself. "Do you like this boy?' Her dad asked.

"Not the way you're thinking. I just really feel like he needs some help and that I can do it. The idea of helping others makes me feel better, it takes my mind of all of the bad things that have happened."

Sarah's dad knew that he couldn't argue with her on this one so he agreed to get his own table.

The diner was an older building that originally opened in the 1950s. It still had the long counter with stools and a hole in the wall behind the counter where the waitress gave orders to the cook. Through the whole customers could see a large grill and a cook. The floor was white tile and the tables all had vinyl booths. The counter had stools in traditional 1950's pink and teal so people could sit at the counter. The food in the diner was good but greasy. A typical 1950s fare from a time before things like heart disease and cholesterol were big worries. Mike had eaten the burgers before. They were good but not great but they always filled the hole. The onion rings were better than the French fries and the malts although touted as a specialty always left him disappointed.

When they went inside Sarah's dad made a beeline for the counter and sat down at a stool near the end of the counter by the door. A waitress led Mike and Sarah to a booth in the opposite corner of the restaurant. They sat down and looked at the menus. "Have you eaten here before Mike?"

"Yeah I've eaten here a few times. The burgers are okay but the onion rings are excellent."

"We have eaten here after church a few times. I like the chicken fingers myself. I like them with ranch."

"I've never had the chicken fingers but those sound good."

"What kind of sauce do you like with your chicken fingers?"

"Barbecue."

"I've never been a big fan of barbecue sauce."

"I love it."

"Apparently. So is that what you're going to get?"

"Either that or the burger and onion rings."

The waitress came back and asked if they were ready to order. "Ladies first." Mike replied with a smile trying to be cool.

"I'll have the chicken fingers meal with a side of ranch for dipping."

"Ranch is an extra thirty cents. Is that ok?"

"I know it's fine."

"And for you sir?"

"I think I'll get the All American Burger with cheese and onion rings instead of fries."

"Onion rings are a dollar more."

"And they are worth every penny."

"Will there be anything to drink today?"

"I'll just have water." Sarah said.

"I'll have a Coke." Mike said.

"Small or large?"

"Large."

Very good, I'll put that right in for you two."

"Sarah, didn't you say before that you were once going to be a doctor?"

"Yeah. Why?"

"Well this isn't exactly the model of healthy food. Shouldn't you have ordered a salad or something?"

"Well like many of my pre med classmates I would preach to others about the dangers of this food but always secretly crave it myself."

"So are you saying doctors are hypocrites?"

"No. Most of the people I knew would eat this food occasionally but not make a big habit of it. Moderation is the key. A little will not kill you but if you eat it all the time it surely will."

"Well I guess I'm in trouble." I used to practically live on fast food when I first started college."

"Do you still?"

"No. But I would bet that I still eat too much of it."

"Well at least you're trying to cut down on it. Remember baby steps always work best. Keep working at it and you'll eat less of it over time."

"Thanks for the tip."

"You're welcome. So what did you think of church today?"

"Actually, it was quite interesting. I've never been to a church like that."

"Is that a good interesting or a bad interesting?"

"It's a good interesting. I really enjoyed the sermon. I'll admit most times in church I don't listen to the sermon. I just let my mind wander while I wait for it to be over."

"That doesn't sound like a good thing to do in church. But anyway, what did you like about the sermon today?"

"Well first the priest's voice was very loud. He was easy to hear and really just a good speaker. I haven't seen too many priests that are good public speakers. It's almost like his voice says to you subconsciously listen to me."

"Yeah? What else?"

"The whole God's ways are not our ways concept. I think it may explain why some of my prayers have gone unanswered all these years."

"Yeah I thought the same thing. What did you come up with?"

"I'm not quite sure yet. It is something I'll have to think about. I honestly do my best thinking either in the shower or while lying awake in bed."

"That's kind of weird. Why do you think that is?"

"There aren't any distractions. It's just me and my thoughts, nobody else is talking to me and putting other things in my mind."

"That makes sense. I think that I do my best thinking sitting out on the patio. It's always quiet and I think nature helps me think but the main point is that it is quiet out there."

"Yeah I like sitting outside too. I can get some good thinking done out there too if nobody else is around. My neighbors are loud though and outside a lot."

"We have a privacy fence so it's not a big deal for me. That fence shields out a lot."

"I wish we had one. That would help.

The waitress came back and brought their meals. Mike and Sarah continued to talk after the food came. "How's your burger?"

"It's good, just what I expected."

"You didn't try the chicken fingers. Why not?

"I thought you might give me a bite of yours so I could have the best of both worlds."

"Well you're lucky we just came from church and I'm in a giving mood. Here, you can have half of this one."

"Thanks." Mike said as he took a bite. "These are pretty good but I think I like the burger better. Although I may like it more if I had barbecue sauce to dip it in."

"Well enjoy your burger."

"Thanks enjoy your chicken."

Mike and Sarah ate their meals in relative silence. Mike was not much for talking while eating and he answered most of Sarah's questions with short closed ended answers. He wasn't trying to be rude; he just never talked much while he ate. Sarah became a little annoyed at this and finally asked, "Why are you being so evasive all of a sudden?"

"What?"

"We were having a nice in depth conversation and now you're barely talking to me. "

"It's nothing personal. I just don't talk much while I eat."

"Is there any particular reason?"

"Not really, I just tend to eat in silence. I think I like to get it down before it gets cold, especially if it's good, like these onion rings."

Sarah accepted his explanation and relented somewhat with the conversation. After they finished, the waitress brought the bill. Mike grabbed it and said, "I've got this."

"No you don't have to. I invited you."

"Don't worry about it, I just got a new job and would like to treat you."

"Are you sure?"

"Absolutely."

"Well can I at least leave the tip?"

"No don't worry about it. Besides this way you can get the next one." Mike decided to flex some confidence to try to impress Sarah, assuming that she would want to see him again.

"Well ok, I can live with that. So I guess that means you'll have to come back again next Sunday so I can return the favor."

"Well I don't have to work so it should be fine."

"Well my dad is motioning to me. Looks like he's paid his bill and is ready to go. Can I call you again this week?"

"Yeah I have the same schedule as this week. I'll be gone Friday night but Thursday I'm off and I should be home every other evening after six."

Mike was nervous, for all the confidence he tried to put forward he was nervous and wondering if she should hug or kiss her goodbye. He couldn't decide but while he was thinking, Sarah got up and said "Great, I'll give you a call before Sunday." Sarah then proceeded to walk out, as she walked by she touched his shoulder, Mike turned around and yelled "bye." Sarah turned, waved, and then walked out with her dad. Mike thought she touched his shoulder and that must be a sign she's interested. He would debate that to himself over the next week. Mike then paid the tab and left.

While driving home, Sarah's dad said to her, "that boy likes you."

"No he doesn't."

"Yes he does. I was watching, maybe he isn't head over heels for you but there's some interest."

"No we're just friends."

"Well maybe you should make that clear to him."

"Dad you worry too much. Now lets change the subject."

They spent the rest of the ride home talking about plans for the rest of the day and the coming week.

Chapter 15
Beginnings and Endings

Sarah walked into Tony's office excited to tell him about her Sunday with Mike. However, before she had a chance, Tony began to speak. Usually Tony waited for a Sarah to get comfortable to begin speaking. It was part of what made Tony such a good therapist; he knew how to listen.

"Sarah, I have some news for you today!"

Sarah hesitated, as she did not quite know how to respond to the abrupt start. This was a rarity for Sarah as she was almost never at a loss for words. Sarah began to stammer, "What? What? Is there something wrong?"

"No, nothing is wrong. I just am so excited to tell you. I received a job offer from Michigan State University to be a professor and I start in the fall semester. I wanted to tell you right off the top before we got into our work for today. Also, come fall, I will be transferring your care to Rick Templeton. I have asked him to stop by before the end of our session so he can meet you. I have given him the information on your case and he is eager to begin working with you. I chose Rick because I think he is the best counselor in the office, even better than I am. You will be in good hands."

Sarah began to think. This was an unexpected setback. She had been doing so well, how could Tony leave just as she was getting better. Then she began to think that she has been doing better and how helping Mike has helped her.

Absorbed in thought Sarah failed to realize that she had remained silent for several minutes. Tony began to notice that Sarah had not spoken in a while and this worried him. It had not been like Sarah to be quiet lately so the sudden silent treatment worried him. Finally, Tony felt compelled to speak and break the silence to be sure his patient was all right. "Sarah?"

Sarah jumped. "Oh what? Yes, I'm fine. Sorry I was just thinking about your new job."

"Are you all right with that?"

"I think so but I have a question."

"What is it Sarah?"

"How can this guy Rick be as good of a counselor as you are? I can't imagine any counselor doing as much for me as you have."

"Well thanks for the ego boost. But Rick is amazing, the man is a miracle worker."

"Well pardon my adulation but I think you are a miracle worker. I remember where I was at Christmas, it has been less than six months, and I am a thousand times better. I could not have come this far without you."

"You give me too much credit, Sarah. I am not a miracle worker just a man. I haven't done much of the work here; you have done most of the work. You have helped you more than I ever could."

"I disagree, I would not be doing as well as I am without your help."

"You are half right. Without my help, or another counselor's help you would have had a much more difficult time getting started. I believe that as strong of a person as you are you would have eventually gotten started on your own. I merely sped up the process. You see Sarah, a good counselor counsels and tries to help their patients, but a great counselor knows that the patient accomplishes true emotional healing.

"That's crazy. You have done more for me than I have done on my own."

"Well Sarah let me ask you this, was in Whitefish Point when you had your huge breakthrough?"

"No."

"Was I there when you decided to help Mike?"

"No. But I told you about it."

"Yes you told me about it but I didn't make you decide to help him. You did that on your own."

Sarah thought for a moment, and eventually realized that Tony was right. "I suppose you're right. I did do all of that on my own. I only told you about them." Immediately a warm feeling began to grow in Sarah's stomach. The warm feeling grew into a burning passion as Tony continued to speak.

"Exactly. I could have told you not to do those things but you were so excited about them that doing so would only upset you and further slow your recovery. That is what a good therapist does. He analyzes the patient and the situation and parcels out small packets of advice when needed. When advice is not needed he keeps it to himself because the risk of unwarranted advice is greater than the risk of no advice."

Sarah was impressed. By this point, the warm feeling had become a raging fire. She knew at that moment that she wanted to be a counselor like Tony, and she knew that she wanted to study under Tony.

"Tony, do you think that I would make a good therapist or counselor?"

"Sarah, you have what can't be learned in any classroom or office and that is life experience. Often times the best therapists are people who have faced and overcome great difficulty in their lives. I think that in time you could be a great counselor if it is something that you wanted to explore."

"I think that even though you are teaching at that 'other school' up north I would like to come up and study under you this year. You would be a great mentor, and then you could continue being my counselor."

"Whoa, slow down Sarah. I know you're doing much better but you are not ready for something so grand yet. Right now, and for the next year, I think you need to stay home with your father and help each other heal. Remember, your dad not only lost your mom, but he also nearly lost you as well, I'm sure he hasn't completely healed from that yet."

Sarah knew that Tony was right but didn't want to admit it. She grudgingly agreed to wait a year before she went back to school anywhere.

"But in a year you would have no problem with me studying up there?"

"I have two conditions that you must meet first Sarah."

"What are they?"

"First, and most importantly you must never again refer to Michigan State as 'that other school up north,' second, Rick will have to release you from care before you begin your first semester. That way if you end up in one of my classes there will not be any conflict of interest."

"Well the second one will be easy, the first a little bit more difficult, but I agree."

Tony and Sarah shook hands on the agreement. Then Tony asked, "So how is it going with the man you met up north?"

"Great! I got him to go to church with me on Sunday and it sounds like he is doing really well. He's doing very well at his job and he is going to be coaching baseball which I know he loves."

"How is your dad doing with the situation?"

"He's nervous. He thinks that Mike is just interested in me as a girlfriend and not as a friend."

"Well I would bet that at some level the thought of being more than friends has crossed his mind. You have to understand that he is a guy and guys think with different organs sometimes."

"I know that. I'm not stupid. But not all guys want to marry every girl right?"

"I'm not talking about marriage."

"But not every guy wants to get married right?"

"You're right but I think you're missing the point of what I am saying."

"No I'm not. I know he probably wants sex. Most men do. But does that mean he is some crazy sex fiend?"

No."

"Exactly my point. Both you and my dad worry too much. Mike is a nice guy."

"But there are a lot of nice guys that want sex."

"Good Lord Tony lighten up. I know how to take care of myself. I'm not thirteen.

"All right. I'll trust you. I just want to make sure you understand all aspects of the situation.

"Don't worry. I'll be fine."

At that moment, a tall hulking man with shoulder length semi curly hair bordering on a mullet appeared in the doorway. He wore jeans and boots with a polo shirt. Somehow, these things didn't seem to go together in Sarah's mind. She was a little worried, then her worry increased when Todd greeted him "Hey Rick, I thought you still had an appointment until one?"

"I did but they cancelled so I thought I'd come by a little early and take a long lunch."

Sarah looked up in the man with awe and trepidation. Rick had to be six foot six at least and weigh well over two hundred pounds. His hair and clothing made him look more like a lumberjack than a counselor. The loudness of Ricks voice also startled Sarah. He wasn't shouting, but the way that he talked must have been shouting for most normal people. She began to worry quietly inside that this man would be helping her heal.

"So is this my new patient Tony?" Rick said loudly.

"Yes this is Sarah. She is a bit nervous but I have assured her that you are our best counselor."

"Well at least you know your role college boy. Good afternoon Sarah, I'm Rick."

Sarah reached her hand out nervously to accept Rick's handshake. Rick's handshake felt like a vice grip tightened all the way. It hurt her hand slightly. She began to think nervously that not only is this man a lumberjack but he is also a redneck. How had he made it through medical school?

Tony could tell that Sarah's anxiety had returned so he quickly attempted to lighten the emotional load for her. "Don't worry about Rick, Sarah. He may not have the best fashion sense in the office but I assure you that he is the best counselor."

Sarah finally collected herself. She said to herself, come on Sarah you're better than this you can conquer this. Finally, she spoke aloud "I'm sorry I was just taken aback by your appearance and mannerisms, Rick."

"Honest little thing isn't she, Tony?"

"That's for sure."

"Well Sarah you are not the first to be put off by my appearance and mannerisms. It took me six months to get my wife to agree to go out on a date with me, but I caught her and got what I wanted."

"Yes Rick, pity is a very strong emotion."

"Hey Tony, it may have been a pity date but it turned out quite well for me. Ultimately I got what I wanted."

"So you did Rick, so you did."

The humor of the conversation between Rick and Tony made Sarah laugh loudly. She didn't mean to laugh, she tried to hold it back until later, but it just slipped out uncontrollably.

Rick stood up straight with a look of satisfaction on his face and said to Sarah, "see got you laughing already. We're going to do fine together. I may be the best counselor here but Tony here is a distant second. You have had and will have all of the best that this office has to offer,"

"Thank you." Sarah said. Her anxiety was now almost gone. She really enjoyed Rick's humor. He could use humor in a way that Tony never could. Not that Tony was unfunny, but Rick was just hilarious. She figured that his sense of humor had to be one of the things that made him such a good therapist. She was now certain that as long as she could get by their weird clothes and hair that she would be all right. She thought getting by all of those things might be the most difficult aspect of healing now.

"Well Sarah, it has been nice meeting you. I look forward to working with you come August."

"Thank you. I'm sure it will be fun just promise to always have a joke ready for me. I'm going to need it to look past your clothes."

"Wow, Tony, this cat has a few claws in her. Well I think I can manage that Sarah. That's how I keep my wife from leaving, maybe I can try out her nightly joke on you before I try it on her, what do you say?"

"Deal."

"Excellent! Well Tony, I will see you after lunch, and Sarah I will see you in August. Be ready for some jokes."

"All right man, I'll see you later. By the way, you still up for drinks Friday night."

"Yes sir! Remember they are on me to celebrate your new job."

"Don't worry, I couldn't possibly forget that."

With that, Rick left for lunch. Tony turned to Sarah, "So he's not too scary is he?"

"No I think I'll be fine with him. He has one thing wrong though."

"What's that?"

"He's the second best counselor. You are the best."

"Well I guess that's a matter of opinion but I will accept your compliment."

Sarah began to look serious again for a moment, and then he figured out why. Sarah looked up at him and asked, "Can I ask you a personal question?"

"Well that depends on just how personal you intend to get."

"I'm curious about the she shooting you were involved in. I'm curious to know what led up to it, how it happened, and how you got from there to here. I can understand if you don't want to talk about it but I would really like to hear the story."

"Well Sarah you just asked a mouthful, but I would be more than happy to tell it. You would not be the first patient I've told the story. I don't go around offering it up to patients but if they ask me as you have I always oblige to tell them in the hopes that it will be a source of inspiration for them, and many have told me that it has been. Some have even told me it is the most remarkable story that they have ever heard. I don't know that I would go that far but I think it is a valuable story nonetheless."

Tony paused for a minute and began to speak, "as a kid I never knew who my father was. My mother often had men over at our house and she would often say that this man might be your new father but it never happened. None of them ever came around for more than a month before someone new replaced them. One day when I was nine, my grandma, who was a respectable woman, took me out of there. She made me go to school every day and I even began to get good grades and play on the middle school basketball team. However, when I was thirteen my grandmother was killed by stray gunfire during a gang shootout at the house next door to hers. I found out which gang had fired the fatal shot that killed my grandma and then joined the rival gang to get revenge. I moved back in with my mom, stopped going to school, and started doing drugs. One night when I was seventeen, I was with a friend named Marcus who was in my gang. We were going to a house to buy some drugs from another member of our gang. Little did we know the rival gang was staking out the house waiting for a few of us to show up so they could take out more than one of us? When we got to the door Marcus knocked, then the shots began ringing out, Marcus was hit right away in the back of the head, then shots started coming from the house we were going into. I turned to try to run away and get to the other side of the house for cover but immediately felt a terrible burning pain in my spine. A bullet coming from the house had hit me and lodged in my spinal cord. I immediately fell to the ground. Suddenly the shooting stopped. In the last few minutes, before I went unconscious I saw a car speed away from the driveway of the house. My own gang members were leaving me there to die. A neighbor finally called 911. When I came to, I was in the hospital. They told me that I would never walk again. I didn't want to live. That is when I met Erin. Erin was a social worker. She got me into a center for homeless teens and helped me study every day for eight months so I could get my GED and make something of myself. When I got my GED, she encouraged me to enroll in college. She even invited me to live with her and her family for my first year at Wayne State. She didn't let me live free; I had to get a job, pay them rent, and get good grades. I got a job at a local McDonald's and after a year, I became assistant manager. I didn't want to impose on Erin and her family anymore so I got my own apartment, applied for a scholarship at Wayne State and got it. The scholarship covered most of my tuition, which allowed me to pay my bills. I graduated with a degree in social work but wanted a masters degree. That is when I went to Michigan State, but before I did, I had to propose to my girlfriend of three years. I couldn't ask her to go to East Lansing without making an honest woman of her. We were married right before my first semester of graduate classes started. She worked at a bank and I worked at a local counseling center part time to pay the bills. After I graduated, Erin helped me get a job here and I have been here ever since."

"That is an amazing story. I can see how it really helps people. I feel rather inspired having heard it. Maybe telling my dad I want to go to Michigan State won't be so hard now."

"You're scared aren't you?"

"Just a bit. You know that both of my parents went to Michigan."

"I do, but don't stress over it. I'm sure there will be some shock but he'll accept it if he knows it will make you happy.

"I hope you're right."

"I know I am."

Sarah and Tony talked for the next half hour. They talked about Mike a little more, her father, religion, school, and the future. As their session was ending and Sarah was getting up to leave she turned around as she walked out the office door. "Tony."

"Yes, Sarah?"

"I will see you up at Michigan State next year. I'm going to make it, and I'm going to be a great therapist."

Tony smiled, "I know you will. I'll see you in July for our next session."

As Sarah walked out of Tony's office and down to her father's car, a sense of nervousness began to grow inside of her. By the time she neared her father's car there was a strong burning sensation in the pit of her stomach. She didn't know how she would tell her father that she was spurning both his and her mother's alma mater of Michigan for their archrival Michigan State. Michigan and Michigan State don't just have a friendly rivalry--they have a deep seeded hatred for one another, a hatred that has cost people jobs, and caused many an immature prank. A hatred that for one week every fall in the state of Michigan turns husband against wife, father against son, mother against daughter, brother against sister, friend against friend, cousin against cousin, uncle against nephew, aunt against niece, doctor against patient, teacher against student, principal against teacher, gambler against bookie. It divides a state in half, which continues with a somewhat lessened fervor the entire year. There is no middle ground in Michigan. Nobody says that they like both teams and just want to see the better team win. There is no such thing as sportsmanship in this rivalry. Every fall fans of both schools will gather together with one another to watch the annual football clash. The entire week leading up to the game will hear nothing but taunts and boos tossed back and forth between the two sides.

Sarah knew this all too well growing up in a house where both parents were University of Michigan alumni. She had seen it many times. Her parents would have a party and invite many of their friends, some who were Michigan fans and some who were Michigan State fans. The taunting would go on all game and even after it was over. The fans of the losing team suffered verbal tirades of the winning teams' fans for the next several hours. Many times these verbal jabs would continue for weeks. Sarah at one point had fulfilled a dream of her parents by attending The University of Michigan, now she was terrified that she would be creating a nightmare for her father by choosing to attend Michigan State. She thought that her mother would turn over in her grave when she looked down from heaven and saw her daughter attending the school that University of Michigan students slanderously call "Little Brother" thus giving every Michigan State student the firepower to call that other school down in Ann Arbor arrogant. However, the moment had arrived she knew the quicker that she told him the less painful it would be on her.

Sarah's dad was waiting down in the parking lot when she finished the session. "How did it go honey?"

"Well on the downside, Tony is leaving next month. He is transferring me to this counselor Rick, who I have to admit scared me when I first saw him, but after talking to him, he has a great sense of humor. Actually, he is hilarious. I think it will work out fine."

"Good, I'm glad to hear that. Your mother must be smiling right now seeing the progress you have made."

"Actually, dad, I don't think she is smiling right now. Actually I think she is mad at me."

Sarah's dad's demeanor completely changed, "why would your mother be mad at you honey? She loves you, she would be happy that you are making such great progress."

"Well dad I think you're going to be mad at me too."

"What? Stop talking like that. What is going on?"

"Well I told you that Tony is leaving."

"Yes. What does that have to do with it?"

"Well he's leaving to become a professor and I want to eventually go to the school he is teaching at and become a counselor as well."

"Your mom and I wouldn't be mad about that as long as it makes you happy."

"He's not teaching at Michigan."

"That's fine, just because your mother and I went there doesn't mean you have to. There are plenty of good schools out there. Where is he teaching?"

"Um, Michigan State." Sarah said meekly.

Sarah's dad slammed on the brakes, swerved, and nearly took out a mailbox, a cat jumped up into a tree screeching, and an old woman sitting on her front porch screamed.

"Michigan State! You're going to be a Spartan? I don't know what to think about that."

At this point, the car idled near the curb. Suddenly, there was a knock on the window. It was the old woman on the porch. "Are you drunk sir? Do I need to call the police? What kind of example are you setting for your daughter?"

"No ma'am my daughter just said something that shocked me. She told me she wants to go to Michigan State."

"Aaah, a fellow Spartan. Congratulations young lady, you are going to get a fine education."

Sarah's dad jumped in, "Both her mother and myself went to Michigan."

"Aah dear, so you are going to live out the American Dream and do better than your parents. You are going to enjoy East Lansing honey; it's an unbelievable town.

"It's no Ann Arbor." Her dad said annoyed.

"You know sir you are right. East Lansing has far fewer freaks than Ann Arbor, and a more attractive student population. Good luck to you young lady." Before her father could respond, the old woman said goodbye and walked back to her porch.

"Dad, are you ok?

"Yeah I'll be fine, just you going to that 'other school' was a bit difficult for me to take. I think you took a few years off my life there."

"Dad can you do me a favor?"

"What?"

"Could you not refer to MSU as that 'other school.' Tony made me promise not to and I would like you to as well. Besides you know as well as I do it's a good school."

Sarah's dad mumbled something incoherently. "What was that dad?"

"Fine," Sarah's dad said grudgingly. Her dad had probably never said anything as grudgingly as he agreed to Sarah's request.

"Thank you dad."

Sarah's dad just mumbled a reply. They drove the rest of the way home in silence. About fifteen minutes later, they reached Sarah and her father arrived home. Sarah went to get out but her dad grabbed her sleeve before she could. She turned to see what he wanted, "Honey, your mom and I are not mad at you for wanting to go to State. I'm sure your mother would be happy that you found a new goal in life that makes you happy, and it makes me happy to, however conflicted I am about you attending Michigan State."

"Thanks dad. Actually, I'm starting to think that the family rivalry will be fun. I think that tomorrow I'll have to go buy a green and white Michigan State shirt. This house could use a little green and white to balance out all the maize and blue. "

"Dear God."

Sarah kissed her dad's cheek, told him she loved him, and then ran into the house. Her dad sat in the car for a few more minutes looking at his University of Michigan air freshener hanging from his rearview mirror. He then shook his head and went into the house.

Chapter 16
Meetings

Mike was working his Tuesday morning shift. Overall, it was a slow morning. In fact, it had been so slow that he had been able to organize the back stock room and get all of his paperwork done. It was shortly past two o'clock when Carrie came back from her lunch. Mike planned to take his break right after Carrie returned. Carrie returned at two o'clock. Mike's shift ended at four so he decided to skip his break and earn a little extra money. However, there was a pizzeria right by the store and he was hungry. Mike decided to run and grab a slice of pizza and bring it back for a snack. He didn't need a full break so he figured why take one. It would take him five minutes at the most to get the pizza and get back and probably less than five minutes to eat. Mike told Carrie that he was going to run down and get a slice of pizza and asked if she would be fine for five minutes in the store by herself. She replied that it would not be a problem and Mike walked down to the pizzeria and got a slice of pizza and a small Coke. He would need something to wash the pizza down with and the Coke itself would not last long either as he suddenly discovered that he was quite thirsty. The pizzeria's pizza was not the best pizza that Mike had ever had but it was not horrible and it would fill the hole until he got home. When Mike got back to the store it was still deserted so he took his pizza and Coke to the back office to eat it. Mike had just finished eating his pizza and wiping his face with his napkin when Carrie called out to him from the store, "Hey Mike."

"What is it Carrie?"

"There is someone here to see you."

Mike was surprised that there was someone there to see him. He couldn't imagine who would be there to see him. He figured it was Todd or one of the other higher ups in the company coming to see how he was doing, or perhaps maybe his mom or his dad wanted to come in and throw some business the store's way. Mike took a quick sip of his Coke and then walked out into the store. He was very surprised to see Sarah standing looking at some Michigan State shirts. He was especially surprised to see her looking at Michigan State shirts, as he knew she had gone to Michigan. He figured she had some smart aleck comment she was working on to say to him when he got over there so he decided he had to beat her to the punch.

"Hey you know, you being a former Michigan student, I don't think I can legally allow you to stand in the presence of such great shirts. And I know it violates a State of Michigan law for me to sell you one, so I'm going to have to ask you to back away from the shirts slowly or I'll be forced to call the police."

Mike was proud of himself for coming up with that little diatribe on the fly. Witty remarks like that usually escaped him when the situation presented itself, but this time it came right to him. Mike assumed it must be divine intervention as a thank you for going back to church.

Sarah laughed and Mike's sense of self-satisfaction only grew with her laugh. "Good one Mike. Actually, my counselor Tony has accepted a position to teach at Michigan State and I have decided that I want to be a counselor to help people that have similar problems as me. I feel with my experience I can really be helpful to people. And seeing as how Tony will be teaching up at Michigan State, I have decided to start there next fall."

"Wow glad to see that you are finally getting with the winning team."

"Well judging by recent football results I'd say I am joining the losing team."

Mike did not have a comeback for that one, as he knew that during his lifetime Michigan had beaten Michigan State much more than Michigan State had beaten Michigan. "Well played." Mike said. "So what brings you into my store?"

"Well I figured that if I'm going to be a Spartan in fifteen months that I'd better start dressing the part and I remembered that this was the store that you worked at so I thought I'd come in, hassle you a little bit, and buy my first Michigan State shirt. It's really going to make my dad mad."

"Is your dad a big Michigan fan?"

"One of the biggest. Both him and my mom went to school there. That is the main reason why I decided to go to school there in the first place."

"So have you told your dad that you are planning on going to MSU? If not I'd like to be there when you do, sounds like it could be entertaining."

"Yes I've already told him. Although I made the mistake of telling him while he was driving. He very nearly crashed the car."

"Wow! That's crazy. Has he kicked you out of the house yet?"

"No. My dad is very upset about it but I know he would never kick me out. But if there is anything that he would kick me out for this would be it. So, will you be coming to church this Sunday?

"Yeah. I think that I will. It was a very nice service last week. As I said last Sunday the priest was quite good and an interesting speaker."

"Good. I'm glad that I'm getting you to go to church. You're not just going to try and impress me and hook up with me are you?"

Sarah's question caught Mike completely off guard. Originally, that was his motive for going to church with her but now he legitimately wanted to go to church. He knew he had to come up with a good answer, but once again, Mike thought quickly on his feet. "Well I'll be honest with you, last week that was much of my motivation, but this week I really want to go. I felt very moved by the service last week and have even begun praying my rosary again. I haven't done that since I was probably ten or eleven." Mike hoped Sarah did not get mad because of his ulterior motive; he waited for her response.

Sarah frowned at Mike's explanation. Mike noticed the frown and grew concerned. He tried to fix the situation. "Sorry. I hope I didn't offend you. Don't be mad, remember I'm a guy, I think we're from a different planet than women."

"I'm not mad at you. Maybe a little disappointed but you're lucky I'm nice; the disappointment will go away quickly. I'm mad because my dad was right. I hate it when he's right. He likes to gloat."

"Most parents do. I think it makes them feel young to prove their children wrong."

"You might be on to something Mike. But before we go any, further I need to make sure that you understand that I don't plan to date anybody anytime soon. Right now, I just want to get better and move on to the next chapter of my life. If you can't agree to that I'm afraid I may have a problem continuing to see you."

"It's cool." Mike said, trying to act unaffected. Actually, Mike did a very good job of not showing any outward emotion of disappointment. Mike had become an expert at that talent through the years of his life.

"Good, I'm glad. I'll be honest; our friendship has really helped me feel better. Helping you, turn back to God has made my day. I hope you don't mind but I am going to take total credit for that."

"Well I guess you have earned it. I would not have gone to church last week and be planning to go this week if you hadn't invited me. Although my mom is going to be a bit jealous of you as I know she would have liked it better if she got me to go back to church."

"Your mom goes to church?"

"Yep, every Sunday she's there, or sometimes she goes on Saturday. I always hated the Saturday mass as a kid because it interrupted my playing. I mean what kind of cruel church would force a kid to stop playing outside on a warm and sunny July afternoon to get all cleaned up and dressed up for church?"

"That would be the Catholic Church, Mike."

"Yeah I know." Both Mike and Sarah shared a laugh. Sarah picked a Michigan State shirt off the shelf and said "Well I had better get going, this is my first time driving by myself since my mother died. My dad will probably send out a search party if I'm not home soon."

"Well we wouldn't want that. Congratulations on your new accomplishment by the way."

"Thanks. I know it doesn't seem like much but it is a huge step for me."

"Hey no problem, remember you can't argue with the little things."

"Very profound."

"Thanks, I got it from an episode of The Simpsons."

"I never really watched The Simpsons."

"You're missing out, I never miss an episode."

"Well maybe I'll have to watch one sometime."

"I don't think there's any maybe about it. Not watching The Simpsons is un-American."

"Well then I guess it's my civic duty."

They both laughed and Mike rang up the Michigan State t-shirt, Sarah paid, said goodbye and left the store. Mike didn't realize it but his conversation with Sarah killed a half hour. Mike was excited now four would be here before he knew it. Mike went back to the office to finish his coke, as his mouth was as dry as The Sahara Desert. As he was sitting at the small desk in the office Carrie came back. Mike swallowed his Coke and said "Hey Carrie what's up?"

"Who was the girl?"

"Just a friend of mine."

"Seems like you want to be more than friends."

"Well I can't say that I would mind. She is pretty hot, and a nice person."

"It sounded like she has had some issues though."

"Yeah her mom died and I guess she tried suicide at one point because she couldn't take the grief. It seems like she's doing a lot better now."

"Well man if you want to get in, just keep being supportive but don't be a complete sap about it. When this is over, she'll remember how much you helped her and that you're not a complete sap. That will give you the inside track."

"I'm not sure that I'm smooth enough to pull that off."

"I could give you some pointers if you want."

"Why would you do that for me? No offense but I'm a bit surprised that you offered to help."

"You showed me a way to make this job fun for me. If you hadn't I probably would have been fired by now, and my parents would have killed me. But you took extra time to give me some pointers to make this job work for me, so I feel I should return the favor."

"Well that would be great. I've never been too good with women so any help I can get I will take."

"Cool. Every time we work together I'll talk to you for a few minutes on my break and you can tell me about your encounters with Sarah and I'll help you analyze them and come up with the best course of action."

"Sounds good. Shake on it?"

Mike and Carrie shook hands and Carrie went back out onto the sales floor. Mike finished his Coke. Four o'clock rolled around quickly and Mike left work. Mike was amazed at the impact his advice had on Carrie. Now he really could not wait for fall to start working with the baseball team and helping them as well.

Sarah made another stop on her way home at a local department store. She picked up a Michigan State air freshener and replaced the Michigan one in her dad's car. She did it partially to give her dad a hard time, but also to take away a reminder of the hardest time in her life. Her career at Michigan had ended in disappointment and heartbreak. In addition, she had met Steve at Michigan and she knew it was childish and petty but she partly blamed the university for Steve's abandonment of her. There were no bad memories associated with Michigan State and she vowed that there never would be any bad memories associated with her new school. Sarah pulled in the driveway, stashed the Michigan air freshener in her bag, and went in the house.

"How did it go honey?

"Good."

"No problems?"

"None at all. I think I'll go try on my new shirt."

Her dad just put his head down at that. She walked over to him and gave him a big hug. "Don't worry dad, I still love you."

"I know you do honey. Those colors are just hard for me to look at. I'll try my best to get used to it."

"I knew you would." Sarah then kissed her dad on the cheek and ran upstairs to try on her new shirt.

Chapter 17
Moving On

Mike got up a little bit early Sunday morning to get ready for church. He didn't mind it this time as he did last time. He actually had enjoyed the talk that the priest had given the week before and even reflected on it, not just, because he thought it would impress Sarah but also because he thought it was useful to his own life. He realized that he needed to give more control over to God to help lead him through the difficult times and going to church every Sunday was a good way to start that endeavor. Mike ate a quick breakfast and headed out the door.

It was a warm and humid Sunday morning, the sun had already been up, and shining for a few hours and the temperatures had already soared to near eighty degrees. Mike knew this would be a hot day. Temperatures would reach the lower to middle nineties with high humidity making being outside somewhat miserable in the afternoon. Mike had a higher tolerance for the heat than many other people he knew did but even he had his limits. He may have been one of the only one's that drove around with his windows down in the heat, but despite that Mike knew he would spend most of this Sunday afternoon indoors in air conditioned comfort.

Despite the warm and muggy morning, Mike enjoyed the drive to the church. The sun was out, the sky was blue, and there was not much traffic. All three factors put together made it a good drive. Mike got to the church a little early. People were just starting to file into the church. Mike drove around the parking lot looking for Sarah's car but did not see it so he found a parking spot in the back and parked facing the entrance so he could see Sarah and her dad pull in. When he saw them, he would get out of his car and go meet them to walk into church. The church was still new to Mike and he didn't feel completely comfortable walking in by himself. In time, he would, but for now he felt better walking in with someone he knew.

It was a typical Sunday morning for Sarah and her dad. They got up, had a small breakfast, got cleaned up for church, then got dressed and left the house. Sarah and her dad didn't talk much on the drive to church. Sarah did notice that the Michigan State air freshener no longer dangled from the mirror but a new Michigan air freshener did. "Where's the air freshener I put in here dad?"

"I don't know what you're talking about honey."

"You know what I'm talking about. I bought a Michigan State air freshener and put it in here Wednesday."

"You didn't put it in this car. If you did you'd never be allowed to drive it again."

Sarah knew that her dad had done something with the air freshener. She also knew that she would be unable to get him to acknowledge that he did anything to it. Sarah just decided to give it up and let her dad have this one. "Well I must have intended to buy it, forgot, and then just thought that I did."

"That would be my first guess. But be warned, if I ever find an air freshener or bumper sticker or anything green and white attached to my car after use it you will have to find your own car. I'm a tolerant man but there are things that even I can't tolerate. Desecrating my car with green and white paraphernalia is near the top of the list."

"Well I'll do my best to remember that."

"See that you do."

By this, point Sarah and her dad were only a block from the church. Shortly, they reached the driveway to the church and turned in. Sarah noticed Mike's car already parked in the back. She was happy he had shown up again. As Sarah's dad neared the parking space and pulled in, she noticed Mike getting out of his car. When Sarah's dad shut off the car and they began to get out Mike had already reached the car. Sarah greeted Mike right away. "Hey Mike have you been here long?"

"I got here a few minutes ago. I've been sitting in the car waiting for a song to end ever since."

Sarah sensed that he was waiting for her and her dad. "You could go in by yourself, you don't have to wait for us. Nobody here bites. Besides it's so hot out here you should get into the air conditioning."

"Heat never bothers me."

Sarah's dad suddenly jumped in and asked Mike a question. "So are you the one responsible for making my daughter wanting to go to Michigan State?" Mike's dad suspected that was the real story but didn't have any evidence.

"Wish I could take credit for that one sir. But it was not me unfortunately. But I've been an MSU fan since I was a kid."

"Well there's no accounting for good taste."

"Dad!" Sarah said loudly. "Don't start that college superiority crap here!"

"Well I hardly think that it is appropriate to use such language in a church parking lot. I think I know where the influence for that came in."

Sarah just laughed sarcastically and all three walked into the church and found a seat. Mike immediately enjoyed the air conditioning in the church. The church that he had gone to growing up did not have air conditioning so this was almost a treat for Mike. Sarah could see the impressed look on Mike's face and couldn't help but whisper to him, "This air conditioning is pretty nice huh?"

"Sure is." Mike said nodding in agreement. Just then, the music began to play and the priest walked in. The mass began and both Mike and Sarah listened intently to the sermon. They had both enjoyed last week's sermon so much that they wanted to be certain to catch all of this weeks. Once again, both Mike and Sarah found the topic very enlightening. Both listened intently as the priest went on, "God gives all people a unique skill set. He purposely equips each of us with a unique set of skills that help us succeed better in some situations better than others. The key for each of us is to recognize what our own unique skill set is and live within our own limits. When I say limits, I don't mean that we are all limited in what we can accomplish. God has given us the skill set to do anything as long as we stay within God's plan for each of us, and while unlimited potential on the path would like us to follow is difficult but once we venture off of God's road we place limits on what we can do. Everything gets more difficult and in many cases impossible. However, when we work within ourselves and within God, we will find happiness and success. I would like to challenge each member of this congregation to go home tonight and listen to what God is saying to them, then analyze what they here against what they are doing in their own life, and then challenge yourself to do what God wants."

Both Sarah and Mike understood exactly what the preacher was saying. They both knew that they had tried to live outside themselves and that it never seemed to work out. They both began to realize that maybe it hadn't been God that caused their problems but in fact, they had caused their own problems by not living on God's path for them.

After the mass was over Mike, Sarah, and Sarah's dad again went to the same restaurant. Just like the previous week, Sarah's dad sat up at the counter and Mike and Sarah sat at a table in the back. "So are you going to take my advice and have the chicken fingers this week?"

"If I do will you stop pushing them? I mean it sounds like you're on some international chicken fingers council or something."

"I promise if you order them this week I will stop pushing them on you."

"Well then I guess my choice pretty much made itself."

Sarah laughed aloud and both put their menus down. Almost immediately, the waitress came over and took their orders. Once she was gone, they began talking about the sermon.

"So what did you think of the sermon today?" Sarah asked.

"It was very interesting. I can see points in my own life where I have failed to live within God's plan."

"Can you give me an example?"

"Well it's like with the whole business thing. I've always assumed that is what I have to do with my life. I never really cared for it personally but it just seemed like the way I would be forced to pay the bills."

"What do you think you would like to do?"

"I don't know. I'm so excited about being the pitching coach on the high school team this year that I almost think that I might want to teach."

"That would be pretty cool. What would you want to teach?"

"Probably history. I always liked history the best. I used to actually read my textbooks for fun."

"Nerd!"

"Thanks a lot."

"I'm just given you the business. History was ok but I was always more into math and science, that's why I was going to be a doctor."

"I couldn't do algebra. I tried but I never could get that crap."

"You see that always came easy to me but sometimes I wonder if I really liked it. I think I was going to be a doctor just because like you said it was the easiest thing for me to do to make money. But after listening to the sermon today, I am even more convinced that social work is the place for me."

"Well that would make sense with the sermon. You would have gone off of God's road and brought in all of the limitations that go with it."

"Exactly. I think that's what I did.

"I was sitting in church thinking that I did the same thing. Aren't we a fine pair?" Mike said with a laugh.

"We sure are." Sarah said laughing. "Here," Sarah said lifting up her Coke, "To bad decisions and making them right."

Mike picked up his glass and clanged it to Sarah's. "Here here."

They both took a drink of their Coke. Mike swallowed his Coke and said, "Does your dad not like me? He's been looking over here constantly."

"He's just nervous that you're going to hurt me. Since my mom died, and with all of the problems that I have had coping with her death he's become very protective, which I can understand. My mom and I were always his two girls and now one of his girls is gone. I know it would kill him to lose me. I think that he thinks you only want try and get in my pants. And just so, you know, in case you were thinking about it right now I'm not anywhere ready for anything romantic. I really just want to be friends for now." Sarah paused, "I hope that didn't sound mean."

"No," Mike said. "I understand completely. I'm probably not in the right condition for a relationship myself. I won't try to force you into anything. Take all of the time that you need to get better, that is the most important thing." Mike was proud of himself. The entire time he was answering Sarah he was remembering what Carrie had said to him and that shaped his response.

"Thank you Mike. Many guys would not be that understanding."

Mike wanted to be clever and came back with "Hey I've always tried to be an understanding guy." Mike thought to himself swing and a miss.

"Thanks again" Sarah said.

Mike thought again trying to come up with something clever but thought better of it and replied with a simple "you're welcome." Right then their food arrived and both began to eat. Once again, they didn't talk much during the lunch. When they finished eating the waitress bought the bill. Sarah grabbed it right away and said "it's my turn this week."

"Thanks. So I guess I'll pay next week."

"Coming back to church?"

"Definitely."

"Great! I'll be looking forward to it. Maybe next week I'll get the burger and the chicken fingers."

"Fine. I've got the cash."

"Good. You'll need it." Sarah looked up and saw her dad standing up. The waitress came over and Sarah handed her a twenty-dollar bill and told her to keep the change. "I hope you don't mind but my dad seems like he is waiting for me so I should get going. Church same time next week?"

"Absolutely. Have a good Sunday, stay cool."

"I'll do my best, stay cool yourself. Bye."

Sarah walked over to her dad and they left right away. Mike waited for the waitress to come back, gave her a twenty for the bill, and told her to keep the change for the tip. "Thank you," She said. "Have a nice day."

"You too," Mike replied.

Mike sat about another five minutes; finished his Coke and left.

In the car, Sarah said to her dad, "Well I told Mike what you told me too."

"Good, how did he react?"

"Actually he was very understanding."

"It was probably a front."

"Dad you worry too much."

"Well honey, you're the only girl I have left. I want to look out for you."

"I know, and I love you for it. You should eat with us next week, you'll see that Mike is a nice guy."

"Thanks for the invitation, maybe I'll take you up on the offer. I'll let you know.

"Good."

By the time Sarah and her dad got home, the temperature was up over ninety degrees with high humidity. They got out of the car and both grimaced when the heat hit them. "Boy thank God for central air" Sarah's dad said.

"I think that is one thing we can both agree on dad, lets get inside and out of this heat."

They went into the house and Sarah went to her room to read her bible and reflect on the sermon while her dad sat in the living room to watch the Tiger's game.

Chapter 18
Changing Seasons

Eventually, June and July turned into August. Sarah's dad finally did eat lunch with Sarah and Mike. This assuaged his fears and he finally stopped being distrustful of Mike. Sarah and Mike continued going to church every Sunday. By the middle of August, Tony was gone and Sarah worked exclusively with Rick. She was a bit nervous about the first session but vowed to go in with an open mind. Sarah sat down in Rick's office. It was much like Tony's only a little bigger and had a window. Rick started the session off by saying, "Don't be nervous."

"I'm doing my best."

"Well what have you been up to? How are things going with Mike? Tony told me you are trying to help him improve his life."

Sarah was surprised how quickly he had changed the subject. This tactic had not helped her calm her nerves. She remained concerned this wasn't going to work. "Well I'm waiting." Rick interrupted her thinking.

Suddenly Sarah's mind shifted gears to answer his question. "It's going well. We're going to church every week and we're both learning a lot about ourselves."

"What were his demons if you don't mind me asking?"

Sarah went into detail about Mike and his issues and how she had interacted to help him.

"Well it sounds like you've got a good handle on the situation. That is impressive considering all that you have been through."

A look of nervousness suddenly appeared on Sarah's face. She had forgotten how nervous she was because she was talking about Mike. Again, Rick interrupted. "Hey there's nothing to be nervous about. You're doing fine. Do you realize you just talked to me perfectly calmly for the last thirty minutes about this guy Mike?"

"No. But aren't we supposed to talk about me?"

"Well that's exactly what we've been doing. Well I should say that's what you have been doing. Excuse me." Rick turned his head and let out a loud belch. "Sorry, just my lunch coming back to say hello."

Sarah was dumbfounded, "but what about all the things that have happened to me with my mom and suicide?"

"What about them? Do you need to talk about them? It seems to me you are at a good place with all of that. Your focus seems entirely centered on helping this guy Mike."

"Well it has been but?"

"But what? Just because you're not talking about it doesn't mean you're not dealing with it. You've found something else to live for, a person to help, and a new career. Whether you realize it or not you have a lot of good going on in your life right now. In fact, if you really look at it you have a lot more good than bad. Yes you've had tragedies in the past but it seems like you have moved on from many of them"

Sarah sat back, thought for a minute, and realized that most of what she had been thinking and doing all summer had almost nothing to do with her mother or her near suicide. "Oh my God. I've barely thought about mom in three months."

"How does that make you feel?"

"Actually I really feel pretty good. I've been busying myself with new adventures. I think that's what my mom would have wanted."

"I'm sure it is, no parent wants their kids to be in pain. They always want them to be happy. We all know that's not possible but yet we still strive for it, it is truly one of humanities greatest traits that we put our kids first and never want them to feel the pain."

"You are completely right. I mean I don't have kids but my mom loved me so much and so does my dad. Neither one of them would want to see me hurting like I was. Wow, this has been such an uplifting session. Thank you so much!"

"Hey that's what I'm here for and why they pay me the big bucks."

"I kind of wish I had started with you instead of Tony. I mean Tony did so much for me but in this one session I think you've changed my life."

"Now stop right there. When you first came here, I reviewed your file. I looked at everything and gave your file to Tony."

Why?"

"Well admittedly Tony and I have two very different styles. Tony is a great therapist and his demeanor and methods were what you needed at the time. Now you are near the end of your journey and you just need someone to kick you in the pants to the finish line. That person is me not Tony, that's why Tony wouldn't release you from care. Even if he had stayed, he was still going to have you meet with me. Now if I had started with you from the beginning you wouldn't be as far along as you are now. That is why we did it like this."

"You guys are both amazing. Thank you so much!"

"Hey it's what we do. Well our time is just about up. See you in September."

"When will you release me from care?"

"If things go like they did today, by Christmas."

Sarah was so excited as she left. She hadn't been this excited since before her mom had died. She got in the car and gave her dad a big bear hug. "What was that for?" he asked.

"Just because I love you."

Well I'll take that. Thank you honey."

The day after Labor Day was the first day of school. Mike had a meeting with the team after school. Coach Stopac had called the meeting to initiate an offseason work program for the team. Mike would be working with the pitchers one day after school each week. He would work outside as long as the weather permitted and then move it inside. Coach Stopac gave Mike a list of seven different players. David was the number one starter, he threw a two, and three seem fastball, slider, change up, and curve. Mark was the number two starter. He threw a fastball change up sinker and slider. Carl was the number three, he threw a two, and three seem fastball, along with a change up. He needed to develop another pitch though. Mike would work with him on that.

Ben was the team's long reliever; he threw a fastball, slider, and curveball. The rest of the bullpen consisted of Kyle, the team's only left hander, Travis and the seldom-used Jack. Mike met with the entire group and said "I look forward to working with all of you. Our practice sessions will be Wednesday's at 3:15 outside on the backfield if the weather is good or in the gym if the weather is bad. These sessions will last for one hour each time. Be prepared to work and have a little fun too, we are going to win that championship this year and you guys will be the reason. We are going to have the best pitching staff in the state. Remember pitching wins championships."

Mike's speech pumped up all of the pitchers and they all told him that they were excited to get started. After the students had left Coach Stopac pulled Mike aside to talk to him individually. "So are you ready for this?"

"Absolutely. Can't wait to get started."

"Good. You are going to need to maintain that attitude all year long. You may not know this but high school kids will follow the moods of their teachers and coaches. If their coach projects a negative attitude, the players will have a negative attitude and their play will suffer. This is our best chance to win a championship since I've been here and I want to win."

"I want to win too. I want to show everybody that I have a future coaching this sport. I know that I will be a great coach."

"Good. I have no doubt you will be. I'll stop buy next Wednesday and check out your first pitching session."

"I'll be looking forward to it." With that, Coach Stopac went back to his office.

The next Wednesday Mike began to work with the pitchers. The first day went well. He really enjoyed it and the kids seemed to like him. They would joke around with him and he would joke right back with them. But when it was time to get down to business the kids did exactly what Mike asked them. Coach Stopac stopped by during the first practice while he was working with Kyle on his throwing mechanics. He hung around for about fifteen minutes and then went back to his office.

When practice ended the kids left and Mike stayed back to put the equipment back in the office. Coach Stopac was sitting in the office when Mike returned.

"The boys looked good out there today Mike."

"Thanks. They seem like a good group. I think there is no shortage of talent in these kids. We just have to tap into their potential. I was working with Kyle on his mechanics and how he plants his foot and trying to get him to generate a little more power in his fastball."

"Yeah I saw that when I came in. So specifically what do you think about the pitching staff?"

"I'm not sure I understand what you want to know."

"Well, think about each pitcher; what do you see as their strengths and weaknesses? Will you work to add any new pitches with any of them?"

"Well I don't know if there is much I can do for David. The kid has electric stuff and knows how to pitch. I think he will mainly require in game coaching. Mark, I would like to develop either a curveball or split-finger to round out his pitches. With Carl I would like to develop an off speed pitch, probably a change or a curveball. In addition, there are a couple of things that I don't like about his delivery. If he threw from a higher arm slot, he could add 5mph easy on his fastball. I'd like to see Ben develop a change up to increase his endurance. I want Kyle to throw harder and develop a split-finger as being our only left-hander I'd like to use him in a setup role, and if he develops a split-finger, he could be almost unhittable. Travis needs to get more movement on his fastball. I think I am going to work with him on throwing a three seam and possibly a four-seam fastball to help him get a little more movement out of his pitches. Lastly, I think Jack has a ton of untapped potential. He has good velocity but not very good command. However, he says he has not been pitching for long so that may be why. Jack definitely needs to develop an off speed pitch. All he throws is a fastball and a slider. I asked him if he would be willing to do a one on one bullpen session every month where I can just work with him and he was all for it."

"Good. It sounds like you have a firm grasp of this pitching staff and a clear plan. I feel confident with you working with my pitchers."

"They really are a fun group of kids." Mike interrupted.

"They are a great group, and they are all nice kids that would do anything for each other or anyone else for that matter. It made me madder than I have ever been in my life when that coach taunted our guys after the game. One of my assistants actually had to hold me back from going after him. You don't treat kids like that. It's just plain wrong on every level. That's why I promised our kids that we would beat them this year, and we will."

"You're right we will."

"You're a good man Mike. I'm glad that you are on the team. You know the game, have an unmatched passion for the game, and I am confident you will do right by these kids."

"I will."

"Well I have to run Mike. I'll see you later."

"Next week?"

"If I get a chance I'll come down and see how things are going, but the beginning of the school year is always busy. If I don't see you next week I'll drop by from time to time and see how things are going."

"Sounds like a plan, have a good night."

Coach Stopac waved at Mike and left. Mike packed up the equipment that he had brought and lugged it back to his car. He threw it all into the back seat and then climbed in, and drove home.

The excitement that he felt on the drive home and the rest of the night made Mike realize that he needed to go down a new career path. Mike wanted to be a teacher. Mike decided that he would begin forming a plan to become a teacher over the weekend. At that point, he could go online and research programs at different schools. He then could contact each school for materials and possibly a tour on Monday morning.

Chapter 19
Autumn

Life went on for both Mike and Sarah. The warmth of summer faded into the first chills of fall and the smell of bonfires on crisp autumn nights. The leaves on the trees began to change from green to bright shades of red, orange, and yellow before eventually turning brown and ending up first on the ground and then either in a garbage can or yard waste bag. Autumn is an interesting time in Michigan. Many people take to the outdoors in droves on warm autumn days to take advantage of the last lingering warmth before the constant cold and grey of winter. However, many people fail to take advantage of the opportunity and spend their time watching football, which is another huge pastime in Michigan whether it is college or the NFL. But those that understand life take advantage of these days by going to cider mills and enjoying fresh apples, cider, and donuts, or by walking down a nature trail on a cool fall day and smelling the one of a kind autumn smell unique to Michigan.

Although the plant life outside was in the process of death and decay, Mike was experiencing a rebirth of sorts. Although he enjoyed working at the sporting goods store and had previously wanted to grow with the company, he now saw the job as a means to an end. He would need the income from the job to pursue becoming a teacher, which because of coaching baseball had become his new passion. He began to save his money to get ready to pay increased tuition payments the following year. Mike decided that he would work full time at the store and substitute teach the one day a week that he did not work at the store. He knew that it would be a tiring schedule but he also knew that it would help him save money for school and give him a little teaching experience.

Mike was not dreading the full schedule but rather he was looking forward to it. He continued to work with the pitching staff through September and it was going well. He had his first one on one bullpen session with Jack on the last day of the month. On September 30, Mike met Jack before school for a half hour pitching session.

"All right Jack you need to develop another pitch. Now you already throw a fastball so we'll start with a split-finger fastball." Mike showed Jack how to properly grip the ball to throw the split-finger. He then let Jack try ten pitches. After the ten pitches Mike said, "All right we need to work on your mechanics. You don't quite throw sidearm but you're throwing at about a three quarter arm angle. I want you to try this delivery." Mike took the ball and threw it from an over the top delivery. "This will give more velocity on your pitches and the split-finger is easier to throw from this arm slot."

Jack nodded his head in agreement and began trying the new delivery. Mike liked what he saw as Jack began throwing from the new delivery. He saw instantly that Jack had better velocity and seemingly slightly better command of his pitches. After about ten or fifteen, more pitches Mike stopped him again. "How does it feel?"

"It feels a little different, maybe a little weird."

"Any pain?"

"No. But why can't I use my old delivery?"

"Take the ball. I want to show you something."

Jack picked up a baseball and stood at the makeshift mound in the corner of the gym. Meanwhile Mike grabbed the radar gun and set it up behind the netting that was serving as their backstop. "Ok now throw a fastball with your old delivery." Jack wound up and threw a fastball; the radar gun read 71 mph on the first pitch. "Was that the hardest you can throw it?"

"I think so."

"Try it one more time from that angle just to make sure."

Jack wound up again and threw another fastball. This time the radar gun ready 70 mph. "All right now try the new way." Jack wound up the way Mike had showed him and threw another fastball. This time the radar gun read 77mph. "See when you use that wind up you generate more power. That extra six or seven miles per hour can mean the difference between the batter hitting the ball four hundred feet or the ball ending up in the catcher's glove."

"What if it was a fluke?"

"Well let's try it again. Throw two more fastballs." Jack wound up and threw two more fastballs. The first pitch registered 75 mph and the second pitch 78 mph. "Well it's no fluke. Now I want you to try something else. When you pitch, I want you to push off the edge of the mound with the back of your foot as you release the ball. I want you to throw three more fastballs with the new wind up and pushing off your back foot." Jack was a little confused at how this would help but he did what his coach said. Jack wound up three more times and threw three more fastballs. The first pitch registered 81 mph on the gun, the second pitch 83 mph, and the third pitch 84 mph.

"You see, with more practice you should be able to throw 85 mph consistently. Bet you didn't know that you had it in you, did you?"

Jack shook his head. "I really didn't, coach. You think I'll be able to get in more games this year?"

"If we keep working on the mechanics and the split-finger you will definitely be used more."

"Awesome! I can't wait. I only got to pitch twice last year and neither of those outings was even a full inning."

"Well, keep practicing like this and you'll probably get in quite a few games."

"Really? You're not just yanking my chain?"

"I wouldn't lie about playing time. I played for a coach in high school who was a complete jerk. He would lie about getting me into the game all the time and then blame losses on me. I will never do that to anybody. Remember, you have to work hard so I can feel comfortable putting you in a close game. If you slack off, even for a minute, you will not make it I promise you."

" I won't let you down." Jack gave Mike a high five and then looked at the clock. "Hey coach the first bell is going to ring in five minutes, can I go?"

"Yeah go ahead, see you on Wednesday."

"Yeah coach, thanks."

Jack ran off and Mike turned around to put the radar gun away. Just then, he saw Coach Stopac sitting in the bleachers.

"Hey coach, good morning." It was not unusual for even the other coaches to call Coach Stopac "coach." Nobody at school called him by his first name. Most staff members in the school didn't even know his first name, just called him coach.

"You did a great job with that kid this morning Mike. The kid took to it very well. You are a natural coach sir."

"Thanks coach, that means a lot. It's been a very rare occasion in my life when I've been told I'm a natural at something."

"Well you're definitely a natural born coach. I've never seen anybody take to it so fast, usually there's a learning curve before solid coaching gets done, but you just get it."

"Well I've had some bad coaches in my life. I basically watched them and learned what not to do."

"Well whatever you're doing just keep it up. You'll be coaching a long time if you do."

Just then, the first bell rang. "Well, Mike I have to go get to my first class. Once again great job."

Mike just smiled and finished putting the radar gun away.

The rest of the fall went just like that for Mike. Every Wednesday like clockwork, he was up at the school working with the pitchers. The kids liked the workout program so much that the hour after school soon became an hour and a half after school. The kids actually wanted to stay longer but Mike could only have the gym for an hour and a half. At the end of practice, he almost had to drag the kids out of the gym. The kids were not being disrespectful; they just loved what they were doing.

By Thanksgiving Jack was consistently throwing 85 mph. The other kids on the team started embraced him as their new friend. Before Jack had been the outcast of the team. Other kids had tried to talk to him but he was always uncomfortable around them. Mike was finishing up a morning session with Jack the day before Thanksgiving when Jack walked up to him.

"Hey coach."

"Yeah Jack what's up?"

"I'm heading to class but I wanted to give you this before you left for Thanksgiving, and since there is no practice after school today I'll just give it to you now."

"What is it?"

"Just a thank you note for all that you have done for me."

"Well you're welcome man."

"Gotta go man." With that, Jack ran off to his first class. Mike put the note in his pocket and finished putting the equipment away. When he got into his car and sat down in the seat he pulled the note out of his pocket and read it.

Dear Coach Mike

I just wanted to thank you for helping me. You see, you don't know just how much that you have helped me, in fact; you saved my life. You see last summer I was thinking about committing suicide. I had no friends here, nobody ever noticed me, and my father had just died. My mom tried to cheer me up but no matter how hard she tried, she was unsuccessful. She tried sending me to a grief counselor but that didn't work either. You see my dad was murdered last December 23 at a local convenience store. He had stopped at the store on his way home from work to pick up some cold medicine for me. As he went to the counter to pay a man walked in with a gun demanding money, after cleaning out the register he turned to my dad and demanded his money. My dad only had ten dollars in his wallet and apparently that wasn't enough for the robber because he shot him in the chest and he was killed instantly. It turned into the most depressing Christmas of my life, and then the most depressing winter and spring. Then at the end of the year you came in and talked to us. I don't know why but something about you moved me. Nothing had moved me in months. I think it was your determination and the fact that you spoke from the heart. But I decided to not kill myself over the summer and see what the autumn would bring. The summer was difficult and there were times I thought about just taking a handful of pills and going to sleep permanently. But I stuck it out, and then you began working with me and I became a better pitcher, and then they guys on the team accepted me as part of the team's family. And slowly, the thoughts of suicide and despair went away. I still miss my dad more than anything but I know now that I can go on, and that is because of you. This Thanksgiving I am thankful that you took the time to work with me and in the process save my life. Now that I think about it with a clearer head I can't imagine what my mom would have done if I had killed myself. Thank you again for all that you have done.

Sincerely,
Jack

Mike sat back flabbergasted. He tried to think of what to do, but nothing came to mind. He had never received anything like the letter that he had just gotten from Jack. What would he say the next time that he saw Jack? His stomach was burning from the sheer shock of what he had just read. He knew that as a teacher, he would have an impact but he never dreamed he would have this kind of an impact.

Meanwhile Sarah was having somewhat of a rebirth as well. She continued to meet with Rick for her therapy sessions. She did miss Tony but she knew that she was in capable hands with Rick. Sarah enjoyed her sessions. Rick made her laugh at least a few times each session. Sarah was also involved in getting as much information as she could about the counseling program at Michigan State. She would keep in touch with Tony via e-mail. She would e-mail him after each session and tell him about it. Sarah being a very detail oriented person would never forget to leave out any small detail of her session in her e-mails to Tony. Sometime she wondered if her e-mails annoyed him. She knew that he would be busy teaching and grading papers of his students, but he always responded rather quickly and would usually acknowledge all of her points in some point or another. So she decided that she would just leave it alone and that if Tony had a problem with her e-mails that he would tell her so. Sarah went for a session with Rick on the morning before Thanksgiving. She felt this was an advantageous time to go, as Tony would have a little more time to read and reply to her e-mail with the Thanksgiving break. "Good morning Sarah and Happy Thanksgiving!"

Rick was in his usual form with his booming voice. "Happy Thanksgiving to you as well Rick."

"What's your favorite thing about Thanksgiving, Sarah?"

She thought for a moment and then answered. "Well it's always been family, and I think it still is. It's definitely different without my mom but I have a big family and we all love each other. What about you? What is your favorite thing?"

"Turkey and football, what's not to like? I'll watch the Lions game and then enjoy my annual turkey leg. I'll eat it just like Henry VIII!"

"I thought the football players were supposed to get the turkey legs."

"Well if the Lions lay another egg and I watch it I'll have earned the turkey leg."

"Fair enough."

"You seem in good spirits Sarah."

"I have been. Things have been going very well. I've been immersing myself in the prospect of being a counselor."

"Well that's a nice concept to immerse yourself in, but how are you feeling?"

"Very good. I can't remember the last time I felt this good."

"How do you feel about spending Thanksgiving without your mom?"

"Well I haven't really thought about it much. I think I've kept so busy with other things and haven't had time to think about it."

"That's good but don't forget her entirely."

"Oh I won't but now I've found balance between her being gone and moving on with life. Surprisingly my main focuses are on my new career and going to church with Mike."

"How is that going by the way?"

"Very well. We have great discussions about the sermons, our faith, and how they are impacting our lives."

"Do you think he wants to be more than friends?"

"Well, I've told him where I stand on that and I think he respects it."

"Well, he may but if he's anything like me he probably wouldn't mind a romp in the hay."

"Rick!" Sarah said horrified at the fact her counselor would say that.

"Hey I was young once. I bet if you gave him the chance he would take it."

"Yeah but I'm not that kind of girl. I never even let Steve. We were saving ourselves for marriage."

"Well that's a rarity in today's age. Good for you."

"Thank you."

"You're very welcome. Well, Sarah I have some good news for you today."

"What's that?"

"If all goes according to plan I will release you from care."

"That's wonderful! I'm surprised. I didn't think it would happen this soon. But I am so excited."

"You have found new purpose in your life. You are doing things you truly enjoy doing. All of this seems to have helped you get over the loss of your mother. I want to see you right around Christmas to make sure you are still doing well. But if all stays as is I will release you from care at that time."

"I can't wait to tell my dad. He'll be so happy! I think I will call Mike tonight and tell him as well. We've helped each other a great deal and I think it would make him happy to hear this."

"I'm sure he will."

Sarah finished the rest of her session with Rick. They talked about the upcoming holiday season, religion, and foods and beverages. Sarah left feeling very happy. When she got to the car, she immediately hugged her dad. Even though Sarah didn't need him to drive her to her appointments, anymore he still insisted. He wanted to protect his little girl at all costs, even though he knew that she wasn't his little girl anymore. Her dad was somewhat surprised at the abrupt hug Sarah gave him when she got in the car. As Sarah was hugging her father he spoke, "to what do I owe the honor of this wonderful hug?"

"Dad, Rick said that if all goes well over the next month, that he will release me from care after my next appointment."

Her dad was silent for a moment and then began to cry.

"Don't cry. This is good news"

"I know it is sweetheart," he said fighting off tears. "I'm just so damn happy to hear it, that I can't help it. This will definitely be something to celebrate at Thanksgiving dinner tomorrow. Are you excited honey?"

"I am. I know I'm ready for this. I bet wherever mom is right now that she is smiling."

"I'll practically guarantee that she is."

Sarah and her dad drove home talking about Thanksgiving tomorrow. Sarah and her father both agreed that they should do a toast to her progress at the beginning of the Thanksgiving meal. It would be a great way to tell the rest of the family the news and give them a chance to celebrate as a family.

Later that night Sarah decided to call Mike and tell him the good news. Mike said that he was very happy for her, but she could tell that there was something wrong by the sound of his voice.

"What's wrong? Something seems off in your voice. Is everything all right?"

Mike thought for a moment about the letter that Jack had given him. He knew that he wanted to tell Sarah about it, but he was not sure if it was his place to do so. He decided that he had to tell somebody and he figured that Sarah would be able to give him good advice on how to approach Jack the next time he saw him. Mike did not realize that he had not said anything for a couple of minutes until Sarah said "Mike, are you still there?"

"Yes, I'm here. Just have something on my mind."

"Well what is it? Is there anything that I can help you with?"

"I got this letter today. Do you remember the kid Jack that I told you about? The one that reminded me a little of myself that I would be working with privately one morning a month?"

"Yes I do."

"Well as I was packing up the equipment at the end of the pitching session this morning he gave me this note. In the note, he told me that last December 23 his father was murdered in a convenience store. He talked about how it ruined his entire Christmas and how that depression had spread into this year."

"Wow...that's sad, is he all right? If you think he needs help I can give you Rick's name and phone number."

"Well let me continue. He said that he had decided that he was going to kill himself; he was going to do it last summer. Then he told me that when I talked to the team last June that something about me made him reconsider. He decided to wait for the next school year and give me a chance. He then said that all of my extra work with him had made the team except him as a brother, which they had not before. He said that he felt better than at any point since his father's murder and that he had me to thank for it. I couldn't believe it. I was literally flabbergasted. That letter has stuck with me all day. I really think that I may have saved this kid's life. It's just such an enormous thing I don't quite know how to process it. Also, I'm nervous to see him next week. I'm not sure what to say to him. Do you have any advice?"

"Well first, do you think there is a possibility that he will consider suicide again?"

"I don't know. I'm sure it's possible. But judging by the letter, right now I think he's good."

"If you ever have any suspicion that he may consider it again you have to get him help."

"I know."

"Let me give you Rick's number, just in case. I'll even call him Monday morning and give him a heads up on the situation just in case you need to contact him."

Mike took down Rick's number, but he still wasn't sure about the situation. "What do you think I should do?"

"Well you don't want to come on too strong. You should acknowledge that you read the letter. Not acknowledging it could push him back into depression."

"That's what I keep thinking but I'm not sure how to approach the situation gently. Damn, this is going to keep me up all night, and I'm tired, plus I have to work all day on black Friday."

"Try this on Wednesday, tell him that you read the letter and that if he ever needs to talk to anybody that you are there for him. Also, let him know that if he doesn't feel comfortable talking to you that you can help him get in touch with someone that can help him. Just leave it at that and don't bring it up again unless he does. That way you have acknowledged the situation, and he knows you care, but also knows that he can trust you to not freak out on him."

Mike thought for a minute and decided that he liked that idea. "I think that might just work. I'll give it a try on Wednesday."

"Good, let me know how it goes."

"Oh I definitely will."

"Are you coming to church on Sunday?"

"I'll be there. I think I need to pray for some guidance on this Jack thing"

"Good then I'll see you on Sunday. I should let you go for now, it's getting late."

They both hung up the phone and eventually went to sleep. The next day at Thanksgiving dinner Sarah's dad gave a toast to his daughter and her good news. The whole family celebrated for ten minutes after the toast with hugs and congratulations. The outpouring of support from the family was almost too much to take for both Sarah and her father. After a few minutes of tears of joy, they were both able to shut off the waterworks and enjoy a wonderful Thanksgiving feast.

Chapter 20
Winter

Mike worried all weekend about what he would do when he saw Jack on Wednesday. He knew that he would take Sarah's advice. Her advice sounded good; it acknowledged that he read the letter and offered an olive branch while not dwelling on the subject. Mike knew that he would do exactly that but the whole situation made him a bit uncomfortable. Tuesday night Mike did not sleep very much. He kept replaying in his mind what he would say to Jack when he saw him. He wanted to be sure that he said just the right thing and didn't do anything to make the situation worse. Finally, around four thirty in the morning when Mike was about to throw in the white flag on going to sleep for the night he drifted off to sleep. It was not a deep sleep rather a dreamless fitful sleep on the edge of consciousness, the kind of sleep that would afford him a few hours of energy early in the day but would have him dragging by noon.

Mike's alarm went off at seven fifteen. He needed to be at work by eight forty five to open the store. It was a very difficult morning for Mike to get out of bed, not only because he was very tired but also because he knew what the afternoon had in store. He willed himself out of bed after lying there for five minutes and went right for the shower. He hoped the water would help wake him up. He was correct on that account. The blast of water from the shower on his body quickly increased his level of alertness. However, that alertness would in fact be short lived. An hour after the shower he returned to feeling dead to the world once again. He worked his shift at the store somewhat like a zombie. He went through the day from one customer and assignment to the next just kind of coasting on fumes. Finally, three o'clock rolled around and it was time for him to go to the school. The drive to the school seemed endless. At this point Mike just wanted to have the conversation and get it off his mind. He was starting to feel sick and he knew the only medicine would be to have the conversation that he didn't want to have but knew that he had to have. When Mike walked into the gym, he saw that Jack was already there early. This actually made Mike happy because he could get the talk over with before practice and not worry about it all through practice. Mike took a deep breath and walked over to Jack.

"Hey Jack how's it going?"

"Good coach. How was your Thanksgiving?"

"It was good. I just wanted to say Jack that I read your letter. I'll be honest it shocked me. If you ever need to talk I'm here, and if you need anything else I can give you the number of a great counselor."

That was all Mike planned to say on the subject. He was surprised when Jack replied, "It's cool coach."

"Are you sure?"

"Completely."

Mike felt he should say something unrelated to the letter at this point, but all that he could come up with was "how does your arm feel today?"

"Ready to work."

"That's what I like to hear."

Mike was surprised at how easy that conversation had gone. Practice went well that day. When Mike got home, he was dead tired. He was so tired that he forgot to call Sarah and tell her what happened with Jack. On Thursday night when Mike came home from work, there were three messages from Sarah, oh crap Mike thought. He grabbed the phone and called Sarah. Sarah answered the phone in an almost frantic voice, "Hello."

"Hey Sarah it's Mike, sorry I forgot to call yesterday but when I came home I was just dead tired and just crashed. I barely managed to stay awake until nine o'clock, which is very unusual for me. Normally I'm up until at least ten thirty."

"Why were you so tired?"

"I had quite the case of insomnia the night before. I laid awake until around four thirty running through my head what I would say to Jack."

"And what did you say? How did it go?"

"Well I think I just wasted a bunch of my time worrying about it. I went right up to him before practice, acknowledged the letter, and told him if he needed to talk, I was there and that if he needed it I could put him in touch with a counselor. He told me everything was cool and I really believed him."

"Why?"

"There was just such a calm about him. He seemed perfectly content almost. I don't think he will have any more problems."

"Well that's great!" But definitely keep an eye on him, with the one year anniversary of his dad's death coming up that could change quickly."

"I know, that's what keeps me a little nervous."

"You really do care about these kids don't you?"

"I never really realized it until I got the letter, but these kids mean a lot to me. I think I'll actually miss them when they are gone."

"I guess you'll be a great teacher someday."

"Thanks."

"How was your Thanksgiving?

"It was great other than worrying about the letter. How was yours?"

"Awesome! My dad told my entire family the good news about my treatments before the meal and we spent ten minutes just hugging, toasting, and crying. Not a sad crying of course."

"I understand."

"So church this week?"

"Yeah I think I'd better be there to thank God after he helped me through the Jack situation."

"I'm sure that one was God's pleasure. He likes to see people helping other people."

"I figured he would. Well I should get going."

"All right Mike have a good night."

"You too. Bye."

"Bye."

On Sunday morning, Mike got up for church. When he went in the kitchen to eat breakfast, his mom was sitting at the table.

"Good morning Mike."

"Hey mom."

"Can I ask you a favor honey?"

"Sure, what is it?

"Just for advent would you mind going to church with me? Your dad never goes to church and at least for the Christmas season it would be nice to have someone to sit with."

"Well I already promised Sarah that I would go with her this week but after this week I should be free." Mike didn't like the idea of going without Sarah over Christmas but he knew that she would understand that this was the right thing to do."

"Well that sounds fair Mike. I'm sure I can handle this week on my own."

"You're welcome to come along with us mom."

"I would love to but I have to serve communion this morning, otherwise I would gladly accept your offer. I think I would like to meet this Sarah of yours."

"I'll talk to her and see what I can do."

"Do you like her?"

"I don't know."

"Is she cute?"

"Yeah she's pretty cute."

"Yeah you like her."

Mike just smiled and put his head down. He was uncomfortable with the line of questioning. His mother recognized this and backed off. Mike ate a quick breakfast of cereal and then headed out. It was a cloudy and cold morning. Mike got in his car, started it up, and thought immediately that he should have allowed time to warm it up. Oh well he figured, it would be warm soon enough.

Mike went to church and sat with Sarah and her father. After church, they had their traditional lunch. In the middle of the lunch, Mike said "Hey about church for the next few weeks, my mom has asked me if I would go with her until Christmas. I feel that I should go with her. It seems like the right thing to do."

"You're right, it is the right thing to do. Your mom would probably love to have someone sitting with her. She probably thinks that I am trying to steal you away from her. Tell her that I am sorry."

"She's not mad. She probably just gets a little bit lonely at church over the holidays because my dad never goes."

"Really? Has he ever gone?"

"He went a couple times at Christmas when I was a little kid. But that stopped probably by the time I was eight."

"That's weird that your mom is so devoted to church and your dad isn't."

"It's always seemed normal to me. That's probably part of the reason that I stopped going for so long. I would see my dad staying home on Sundays and sleeping in and somehow it seemed all right. After all if he could do it why couldn't I?"

"I can see how you would think that. Do you think that you would ever go back to not going?"

"I don't think I could not go anymore. I've seen too much how God works in our lives. I've seen the miracles that he can create. I think I would feel way to guilty if I stopped going."

"That's the Catholic guilt for you." They both laughed at the comment.

"Hey Sarah, when my mom was talking to me this morning she said that she wanted to meet you. I said I would talk to you and see if we could work something out."

"You did tell her we were just friends right? I hope you didn't tell her we were engaged or anything."

"No I told her we were just friendly. I don't know if she believed me though."

"And why is that?"

"I've never hung out with many girls. It's rather unusual so the fact that I've spent so much time with you is raising her suspicions."

"I understand completely, what church does she attend"

"St. Anthony's."

"I've seen that church before. I've never been in it but it looks beautiful from the outside. Is it just as beautiful on the inside?"

Mike didn't know how to answer that question. He wasn't in the business of judging the beauty of buildings. He always thought the church looked nice enough but never really thought it was anything special so he just said, "Yes."

"I'll talk to my dad and see if he'll come to St. Anthony's next week. I'll let you know by the middle of the week."

"Sounds good."

Sarah and her dad did meet Mike and his mother for church the next week. Sarah enjoyed the Victorian architecture of the church and was certain to mention it to Mike. Mike, not really getting the big deal, again just agreed. The rest of the winter went well for Mike. He continued working with the baseball team, enjoyed a nice Christmas with his family, and applied to a local university to begin teacher education classes. He planned to start his coursework in the fall.

As for Sarah life continued to progress nicely. The holidays were difficult for her but she handled them quite well. On the twenty third of December she had scheduled what she hoped would be her final appointment with Rick. She felt confident that it would be but there was a small part of her that was nervous. In her head and even her heart she knew that she was ready to be on her own again, however there was still some nervousness. Still she managed to psych herself up before the appointment and convinced herself that it would be her final session.

"Well Sarah, Merry Christmas!"

"Merry Christmas to you too Rick."

"Good I'm glad you said Merry Christmas. After all there wouldn't be any celebration at all had the Christ child not been born in the manger all those thousands of years ago."

"Well I couldn't agree more but what's with the diatribe?"

"The greeting Happy Holidays annoys me. It just seems so impersonal and of course secular. When I was a kid, everybody said Merry Christmas and nobody got offended. I can understand if you don't celebrate Christmas that is you're right as an American. However, don't try to inhibit me from celebrating Christmas."

"I understand, but I don't think anybody's physically trying to stop you from celebrating Christmas."

"It's not physical it's psychological. But anyway enough about me, I'm getting ahead of myself, this is my last appointment of the year so I'm thinking about some time off."

"Well I'm eager to be done as well. I have all of my applications ready to apply for school. I can't wait."

"Well sounds like there haven't been any relapses."

"No. I'll be honest it's been a little tougher over the last month because of the Christmas season but I think I'm managing."

"No thoughts of the unthinkable I trust."

"Thankfully no. I do miss my mother, I miss her more than anything but suicide is definitely not the answer."

"What is the answer?"

"Just living my life, doing the best I can helping my father, helping Mike, being a good Christian, and doing what I believe God put me on earth to do."

"That may be the best answer to that question that I have ever heard. You've come a long way Sarah; this truly is a momentous occasion. You have been reborn this Christmas. There is nothing I or any other counselor in this office likes to see more than a patient get better."

"Thank you."

"Sarah, Tony and I didn't do anything special. Did we help you? Yes. Ultimately getting better was all you. You made the decisions that got you better. Neither Tony, I, or anyone in this office could make the decisions for you. You did it all on your own. That's what this job is all about."

Sarah really felt that she had learned some important lessons. She also felt Rick gave her this speech for a reason related to her new career choice. He was giving her the first training that she would receive. "Thank you so much for all that you have done. I know you say it was me and I know it was but I couldn't have done it without you and Tony. You guys are awesome! I hope once I have my degree that I can get a job here."

"Well Sarah, people that have gone through struggles like you often make the best counselors because they really understand their patients better than others. I am a rarity in this line of work not having had the great calamity that helps me help others. For me helping others with their problems just seems to be a God given gift that I am thankful for every day. Now I just need your signature here and we will be all set."

Sarah signed the paper and shook Rick's hand. She then left the office and walked to tell her dad the good news. Sarah and her dad must have hugged for ten minutes in the front seat of the car. They were both elated about Sarah's release. To celebrate they went to dinner at Sarah's favorite restaurant. All of her aunts, uncles, and cousins were there. Sarah asked why they didn't just wait the two days to Christmas when they would all be together for the holiday and every single family member without fail told her that this was to momentous of an occasion to wait the two days. Sarah enjoyed her special night reveling in the glow of the love of her family. Two days later, she felt doubly blessed when her entire family gathered once again, this time at her Aunt's home and celebrated Christmas together. Sarah got her father a Michigan State sweatshirt. The entire house went silent when he opened it but she then handed him another box with a University of Michigan sweatshirt. Her father thanked her for the gift. Then one of her cousins could not help himself and broke the ice. "Way to be a traitor Sarah or should we just call you Benedict Arnold?"

All eyes immediately focused on Sarah who in turn replied, "Just call me Sparty, it's better than being called arrogant"

Sarah received a few chuckles for her comment but mostly just stares of disappointment. Her father had done a good job of playing the part of the wounded father and gaining the family's sympathies, although that wasn't much of a challenge since the majority of the family were Michigan graduates. None of that seemed to bother her though; Sarah enjoyed being in the minority.

The rest of the winter was a time of change for Sarah. She applied to Michigan State in January. In February, she received her acceptance letter. She started looking for work in East Lansing as well as an apartment. She was able to find an apartment near campus that she liked. Her dad would take care of the rent for her until she found a job and could help pay for it. Sarah marveled at the difference a year had made. A year ago, she was on the precipice of disaster and now everything seemed completely reversed. She could not believe in her good fortune. She now really believed that in the end everything would be just fine.

Chapter 21
Spring

Winter dragged on for both Mike and Sarah. The depressing doldrums of January and February replaced the bright glow of the Christmas season. A time of year in Michigan, that sees little sunshine and takes away the bright and festive lights of the Christmas season. The landscape often looks bleak and grey with the exceptions of the precious few sunny days, and the times when there is freshly fallen snow which transforms the landscape into a beautiful tapestry of white. However, that beautiful tapestry lasts only a short time, as the beautiful white snow transforms into brown slush and rock salt. These turn any snow near a curb into a grayish blackish brownish combination that almost makes one want to vomit. It is a depressing time of year to say the least. The cold winds coming from the north chill a person straight to the bone. The extra long nights get even colder and make a person just want to snuggle under the covers of their bed to take the chill out, and even that takes a good half hour under the covers on the coldest of nights. Those that have fireplaces and can curl up next to a warm fire become extra popular at this time of year, as a roaring fire has much more warming capacity for the body than a gas forced air furnace. Only the most hearty and rugged of people enjoy being outdoors at this time of year in Michigan. However, Michiganders own a deep sense of pride like most northerners in the fact that they survive the cold, snow, and ice of winter every year and emerge renewed and reinvigorated in the spring.

On the other hand, Mike's first full squad practice did little to reinvigorate and renew. The team's first practice took place in early March. Unfortunately for Mike and the rest of his team, the first practice did not occur during an early March warm spell. The weather for the first practice seemed much more appropriate for football than baseball. There was a strong wind blowing, with a mostly cloudy sky, with brief breaks of sun that offered little warmth, a temperature of about forty-two degrees, and a wind chill probably in the twenties somewhere. Most kids hate practicing in this weather largely because of the aluminum bats. Every kid in Michigan knows just what it's like to hit a baseball with an aluminum bat on a cold day. You are standing in the batter's box already cold, your hands are red, in some cases in pain, and in other cases numb. Every batter knows in their head that they don't want to hit the ball because of the shock and pain that reverberates up their frozen limbs when the ball hits the metal bat. This is probably the only time that they don't want to hit the ball. However, they also don't desire of being labeled a crybaby. They know they can't cry as that would show weakness and subject them to taunts and jeers from their teammates for the rest of the season.

So with grim determination they stand in the batter's box, dig their feet in and lock their eyes on the pitcher. Then the pitcher throws the ball, and with the diligence of a soldier fighting in a war they swing their bat, the ball hits the bat, the bat vibrates like nothing on earth, the vibration travels into the batters hands and magnifies the pain already in the hands. The coaches knew the reason nobody wanted to volunteer for batting practice. On warmer days, there would be arguments about who would hit first. Today those arguments were about who would hit last. Maybe if batting practice happened right away it wouldn't be so bad but usually it started about a half hour into practice, and by then everybody's hands were cold.

Coach Stopac had ways of getting around this problem. The coaches having just hit grounders and fly balls to everybody on the team for the previous twenty minutes gave him an easy solution. "All right since none of you ladies wants to volunteer to hit first we are going to go around the horn. Gary, you're up first. Joe you're the backup first baseman and you'll be hitting next."

Gary grimaced, "Come on coach, can't you start in the outfield?"

"Get in here son, this is no attitude for a championship team. I'm glad the weather is like this today. I hope it stays like this for all of our practices. It will toughen you guys up."

One by one, each kid got up and took their swings. One by one, each played the part of the good soldier, willing to take their punishment for a shot at glory. Mike was anxious to see Jack pitch. After Jack had taken batting practice, it would be his turn to pitch. Mike was hoping more than anything that he would make some guys swing and miss. He was hoping that Jack would do well and gain acceptance by the team. He was worried that if he didn't do well he may fall back into depression and that scared Mike more than anything.

The first person Mike would pitch to would be David, the team's star pitcher. David was that rare breed who was both a great pitcher and a great hitter. Often times it's one or the other, but in David's case, God blessed him with both abilities.

In the first part of every session of batting practice, hitters receive about ten pitches mainly fastballs over the plate so they can get some good swings in. Then the next ten or so pitches are the pitcher trying to throw his best stuff and getting the batter to swing and miss. Finally, there is one final showdown, each batter gets three strikes, or four balls, when they hit the ball, and they run. If they get on base, they stay there and the pitcher has to work through the trouble when the next batter gets there three strikes or four balls.

Jack went through the progression of his first ten pitches. David being the great hitter that he was walloped them all over the field if they were in the strike zone. The entire defense received a huge workout. After the tenth, pitch Coach Stopac instructed Jack to throw whatever he thought he could get David to miss. Mike jogged out to the mound to have a quick conference, "what's up coach?"

"Throw him your split finger on the first pitch."

"Really? I thought I should start him off with a fastball or slider off the plate."

"Not now. Now is the time to show everybody what you can do. Throw the split finger first, then throw whatever you feel is best. He won't be expecting a split finger right out of the gate."

"Whatever you think is best coach."

Mike ran back over to the bench. "What did you tell him Mike?" Coach Stopac asked.

"Watch and see."

Coach Stopac looked over at Jack in great anticipation. Mike had worked tirelessly with Jack on this pitch and he had helped him develop an especially nasty split finger fastball. Jack wound up and delivered a beautiful split finger pitch that might as well have dropped off the edge of the earth right before it got to home plate. David already having committed to swing swung and missed badly, which was an accomplishment as David seldom missed badly at the plate. The entire team's jaw dropped simultaneously when David missed the ball. Suddenly the silence was broken by congratulations from his teammates, "Way to go, Jack," came from his catcher.

"Way to pitch Jackie," from Coach Stopac.

"Holy crap," came from somewhere in the outfield.

Simultaneous compliments of great pitch came from all over the field.

Even David, the hitter who had just missed embarrassingly smiled at Jack and tipped his helmet. Jack went through his next ten pitches going through his entire repertoire, and getting David to miss on six of the next nine pitches. Then in their showdown was able to strike David out on a two and two split finger pitch in the dirt. Even though David was expecting it, he just couldn't locate it.

After missing the ball, David started walking to the mound with a determined look. Mike was nervous thinking David was going to hit him. Instead, David held out his hand and shook Jack's hand and then gave him a hug and yelled, "that pitch is awesome man," and went back to the bench.

Jack experienced even more success against his next two hitters. He seemed to lose a little bit of movement on his split finger against his third hitter but was still able to get him to ground out. As he walked back to the bench and headed for the locker room Mike stopped him and said "two strikeouts and a groundout, great job!"

"Thanks coach. Thanks for the advice too, I never would have thrown the split finger unless I had a two strike count. I wouldn't have had the confidence to do it if you hadn't told me to."

"No sweat Jack, just doing my job."

Just then, David walked over to Jack. "Hey man what are you doing Friday night?"

"I don't have any plans."

"Well there's going to be a party at my house. You should come."

"That sounds cool. What time is the party?"

"Starts about seven, so you can come anytime after that."

"Sounds cool, I'll be there."

"All right, cool."

Mike overheard the entire exchange and felt a great sense of pride. He knew that Jack had achieved something great today and didn't want to take anything away from that but also knew that he had helped Jack immensely. While Mike was standing there, Coach Stopac came up to him. "Great job working with that kid Mike. He is a completely different pitcher because of you. He could even be our closer with that kind of stuff."

"No big deal coach."

"Don't be modest, you have definitely helped him and definitely helped our chances at a championship. If I could I'd give you a raise."

"Can you?" Mike said laughing."

"No money in the budget kid. Welcome to public education. Your raise will have to come from the satisfaction of a job well done."

"Well I can live with that."

"Good. You're going to have to. Now pack up and get out of here. You've earned a break."

"Yes sir coach."

With that, Mike began to gather up equipment and put it in bags. When he had finished, he walked back into the gym and took down his pitching area while Coach Stopac went to his office. Mike drove home feeling on top of the world.

Chapter 22
Sarah's Spring Interview

Sarah's family worried about her a great deal during this time. There is not much to get excited about in the dead of winter in Michigan. Sarah however, was adept at finding her own excitement. In this case, her excitement came from meticulously planning every detail of her move to East Lansing at the end of summer. While this ritual may seem mundane to the casual observer, to Sarah it was as exciting as seven Super Bowls. Sarah would lay out brochures about the social work programs from Michigan State and look through the painstakingly trying to map out her best course of action for the fall semester and beyond. She would also spend hours on the computer looking at jobs and apartments in the East Lansing area. Sarah was going to be certain that she had all of her ducks in a row before she had to move. She wanted to have a job and an apartment by July 8. This way she could move out to the area ahead of time and be settled in when the new semester started. In addition, July 8, gave her easily a six-week cushion in case things took a little bit longer than expected. Sarah spent many a afternoon doing just that.

Eventually the weather began to break and Sarah began spending more time outside. She reveled in the rare days in March when the skies cleared up and the temperature soared to near seventy degrees. She enjoyed walking through the neighborhood on these rare days and taking in the sights and the sounds. Sarah thought that she had stopped to notice the little things before but since her mother's death, she now took it to a new level of awareness. She would walk down the streets pausing for several deep breaths to smell the fresh early spring air. She noticed freshness to the air that she had never noticed when she was younger. She wondered how this smell had escaped her for so long. She knew now that she would notice and appreciate this smell every spring for the rest of her life. As she walked through the neighborhood on a sunny but cool late March afternoon she began to feel a little apprehension about finding a job in time. She decided she had to find a job as soon as possible. Her original plan was to wait until the summer to look for a job but she was worried that she would have a difficult time competing with all of the other college students out there that were sure to be looking for jobs as well. She decided to e-mail Tony and ask him if he knew of any jobs in the East Lansing area.

Two days later Tony sent her a reply and she was shocked when he told her that he knew of a job that would be open come August that he could help her get. Tony told her that a secretary in the social science office would be graduating and that there would be a position inside the social science office coming open. Because he was a friend of the department head, he could make a recommendation that would pretty much guarantee her the job. Tony was sure to mention that as a result of the lower workload in the summer she would not be able to start until August and she may not have routine work through the summer months. Sarah thought that would be perfectly fine as she could come home and spend the summers with her dad. She also knew her dad would like that idea as well. Sarah e-mailed Tony back and said she would love the opportunity to work at the college. Tony made a couple of calls, and on the last day of April, Sarah was driving out to East Lansing for a job interview. Sarah would be interviewing with Dr. Henry Schlemmingstodt who was the dean of the social sciences department. When she arrived at his office, the current secretary let him know she was there for the interview. Sarah had arrived twenty minutes early and thus would have to wait. Sarah began to strike up a conversation with the secretary. Sarah found out that her name was Clara Horning and that she was about to graduate with a degree in History for secondary education. Clara told Sarah that this was a relatively easy job and that the main duties of the job consisted of answering phones, taking messages, making copies, and typing up reports. Sarah thought that sounded easy enough. Clara also told her that Dr. Schlemmingstodt was easy to work for and flexible. He was a very nice man as long as you always called him Doctor before you said his name. Sarah said that would not be difficult to remember as that's what she had planned to do anyhow. After about fifteen minutes, the door to Dr. Schlemmingstodt's office opened and Clara told her that Dr. Schlemmingstodt was ready for her. The office was a very dark room decorated with a lot of brown oak. Dr. Schlemmingstodt was a very tall man, at least six foot five. He had mostly grey hair with a little bit of brown still hanging on for dear life. She could tell that he was an older man but knew better than to ask his age. She assumed he was probably in his late fifties or early sixties. She also assumed that he would probably be considering retirement in the next five to ten years, but by then she would have completed her degree and would not need this job. She already had all of her prerequisites completed from Michigan and would just be taking classes in social work at Michigan State. She figured that it would take her two years at the most to finish the program and that she would then look for a full time job and begin a masters program. Sarah shook Dr. Schlemmingstodt's hand and sat down.

"So Tony has told me quite a bit about you. He says you have had quite the struggle but vouches for your character one hundred percent. So tell me a little bit about yourself."

Sarah decided that it was best to just be an open book and began speaking. She told him about her career at the University of Michigan and the death of her mother and it's aftermath. She went on and told him about how Tony and Rick had helped her and about why she was now coming to Michigan State. Through her entire speech, she noticed that his demeanor did not change at all. She could tell that Dr. Schlemmingstodt was a very serious man and that there would not be much room for humor. As she was talking she also noticed old black and white photos of a young man in a football uniform and a couple of action shots plus a team photo. The team photo said 1963 Michigan Sate football team. Sarah concluded that he had played football for the Spartans and began to hope that her past affiliation with The University of Michigan would not hurt her chances of landing the job. Sarah finished speaking and Dr. Schlemmingstodt began to speak. He began to tell her about then job, what her responsibilities would be, and what the pay would be. He then said that he would offer her the job as long as she could start on August 1. Sarah said that would be fine and they shook hands. Sarah thanked him repeatedly for the opportunity, Dr. Schlemmingstodt told her she was welcome and forced a smile onto his face. As Sarah was getting up to walk out he jumped in and said "just one more thing. I know that you went to that school down in Ann Arbor in the past but I just want to make sure that you know that this is a maize and blue free office, do you understand?"

"Completely." Sarah replied.

"Good that will make both of our lives much easier. Have a good day."

"Thank you, you too."

Sarah walked out of the office and went outside. She decided that since her interview ended early she would go check out a couple of apartments. She quickly found one that she liked about six blocks north of campus; it was a one-bedroom apartment. A second floor unit with a balcony that over looked a courtyard and a grouping of trees in the distance. She stopped short of thinking it was a forest as there probably was not enough room for a whole forest there. The rent would be five hundred and twenty five dollars per month plus utilities. She told them that she would bring her father out soon to see the apartment.

When she returned home, she told her dad about both the job and the apartment. The job would pay eight dollars and fifty cents per hour and that she would work thirty to thirty five hours per week. That would provider her with enough money to help her dad pay some of the rent. Her dad sounded enthusiastic and told her that they would take a ride out there that Saturday to check out the apartment. Sarah went and called the apartment complex to let them know that they would be coming up early Saturday afternoon. She was so excited that she could not contain herself. Right after she got off the phone with the apartment building she called Mike to tell him the good news. She was lucky enough to catch Mike on a rare day on which he did not have to work or coach. Mike had become quite busy in the spring as well. It was now the baseball season and he spent most evenings either at practice, or at a game. The games had just begun and Mike's team was doing well. They were off to a 4-0 start and were seemingly on their way to big things. Not only did Mike not have practice or a game on this day but he also had the day off from the store. Mike was spending his day off doing pretty much nothing.

The rigor of his recent schedule had made him quite tired. So on his day off he slept in until eleven o'clock and was pretty much lying around watching television when the phone rang.

"Hello."

"Hello Mike, it's Sarah"

"Hey Sarah, how are you? Are you enjoying the warm weather?"

"Loving every second of it, I also have some news!"

"What?"

"I got the job at Michigan State!"

"Hey that's cool." Mike was happy for Sarah but there was a part of him that was a little upset about her move. He knew that drastically decreased his chances of dating her because of the distance. However, at the same time Mike knew that if they destined to be together God would find a way to make it happen. He had known God would put the perfect person in his life at some time or another. "When do you start the job?"

"It starts August 1, and I think I found the apartment that I'm going to get. It's a one-bedroom apartment for $525 per month plus utilities. It has a beautiful courtyard and my apartment has a balcony that overlooks the courtyard and some trees."

"That's cool." Mike didn't like apartments. The thought of living in an apartment did not appeal to him. He wanted a house with his own backyard to sit out in when he moved out. Apartments were nice for some he thought, but not him. That is also, why he never tried to go away to college. The thought of sharing a tiny dorm room with another person was about as appealing as getting a root canal.

"I'm so excited. Everything is just falling into place for me. I can't believe how easy this is all working out."

"Well you may want to knock on wood when you say that. You know when you start saying how easy things are they tend to get much more difficult real fast."

"I'm sure everything will go great. I really feel like I am doing what God wants and that's why things are going so easily. In the past things were always more difficult but now that I think about it I don't think I was doing what

God wanted me to do so that's why things were so difficult. How are things going with you and the team?"

"Great we're 4-0 and all the kids are playing hard. It's actually been a fun experience. I love working with these kids. Between that and work I'm exhausted but at the end of the day it's worth it."

"I've missed you at church. It's not the same sitting and having lunch with my dad after church.

Mike felt a sudden surge of pride because of what Sarah said. He knew that he was high up on her priority ladder if she was saying things like that about him. Mike began to think that Sarah moving to East Lansing would not kill his chances of dating her. Mike knew he had to talk soon; he had created an awkward pause in the conversation with his thinking to himself. "I've missed it too. However, because of baseball I've head to pick up a Sunday shift at work to maintain my hours. It sucks but I've got to do it."

"I know you do Mike. Are you making it to church?"

"Yes. I'm getting off between four and four thirty on Saturdays and then heading straight to St Anthony's where I meet my mom for the five o'clock mass."

"Wow that's a lot of running around but God will reward you for it. You are doing great things and God has a reward planned for you. I know it."

"I hope so."

"You know he does."

"Yeah I do."

"So how is that kid who wrote you the letter doing?"

"Really well. He's started closing games for us and the team has adopted him as one of their own. He's being invited to parties, having fun, and becoming one of the guys. It's almost like he's a different kid than when I met him. I feel a little bad that I feel some pride in his transformation."

"You shouldn't feel bad, you obviously helped him quite a bit."

"I did but he did all of the work, all I did was put him in a position to do the work."

"And that's what you should be feeling the pride for. You put him into a position to succeed and he did. You believed in him when nobody else did. He may have done the work but he wouldn't have done it without your help."

"All right that makes me feel better. I see your point and I know that I did help him. So I guess I'll sit back and enjoy it. Thanks Sarah."

"You're more than welcome. So when does your season end?"

"It will end sometime in June depending on what happens with the playoffs and how far we go. I really like our team's chances. There is a ton of talent on the team and they play as a team. We don't have a couple guys all trying to be superstars and do everything. This team supports and relies on each other and that is why I think we have a good chance."

"Awesome! Well I should get going. We're going Saturday to see the apartment and if my dad approves I'll have my apartment and job all set three months ahead of schedule."

"That must be a great feeling. I know you were stressing out about that."

"I was but it seems like it is all working itself out now. Oh and by the way, if you guys make the state championship let me know when and where it is, I'd love to see you in action."

"I definitely will. If we get that far we can't have too much support."

"Well good bye Mike. I'll let you get back to enjoying your day off. Make sure you relax and take it easy."

"That is not an issue. I haven't done a thing all day except get up late, eat, and watch TV. I don't think I'll leave the house at all today. Don't forget to let me know if you get the apartment and congratulations on the new job."

"I will give you a call Saturday night. Keep relaxing. It sounds like you need all the relaxation you can get."

"I do. Take it easy Sarah"

"You too Mike. Talk to you Saturday."

"Talk to you later Sarah. Bye."

"Bye."

Mike enjoyed the rest of his day off. He was true to his word and did absolutely nothing the rest of the day. His parents weren't even mad about it because they knew how hard he'd been working the past couple of months. They even bent over backwards to make sure he had an easy day. Mike really did need the day to recharge his batteries, as he knew he would not have many more like it.

Mike's team continued to do well. Everybody on that team contributed, even Jack got into more games and pitched well. It warmed Mike's heart to see the kid succeed. Mike often sat and wondered after games what his life would have been like if a coach had taken him aside and helped him develop his pitches. He wondered if he could have gone farther than single A ball. But still every time Mike began to think about the what ifs he couldn't get over the fact that he was really truly happy doing what he was doing and that he would not be in the situation that he was in if all of the bad things didn't happen to him.

Mike's team continued to do well. By the end of the season, they had tallied up a record of 14-1. They qualified for the playoffs and there was a great deal of confidence among the team. Their only loss had been the result of a controversial call at home plate in the bottom of the 9th inning of a game that could have gone either way. If the runner were safe which everyone in the stadium thought that he should have been, they would have tied the game and had runners at second and third with a chance to win the game. The team wondered why Coach Stopac did not argue the call. He told his team after the game in an emotional speech "we had many opportunities to win that game that we did not cash in on. If we had played better, in innings one through eight we wouldn't have needed to bat in the bottom of the ninth and the call would have never had the opportunity to be made. Let this be a lesson to you guys to always play hard and never let up."

The team got the message loud and clear. They won their final eight games, each game by at least five runs. They even beat the team they lost to in the final game of the season. This time the team scored nine runs in the first three innings and David had a one hit shutout through the fifth inning. Mike decided to pull him after the fifth so he could rest up for the playoffs. He then let four different pitchers each pitch an inning so nobody was overworked.

The team ended up with a 15-0 victory in the game. After the game, Coach Stopac praised the team's hard work and dedication.

A week later the playoffs started. Mike's former high school team was ranked number one in the state, but the way the brackets were set up Mike's team would not have to play that team until the championship game. That was the only team Mike feared. He felt they could beat any other team easily but that team was loaded with talent. He was also nervous at the prospect facing the coach who publicly humiliated him every chance he got. Nevertheless, Mike knew he could not show any fear, he knew he had to be tough or it would reflect in the confidence of his pitchers. After all, how could he expect them to be confident if he wasn't confident?

David started the first game of the playoffs. David went out there like a man on a mission. He was a senior and really wanted a championship. He had already received a scholarship to play college ball at Arizona State University, one of the best baseball schools in the country. David asked Mike if she should take the scholarship or go right to A ball. Mike advised him to take the scholarship and refine his game in college. Mike told him that he would learn so much more about pitching and the game in general before he even got into professional ball. David took Mike's advice to heart and opted to go to college. However, he had the mentality of a winner and did not want to go out any other way than a champion. He willed himself, and the team to push themselves to the limit. He was an inspiration to watch. The entire team responded and played the best baseball of their lives in the playoffs. David pitched eight innings of shutout baseball and Mike's team won their first playoff game 7-0.

The second game was much tougher than the first. Mike's team fell behind 4-2 in the seventh inning. Mike didn't know what was going on, his team seemed like they were running out of gas. Coach Stopac gave an emotional speech when the team came up in the bottom of the eighth down by two runs. He told the team this game would define the rest of their lives and challenged them to shape their lives in the mold of a winner. The team scored six runs in the bottom of the eighth and won 8-4. Coach Stopac's speech had resonated all the way into the third game of the playoffs. If the team won this game, they would be back in the championship. The team fell behind 1-0 in the first inning. However, Coach Stopac remained calm. He must have known his team would rise to the occasion. The team came back with two runs in the bottom of the third to take one run lead. However, the other team was scrappy and tied the game in the fifth inning. Mike looked over at coach Stopac and saw that he looked a little pale and sweaty.

"Hey Coach you all right?"

"Yeah just a little indigestion, I'll be fine." Reassured, Mike thought nothing else of the situation.

In the sixth, the team scored four runs on a two out grand slam that put them ahead for good. Mike looked over at Coach Stopac after the grand slam and he looked fine just sweaty. Mike thought the coach was a bit nervous. After all, he loved the team like they were his own children. They hung on for a 7-3 victory and a trip to the state championship.

After the game, the team rode back to school on the school bus. In the locker room, Coach Stopac called the team together. "Great game today guys. Enjoy it but remember we haven't won anything yet."

David interrupted him. "That's right coach."

"David I love your enthusiasm but don't ever cut me off again." Suddenly, the coach began to breath very heavy, his face turned almost white and he began to stagger a bit. Almost simultaneously, the entire team asked him if he was all right. He then fell to the ground and the entire team rushed to his aid.

"Somebody call an ambulance!"

Chapter 23
Summer

An ambulance came and rushed Coach Stopac to the hospital. The doctors did a battery of tests and it was determined that he'd had a heart attack. Luckily, he made it to the hospital quick enough that they could save him. The team probably saved his life the doctors said. The blockage in Coach Stopac's heart was sufficient that he would require surgery, which meant that Coach Stopac would not be able to coach the championship game. The game was two days away and Mike got a phone call from the coach's wife. She told him that the coach wanted to see him at the hospital right away. Mike drove immediately to the hospital and went to the coach's room.

Coach Stopac looked week. The heart attack had obviously taken much of his strength. When he saw Mike, he started to speak. "Mike I'm glad you're here,"

"What is it coach?"

"Mike I want you to manage the team in the championship game."

"Me? I wouldn't know where to coach and the other guys have more coaching experience than me."

"You're right but they don't have your heart kid. You will inspire these guys more than they can and they know it. Plus, you have a personal experience with the other coach. I know you'll take your emotion and harness it in the right way to inspire the team. I've talked to the other coaches and they all agreed. They will give you any help you need. Please don't hesitate to ask them, they are all good men and will help you in any way you need it."

"If that's what you want coach I will honor your request."

"Good I'm glad. Now get those boys ready."

"Feel better coach."

"Don't worry about me, worry about the team. I know you'll do the right things."

Mike went out into the hot early summer night. This was the first heat wave of the year and it was going to last through the game on Saturday. Mike had been worrying about how he would use his pitchers in the heat but now he had a whole slew of other worries. He went home and called Sarah. "Sarah?"

"Hey Mike how is it going?" Did you make the championship?"

"Yes we did, but the coach had a heart attack after the game and can't coach the championship."

"Oh my God! I'm so sorry. Is he all right?"

"They are going to do surgery."

"I hope he pulls through. So who is going to manage the team for the championship?"

Mike paused, took a deep breath, and said, "You're talking to him."

"Wow! Congratulations!"

"I'm so nervous, I'm not sure I'm ready for it."

Suddenly Sarah got stern, "Mike, you will do great. You love these kids and will do right by them. And remember I believe in you."

"Nobody ever told me they believed in me before, thank you."

"I'm going to let you go now Mike. I don't want you dwelling on this any longer and if you keep talking to me, you will. Just remember, I believe in you."

"Thank you."

"Good bye Mike."

"Good bye Sarah."

Mike felt a new surge of confidence because of Sarah's comment. The task somehow seemed a bit more manageable but he still wasn't convinced so he called Todd.

"Hey Todd it's Mike."

"Hey what's up buddy? How's the baseball season going?" Mike told Todd about Coach Stopac, the heart attack, and the coach's request of him. Then Mike began to talk about how he wasn't sure he was ready for it. Finally,

Todd interrupted him, "Whoa take it easy buddy, if you're not careful you'll give yourself a heart attack and I'm not in the mood to go to any funerals. Unfortunately, I'm not the guy who can help you here, call Coach Cleary, I'm sure he would be happy to help you."

"I can't call him he's too busy, besides he wouldn't have time to talk to me."

"Hey Mike, remember when you applied at the store?"

"Yes."

"Remember you put Coach Cleary as a reference?"

"Yes."

"Remember? I couldn't pass up the opportunity to talk to a former major leaguer so I gave him a call. Besides, I do check references. He told me that you were a great kid and that he would love to hear from you. Give him a call; you'll both be glad you did. I can't help you in this area. I'm not a baseball coach, I'm a hockey guy."

"I don't know."

"Just call him! It will help you and I promise he won't care. I gotta get running buddy but I'll be sure to come up for at least part of the game Saturday."

"Thanks man."

"You got it, see you Saturday."

"Bye."

Mike went into his room and got Coach Cleary's phone number. He then sat in front of the phone for a half hour debating whether he should call or not. Finally, he took the plunge. He dialed the number and the phone began to ring. Someone on the other end picked up and said "Hello?"

"Coach Cleary?"

"That's me. Who is this?"

"Mike Larson."

"Well I'll be! Hey Mike how's it going? I've been wondering about you. Did you get the job at the sporting goods store?"

"Yes I did."

"Well good for you. What else do you have going on in your life right now?"

"All good things sir. I've decided to become a teacher and I'm currently coaching on a high school baseball team."

"Well that's great. You sound like a completely different person than the last time we talked."

"Believe me it's been a long road with many twists and turns, some for the better, and some for the worse but lately all for the better."

"Well that's great. What brings you to my phone this night?"

"I started as a pitching coach for the varsity baseball team at Harper High School this year. I've been working with the pitchers all year and I've had success. This experience has convinced me to become a teacher. We are playing in the state championship tomorrow and the head coach just had a heart attack and named me as his replacement for the game. I'm nervous, I don't know what to do."

"Well first off congratulations. Second, don't worry about what to do. You know more about the game of baseball than many minor league coaches that I have met over the years do. Just go out there trust in God, and yourself and you will make the right decisions. Go with your gut. You know when a pitcher needs settling down, when to leave a pitcher in for one more batter, and when a pitcher has had enough. Trust those instincts, ask your other coaches for help in the other areas and you will do fine."

"Thanks for the encouragement but the game is against my former high school coach."

"The same coach that blamed you for losing the championship?"

"Exactly."

"Well that should give you all the motivation you need. Here is your shot for redemption. The Lord is putting you in a situation to come full circle and exorcise some personal demons. Trust in in The Lord and I have no doubt your team will win. Do you still have The Bible verse that I gave you all those years ago?"

"Yes. I put it in a drawer in my room after you gave it to me. A girl I know recently gave me a bible and when she did I put it in the bible for safe keeping."

"Have you read it?"

Mike felt a little ashamed here but knew he had to tell the truth. "No."

"Well after you get off the phone with me I want you to read it, and maybe go through the bible and find some other passages. You may find one that inspires you more than the one I gave you. But I promise the answers you seek lie somewhere between the covers of the book."

"Thanks I'll do that."

"Well son. I'll give you one last piece of advice. I've been coaching a long time and I can assure you that there is not a set formula for being a good coach at any level. The formula for being a good coach changes with each group of players. Each group has different talents and personalities. The key is working with them individually, discovering what they are, and then meshing them into the group. From what you've told me it seems you have done that with the pitchers. Being it's the championship game, you don't have much of a chance work with the team but it sounds like the team has gelled already. That being the case Mike, you have a great understanding of the game. You know how to play the game the right way and get your players to play the game the right way. Just go with your instincts and you will make the right decision more often than the wrong one and that being said, you'll have a chance to win the game."

"Thanks coach, that really does make me feel better. But you did already say some of that"

"I know I was hoping that you would notice that. In case you don't realize it yet that is the most important advice, I can give you. Hence why I said it twice"

"Hence?"

"Hey, just because I'm a baseball coach doesn't mean I don't know any fancy words. Well Mike, I have to go. My wife is calling me. My daughter just arrived with our new grandson and will soon experience many loud female voices yelling in my ear if I don't go meet my newest family member. Promise me you'll call me on Sunday and tell me about the game. I don't want to wait five years to hear about it. At my age I may not be around in five years."

"I promise. I'll call Sunday afternoon."

"Great. Take care, good luck, and read your bible."

"I will. Thank you for everything."

"You're welcome. Bye now."

"Bye."

Mike felt his anxiety leave him. If Coach Cleary, a man who knew the game better than anybody he had ever known, had confidence in him, he must be a good coach.

Saturday afternoon Mike met the team at the school to go to the game. Before the game, he gave a short speech and told, them to just play the game the right way, to play as a team, and to not try to do too much. He also dedicated the game to Coach Stopac. The entire team, coaches included cheered at the dedication. The team got to the field and began to warm up. Mike looked over to the sands and saw both Sarah and Todd already sitting in the seats. He waved to both of them and they both waved back. Then he saw his former coach across the diamond. When it came time to turn in their lineups Mike walked his out there. When his former coach saw that he was managing he handed in his card, laughed, turned back to his team and said, "this one is in the bag guys. There is a lazy, untalented, piece of crap coaching the other team." Mike ignored the comment and went back to his team. David walked up to him, "Don't worry about it coach, I've got this."

"Go get 'em Dave."

The team ran out on the field and began their warm ups. Jack came over to Mike, "Don't worry about him coach."

'Thanks Jack, I won't."

The truth is Mike wasn't worried. He was mad. A red-hot flame was boiling inside. Finally, the first batter came to the plate. He quickly smashed a double to left. David walked the next batter, and then the number three hitter came up and hit a three run home run. As he was rounding the bases Mike's former coach said, "See guys, I told you it was in the bag."

Mike was seething at this point. He knew the next hitter was one of the best in the state, and his pitcher was nervous. He called time and went to the mound.

"Sorry coach, I'll settle down."

"David, you're overthrowing, hit this guy."

"What?"

"Hit him. Then throw your next pitch inside, and then play your game.

"But coach, that puts another runner on and the umpire might throw me out."

"He won't yet. You're wild it will look like an accident. Just let me worry about the rest."

"All right, if you know what's best."

"Just trust me."

The umpire came up to break up the conference. Mike ran back to the bench and David stared down the batter. He threw a fastball that hit the batter in the hip. The umpire told the hitter to take his base. Just then, the other coach ran out, "come on ump he threw at him, eject his ass."

"Hey get back in your dugout," the umpire yelled. "I'm warning both teams right now, if anyone else is hit, the pitcher faces ejection."

The next pitch came inside and the batter backed off. On the next, pitch the batter reached for a pitch on the outside part of the plate and grounded into a double play. David struck out the next batter and the inning was over. However, Mike's team struggled to get offense going. It was the bottom of the fifth inning when Mike's plan came into focus. Jeremy, one of the team's best hitters was leading off. Jeremy had already hit ten home runs during the season. The other team's star pitcher responded by throwing a fastball that hit him in the shoulder.

"Batter take your base. Pitcher, you're out of here."

"What! That was the first batter he hit! This is terrible! Where did you learn how to ump?"

"Hey I warned both teams. He almost took the kid's head off. Settle down or I'll throw you out of the game."

He went to scream at the umpire some more but his coaches pulled him back into the dugout. This brought in a new pitcher who was cold. He walked the first hitter he faced. David came up next and drove a fastball down the middle of the plate into the left center field gap. Both runs scored and David wound up at third. He would later score on a two out single that tied the game at three. The game remained that way until the eighth inning. With two outs and nobody on in the bottom of the eighth Jeremy, hit a solo home run that put Mike's team ahead 4-3. David came out to pitch the ninth, he looked tired, but Mike decided to leave him in the game. He got the first hitter to fly out to deep center field.

"Don't worry, we've got the heart of the lineup now and this guy is done, his arm is jello, we've got this game."

Mike told Jack to warm up. He had a hunch. The next batter singled. The batter after that singled. David struck out the next batter but then walked the next batter. Mike called time and ran out there.

"How do you feel?"

"Tired but I can get the next guy. "

Mike quickly thought back to his high school championship. "No, you've pitched a great game, we'll get this guy for you." Mike motioned Jack to come in. Jack ran out to the mound. When he got there, Mike handed him the ball.

"All right keep everything down, throw a first pitch fastball then all split-fingers got it?"

"Got it coach"

Jack took his warm up pitches and was ready. He threw the first pitch fastball and the hitter shot it inches foul down the right field line. The other team was now very confident they had the game won. When scouting, Jack they had not made note of his split-finger fastball, Mike hadn't had him throw it much because he wanted to save it for the championship. Jack wound up and delivered his split-finger and the batter swung and missed badly at it. They were one strike away. Jack looked back at Mike and he just nodded his head. Jack wound up and threw another split-finger fastball. The batter tried to adjust but hit a slow grounder back to the mound, Jack fielded it threw it to first and the game was over. The team mobbed Jack on the mound. Then they all came over to Mike and mobbed him. Mike was elated. He knew he would be a coach and teacher for the rest of his life. He looked up into the bleachers and saw both Todd and Sarah smiling approvingly. He felt he had finally made it. He was on top of the world.

Chapter 24
Good Byes

After what seemed like an eternity but in reality was around ten minutes, Mike finally made it out of the mob of students. Although it left him smelling like a jock strap, he didn't mind. Really, he was just happy for his kids and the fact that they had managed to overcome the odds and win the championship. He knew this was something they would remember for the rest of their lives, and that whenever they thought of the game they would think of him. He was especially happy for Jack. Since Mike had slipped out of the pile, they had switched from mobbing him to mobbing Jack. Jack was an instant celebrity and Mike knew he had a huge hand in making that happen. He thought about Jack's note and how he had contemplated suicide. When he saw the giant smile on Jack's face, he knew that suicide was the furthest thing from Jack's mind.

Mike finally made it over to the bleachers where both Todd and Sarah were standing and waiting to congratulate him. Mike walked over to Todd first as he figured he would have more to say to Sarah and he didn't want to keep Todd waiting while he talked to her. "Hey coach great game, you keep this up and you'll be in the hall of fame in no time."

"Thanks Todd but the kids did all the work, I just encouraged them."

"No you did much more. The way you settled down your starting pitcher and at the same time goaded the other coach into doing something stupid and getting thrown out, that was all you buddy."

"Well I still think it was the kids but I will accept the praise. After all it hasn't been often in my life I've gotten this much praise."

"Well get used to it, if today is any indication, you will get much more over the coming years. Remember, you are now 1-0 in championship games. Most coaches would kill for that record."

"That is true."

"I've been talking to some of the upper management guys in the company about you and they have their eyes on you for some rapid advancement, especially when you finish your degree. When do you think that might be?"

"That's right I haven't told you. I'm switching my major to education. I want to be a teacher. Working with these kids has changed my life in ways I could never have imagined. This is what I want to do for the rest of my life. It's the one thing business never offered me; the chance to make a positive difference in the lives of others and go home every night feeling like I've changed things for the better just a little. I start at Madonna University in September. So I think for the next couple of years I'll just keep my management position, coach these guys, and get my degree."

"Well good for you man. That sounds like a great plan and the position is yours as long as you need it."

"Thanks."

"You're welcome. Well I have to run. Once again, great game and congratulations. We'll have to get together and celebrate in the next couple of weeks. Maybe the Tigers will win for us this time."

"Lets hope they do. That sounds great, take it easy."

"Yeah, talk to you later."

Todd walked off to his car and Mike turned to talk to Sarah. Sarah greeted Mike with a big hug and an emphatic "congratulations."

"Thanks but like I told Todd the kids did all of the work, I just coached them."

"Don't be modest, you did more than coach them; you lead them. You took control of the game and said without speaking this is what we are going to do and how we are going to do it. The kids responded to it and every single one of them followed your lead. You have their respect and admiration which is more than most coaches can say."

"Well thank you. You really know how to stroke my ego. I like that."

"Well if I'm going to be a social worker I think I need to be able to do that. Don't take this the wrong way but you have been good practice for me in that area."

'So I was just practice for being a social worker" Mike said jokingly.

"You know that's not true, you were much more than that."

"I know I just like to give you a hard time."

"I've discovered that, but for some reason I don't mind. So you're all set to begin your teaching program."

"Yes. I've registered for classes and I start the day after Labor Day. What about you, are you ready to move up to East Lansing?"

"Yes. Actually, I'm going to be heading up early, right after the fourth of July. They said I could start two weeks early so I'm going to take a week and get settled then start work in the middle of July. The professor wants me their early so the girl that I'm replacing can train me and I can hit the ground running on August 1. So that means we will only have a couple more masses together. Will you be coming to church tomorrow morning?"

'How could I miss it? God has helped me out in so many ways over the last year and today that I feel going to church is the least I can do to thank him."

"Solid reasoning."

"Thanks, I thought so."

"You would. But in this case you are right."

"You just hate to admit it don't you?"

"Of course I do."

"So how is your dad reacting to you leaving early?"

"He's at a good place with it. I think that he would feel better about if I were going to Michigan but I think he has come to accept my decision."

"Are you sure about that? I mean you spurned Michigan for Michigan State. I think that violates a law in some counties in this state."

"Well I can't say the acceptance came easy. It really was like pulling teeth to get him to accept it. But I think when he looked at the fact that Tony would be there and my relationship with him I think he understood that Michigan State was the best place for me and that was what really mattered. Although he's already dropping hints to me about doing my grad work in social work at Michigan."

"That's probably not going to happen is it?"

"No, probably not."

"I didn't think so."

"But then again, he doesn't need to know that. If I let him think there is a chance that I may go back there it will keep him happy at least for a couple years until I end up back at MSU or somewhere else."

"Well I have to get these kids back on the bus but thank you for coming out and supporting us. I really appreciate it."

'Hey I wouldn't have missed it for the world and once again congratulations."

"I'll see you bright and early at church tomorrow."

"I'll save you a seat."

"Thanks."

With that Mike walked over and corralled up the players, "lets go guys, on the bus."

The team didn't want to listen to him. The adrenaline was still pumping through their brains at a very high level and it was difficult for them to get themselves under control. Finally, with the help of the other coaches Mike was able to get them all onto the bus. When everyone was on the bus and the bus was heading back to the school Mike got up and addressed the team. "Gentlemen, listen up. I've got something to say to all of you." Mike was talking in a serious tone that the guys had never heard so he had their undivided attention out of sheer curiosity.

"Men, you played a great game today. You guys are champions now and nobody ever can take that away from you. No matter what you do in life, you will always be a champion. Whether you are pitching in World Series, negotiating a multi million dollar business deal, working in a factory, or driving your own child to their first little league game you will always be a champion. Don't let anybody, regardless of who they are take that away from you. Every one of you accomplished something amazing this spring. You started the season an underdog, and through hard work, perseverance and teamwork you defied the odds and became champions. Enjoy it. Look back on it fondly, and most importantly take that same attitude with you into whatever you do in life and you will succeed. You guys have changed my life. I only hope that we, your coaching staff have changed yours."

The team thought about what Mike said for about thirty seconds and then all began cheering in unison. The cheering lasted a good fifteen minutes. Eventually, the team settled down and they rode back to the school in relative quiet. When they got back to the school most of the students' parents were waiting to take them home. One by one, they walked over to the congratulatory handshakes and hugs of their parents then got in their cars and drove away. They had all left and the coaches were saying their good byes when a car pulled back into the parking lot. It was Jack and his mother. His mother got out of the car and approached Mike. "You're Coach Mike correct?"

"Yes I am."

" I am Jack's mom and I would just like to thank you for everything you have done for him.

"You're welcome ma'am it was my pleasure, he's a great kid."

"No you don't understand, his father was murdered a year and a half ago right before Christmas and Jack never seemed to get over it. We were all worried about him and were scared that he may try to commit suicide. We all tried feverishly to cheer him up but nothing worked. He was in such a deep and dark depression that we were afraid he would never come out. Then you came along. Suddenly he stopped talking about being depressed and started talking about how you were working with him and how you were the only person other than his father that ever believed that he could be successful. After the game tonight a college scout from The University of Iowa approached him about perhaps offering him a scholarship to pitch at their school. Now all he can talk about is baseball, college, and what he wants to major in and I have you to thank. I just wanted to thank you for everything you've done."

"Well he's a great kid and I'm glad he is doing so well. I hope he comes back and visits me here next year. I will definitely be here.

"I'll be back coach!" Jack shouted from the car.

'I'll be looking forward to it buddy."

Mike looked up and saw Jack's mom crying, not tears of sadness but tears of joy. She reached over and gave Mike a hug, thanked him one last time, got in her car, and drove away.

Just then one of the other coaches shouted to Mike "hey we're heading out for a celebratory drink you want to come?"

"No, you guys go ahead, I'm going to go celebrate with my family. I'll see you guys in the fall."

"All right you take it easy."

"Have a good time guys, don't drink too much."

With that, Mike got into his car and drove home.

Chapter 25
Eulogy

So, that was it. I closed my journal of notes from my last conversation with Mike and stood in the narthex of the church. I had excused myself to go review my notes during the priest's sermon as I still was unsure as to what I was going to say. My last conversation with Mike came exactly one week before his death. A couple of days earlier he had asked me to give the eulogy at his funeral. Despite my initial objections, Mike was most insistent that I give the eulogy. I didn't think that I was the best choice to give the eulogy but Mike said it had to be me.

"Why?" I asked.

"Because we saved each other's life in our twenties. It seems fitting to me that the person who saved my life would give my eulogy in the end."

Part of me still wanted to protest but I knew that I couldn't. "Fine." I said. "I just have one condition."

"You name it." Mike replied.

"That we sit and talk about your life over the next couple of days, so you can help me give the best eulogy possible. I was never the greatest writer but if it is your dying request I will honor it."

"Agreed. We can start now if you like."

And just like that, we began talking and I began taking notes in the notebook that I held in my hand and read countless times over the last week. Part of it still didn't seem real to me. A year ago, Mike seemed perfectly healthy. I remember seeing him last October at a Halloween party and nobody would have guessed that he would have been gone in a year. He felt great, he laughed, joked, and seemed perfectly healthy.

However, in March of this year Mike began to experience pain when he swallowed. The pain was minimal at first but increased over time. I remember him telling me about it in early April, and I suggested that he go see his doctor, but he said he was too busy with baseball season and school and that he would get checked out when the season and school year was over in June. The symptoms only got worse; by the end of the season, Mike was having bad heartburn and indigestion daily, very painful swallowing, hoarseness in his voice and a persistent cough that never seemed to go away.

As soon as school and baseball ended for the year, he went to his doctor. His doctor immediately sent him to the hospital for tests. When the tests came back, they showed that Mike had stage three-esophageal cancer and that the cancer had spread to his lymph nodes. The prognosis was not good. Both chemotherapy and radiation were attempted beginning in July and stretching into August but it was to no avail. By September the cancer had spread into Mike's lungs and the doctors told him that there was nothing more they could do. They gave him one to two months to live in September. I still remember crying on the phone with Mike when he called to tell me. I couldn't believe it. He was only forty-nine years old, too young seemingly for all of that cancer, but it happens. I told Mike that I wanted to see him before he died and he said that he also wanted to see me to ask a favor. That favor turned out to be this eulogy, which I'm still not exactly sure how to address.

I met with Mike three days in a row the week before he died. The last of the three days I spent with Mike came exactly one week before his death. I thought we were going to talk about Mike's entire life but we mainly focused on the year immediately following when we met. Back when I still couldn't cope with my mother's death and Mike couldn't come to terms with many things happening in his life. Mike revealed to me many of his innermost thoughts and feelings from that time that I would never have guessed that he had. He even told me that he considered the possibility of us being more than friends at the time. I was shocked. I couldn't picture him with anybody but his wife Caroline whom he met in his first semester of the education program at Madonna University. The two had an instant connection and got married three months after Mike finished college. He already had a job lined up teaching history at the high school he had been coaching at so it wasn't difficult for them to start a life together.

I felt intense sadness for Caroline. I thought of my former fiancée Steve and how much it hurt when he left me after my mom died and knew that the grief I felt from that couldn't come close to what Caroline must be feeling. She is such a nice woman, a caring compassionate kindergarten teacher who sings in the church choir and gives money to charity whenever she can. Then there are their two sons. Andy just graduated from high school a little over a year ago and Theodore who is currently in his senior year of high school. It's going to be toughest on him.

That's why Mike wanted me to focus on our time together right after we met. We had both hit a literal and metaphorical bottom with the help of each other and God came out stronger on the other side. He hoped that the tale could help his sons and wife deal with his death and make something positive out of it.

I looked back into the sanctuary and Dennis was looking back, trying to find me. I had met Dennis in my final year at Michigan State and we married two years later. While Dennis knew and liked both Mike and Caroline, he didn't know anybody else here and was starting to get uncomfortable. Also, I could tell the priest was wrapping up and it would soon be my turn to speak. I slipped quietly back into the sanctuary and sat back down next to Dennis.

"Figure out what you are going to say?" Dennis asked."

"No. Hopefully I'll figure out something quick."

"You'll be fine, just stop worrying about it, I'm sure God, and Mike will both help you say something amazing."

"Thanks." Easy for him to say I thought, he doesn't have to get up and give a speech in front of a packed church.

Suddenly I heard the words that I had been dreading for the last week and a half. "Now Mike's long time friend Sarah will say a few words about Mike's life for us."

As I got up and walked to the podium near the alter I began to get very warm. Then I stood and looked around the church and realized that I didn't know ninety percent of the people in the church, and that since I would probably never see most of these people again that maybe this wouldn't be too bad. I looked around at all of the people in the church. I heard a couple coughs; a few sniffles, and a couple people clear their throats. Then it hit me, and I began to speak.

"My name is Sarah Carson. I first met Mike on a chilly beach in Paradise, Michigan on Memorial Day weekend twenty-five years ago. Two people died on that beach that night."

At this point, I paused for effect as people looked around and mumbled under their breath in surprise. "No, physically nobody died, but mentally two sad, angry, and lost individuals died and were reborn as loving, confident, and devoted followers of Christ. You see for different reasons both Mike and I had lost our way on God's journey. We had both strayed far away from God and were teetering on the precipice of ruin. Then we found each other. Over the next year, we talked and went to church frequently. We discussed the sermons and God's role in our lives, and by the end of that year, we were both back to walking hand in hand with God on our journey through life. Because of this, I became a social worker and touched many lives. Mike became a teacher and baseball coach, and judging by the standing room only crowd in this church, touched many more lives than I did. I owe a great deal to Mike, probably more than he could have ever known in life. Now I am sure he is up in heaven looking down on us smiling, and feeling a great deal of love and satisfaction. I'm sure right now he is basking in the love of God's kingdom and lobbying God, for a little divine intervention to help The Detroit Tigers win game 7 of the World Series tomorrow night. I met with Mike for three days the week before he died, I thought we were going to talk about his entire life, but he insisted on focusing on the year directly following when I first met Mike. It was a dark time in both of our lives and through each other and Christ; we helped each other become born again. He wanted to focus on this point because Caroline, Andrew, Theodore, he hoped it would help you find your way through this most difficult time. Even in his dying moments, he thought of his family before himself, as he had done many times with his students and his players over the last twenty-five years. So I could stand up here for the next fifteen minutes or so and talk about my journey with Mike

I think it would be more appropriate if people in the audience came up and said a few words. I know Mike is watching us right now and I know he would love to hear what everyone has to say. So rather than think of just myself and my thoughts on Mike, I'm going to sit down, and if you like come on up and tell us how Mike helped or affected you."

I walked back to my seat looking around the church with one eye looking to see if anybody in their seat about to get up. I returned to my pew and sat back down next do Dennis. I again looked around to see if anybody was even stirring. I took a calculated risk here and I was praying that it would pay off. When at first nobody moved I began to get an extremely warm feeling in my stomach. A feeling I think most of us know as we have all embarrassed ourselves at some point or another in our lives. I was almost to the point of being horrified and bursting into tears when suddenly, a man with graying brown hair, who looked to be in his late thirties or early forties got up and walked to the podium. He straightened his tie and then began to speak. "My name is Jack, and I had the privilege to be one of the first players that Mike ever coached. He didn't just coach me; he saved my life. Not even my wife knows what I'm about to tell this crowd gathered here today, but like you, she will in a minute. At the end of my junior year of high school, I may have been the unhappiest kid on the planet. My dad had been murdered less than a year earlier, I didn't have many friends, and I was going to kill myself. I was going to do it right after school ended. Then my coach brought Coach Mike in as our team's new pitching coach. I remember listening to him speak that June afternoon and something about him made me optimistic for the first time in months. I decided to put off suicide and see how things went in the fall. Mike changed my life that fall. He believed in me like no other person that I had ever known. He was the only coach ever to care enough about me to work with me one on one. He made me part of the team and as a result by next spring I was going to all of the parties that the other guys were going to. I got a college scholarship to The University of Iowa because of his help. He changed my life forever. I would not be standing here the proud husband of a beautiful wife, the proud father of two boys and a girl, and high school teacher and baseball coach myself in the state of Iowa if it were not for Coach

Mike. He was the best mentor and leader that any kid playing baseball would be lucky to have. Thanks coach you saved my life."

Jack returned to his seat. He sat and immediately hugged his wife. I knew his wife had not known about his thoughts of suicide as she had not cried once the entire service but immediately fell into her husband's arms sobbing when he returned to his seat. There was an old man waiting up front to speak. He walked up slowly as if it pained him. He must have been in his eighties.

"My name is Mark Stopac. I hired Mike as a pitching coach. He had a way of showing kids baseball that I've never seen in forty plus years of coaching. Kids loved him and he loved them back. He would go to bat for any of his players at any time. I don't know why he had to be taken so young while I hobble around so old. The world has lost a great man." With that the old man walked slowly back to his seat.

The next person to get up and speak was a person everybody knew. Bob Mack was one of Mike's former players. He had played the last twelve seasons in the Major Leagues, splitting time with The Houston Astros, Seattle Mariners, and Boston Red Sox. Two years ago, he had signed a four-year contract with The Detroit Tigers in the hopes of finishing his career with his hometown team and winning a World Series. Bob had lead the majors in home runs the previous two seasons before signing with The Tigers. Over his first eleven seasons, he never hit fewer than 25 home runs or had fewer than 90 RBIs. However, an injury in spring training this year had kept him out until the end of July. When he came back, he just never seemed to have his swing. Despite playing almost every day he hit just 2 home runs, had just 16 RBI's and was hitting just .213. All of those numbers were well below his career averages. Many thought that this was the end of the line for him. Many called for the Tiger's manager to sit him in game 7. The manager said that even though he's struggling we can't go against him. Bob wasn't a man of many words so his speech at the funeral was short.

"Coach Mike was by far the greatest coach I ever played for. He taught us to play the game the right way. He taught us sportsmanship, and above all, he taught us about life. Coach Mike, wherever you are, tomorrow night is for you. We're going to bring the title home for you coach."

For the next hour, person after person came up to share their memories of Mike. Many former students and players pointed to him making a huge positive difference in his life. Finally, Mike's wife Caroline made her way up to the podium. She stood there for a moment trying to fight off tears but finally spoke. "Thank you. Thank you all for coming and sharing such beautiful words about our dear husband and father, and a special thank you to you Sarah. What a perfect gift for us to hear all the wonderful things that Mike did. I know Mike is looking down right now with his parents and his Grandma Sophie who I never met but he never stopped talking about, and I know that he is smiling right now. I know his parents are smiling, and I know that his Grandma Sophie is smiling. He is with God now and I know someday, we will all be reunited with him. I know he doesn't want us to be sad, and I know he'll be watching from heaven tomorrow night when The Detroit Tigers play The Los Angeles Dodgers in game seven of the World Series. He always said he wanted to see the Tigers win another World Series before he died. Once again thank you all."

I was waiting at the altar when Caroline was done speaking. She walked over to me and we embraced. We cried into each other's shoulders. When we let go, Caroline went back and sat with her sons. I went back to the podium to say a few final words. "Thank you all for your kind words. I know Mike is smiling down from heaven right now. There will be a luncheon at Marco's Italian restaurant immediately following the service."

I went back to my seat, we had communion, the priest said a final blessing, and we went to have lunch.

Mike's body was cremated and Caroline already had the urn with the ashes when Dennis and I and our three children arrived at Caroline's house to watch game seven. Caroline had Mike's urn on a table facing the television for the game. It was her way of coping as neither her or her children could imagine watching the game without him. As long as I live, I'll never forget what happened that night. I can still recite word for word what the announcer said.

"Well here we go bottom of the ninth two outs, runner on first, Tigers down a run and Bob Mack coming to the plate. Mack's struggles have continued tonight. He's 0 for 4 with two strikeouts, a pop out, and a ground out to second. And the first pitch, Mack takes a ball outside. Terrence Martin on the mound for The Dodgers has converted twenty-six consecutive save opportunities. Martin winds up the pitch, fastball, swung on and missed by Mack."

"Well I'll tell you Jim, Mack's swing just hasn't looked the same at all since he's been back. I have to question the manager not putting in a pinch hitter here."

"His numbers have been way below his career averages ever since he came back in late July. Now Martin ready again, here's the pitch, Mack takes a strike on the inside corner. Nice pitch by Martin there. Great movement on the cut fastball"

"Mack didn't have a chance at that one Jim."

"The wind continues to blow hard from right to left field across the diamond. Mack's power is to left he needs to just try to poke a single the other way as a fly ball to left will either hang up and be caught or go foul." Now the one two pitch, fouled off, Mack just got a piece of that one. Now Mack is calling time. He steps away and looks up at the sky. He's pointing up at the sky now."

"Jim, Mack's high school baseball coach passed away earlier this week He made a short speech at the funeral that the Tigers would bring the title home for his coach who was a lifelong Tiger's fan. If they're going to do that now is the time."

"Well Mack stands back in. Martin is ready, and the pitch, high fly ball to left field, it's hooking, looks like it's going to go fall, wait the wind just changed direction, the ball is hugging the line and it is gone, home run, I don't believe it the Tigers win! The Tigers win! Look at the flag; the wind has changed back. I have never seen anything like this in all of my years of baseball. They are now mobbing Mack at home plate."

At that moment, we all looked down at the urn. Mike's oldest son picked up the urn, held it up, and said "M-V-P." Just then, we all heard a horn honk come from inside the garage. Well went out to look. Caroline opened the garage but there was nothing there. Mike's car sat locked in the garage, nobody could have honked the horn. We all had heard the sound of the horn from the garage but none of us could believe what we had heard. We knew it was Mike. There was no other explanation. We all huddled together and cried briefly. Then we went inside and celebrated The Tigers' victory.

Epilogue

Time went by and erased some of the pain of Mike's death. The pain would never completely go away for Mike and his family, but it would get better. I became good friends with Mike's widow Caroline. We had always been friends but I guess we were never good friends. After Mike's death, I made it a point to try to have lunch with Caroline at least once a week. At first, it was mainly for support but after the first few weeks, we discovered that we had more in common than we ever thought. The lunches became a fun diversion from the rest of life. Caroline misses Mike dearly. I sometimes ask her if she would ever consider remarrying. Her answer is always the same, "It's not up to me, it's up to God." When I ask her what that means she just tells me that if God and Mike want her to, she will, but she's not actively pursuing that. She still misses Mike deeply but over these past six months, her spirits have improved. I think she's handling everything pretty well.

Mike's two sons while obviously shaken by their father's untimely death seem to be dealing with things well also. Their oldest son is in his second year of college. Their youngest son has begun college up at Michigan State. He has decided that he wants to go into medicine and try to cure cancer. I told him that was a very lofty goal, and his response is always the same. He says, "It's not just a lofty goal it's the loftiest of goals. Just think of how many people die of cancer. If I can prevent even one family from feeling the pain that mine did than my life will be worthwhile. I know if God wants to take someone that it is their time. However, if I can help just one person not die before their time then it will be all worth while. Or even if I can find a way to make their lives more comfortable while they fight cancer, then again, my life will be worthwhile."

When I hear Mike's family talk as they do, I know that he is looking down and smiling. He is smiling at the realization that his wife and children have followed what he tried to teach them when he was alive. I sometimes look up and wonder when I will see Mike again. While I do miss him I hope it is not for a long time. Then again, such matters are not up to you and I; they are up to a much higher and more knowing power.